THE UNEXPECTED MISS BENNET

Who will give consequence to a young lady slighted by men? Mary Bennet's elder sisters are beautiful and full of fire and spirit. Her younger sisters, though very silly, are popular wherever they go. Everyone believes that Mary, who likes to read books and play music, will die an unloved spinster; not being handsome enough to tempt suitors. However, when an opportunity arises for her to embark on a new life, she grows new friendships. Mary realizes her own strengths and discovers just how much a woman of understanding and fortitude can shine in the eyes of a good man.

Patrice Sarath has written many novels including short stories that have appeared in magazines and anthologies, including *Alfred Hitchcock Mystery Magazine.*

Her novels are enjoyed by readers who love fantasy, horses and romance, with a dash of mystery thrown in. Patrice lives in Austin, Texas, with her family. *The Unexpected Miss Bennet* is her first novel published by Thorpe.

PATRICE SARATH

◆

THE UNEXPECTED MISS BENNET

Complete and Unabridged

ULVERSCROFT
Leicester

First published in Great Britain in 2011 by
Robert Hale Limited
London

First Large Print Edition
published 2012
by arrangement with
Robert Hale Limited
London

British Library CIP Data

Sarath, Patrice.
  The unexpected Miss Bennet.
  1. Single women- -Fiction. 2. Regency novels.
  3. Large type books.
  I. Title
  813.6–dc23

  ISBN 978–1–4448–1212–1

Published by
F. A. Thorpe (Publishing)
Anstey, Leicestershire

Set by Words & Graphics Ltd.
Anstey, Leicestershire
Printed and bound in Great Britain by
T. J. International Ltd., Padstow, Cornwall

This book is printed on acid-free paper

1

It is a comforting belief among much of society, that a plain girl with a small fortune must have no more interest in matrimony than matrimony has in her.

Mrs Bennet was not a particularly doting mother, but she did have one object, and that was to see all of her daughters married. She was the most often bemused by Mary, her third daughter of five, and the one with the fewest prospects.

It was not that Mary was plain, exactly, for she was a Bennet, and the Bennet girls were known as the prettiest in their small neighbourhood. But she said the most alarming things and was full of dire pronouncements on the base leanings of men, of which men were not eager to hear, and though she applied herself diligently to the piano and singing, she was not as accomplished as many another girl who approached the task with rather more gaiety than determination.

It might have been with something like relief, then, her two eldest daughters having made quite eligible matches, that Mrs Bennet could surrender her vigilance with regards to

Mary. For Kitty, some effort must still be made, of course, and that was a daunting enough task in itself, but Mary — Mrs Bennet owned herself unequal to the task.

She confided as much to her eldest daughter Jane on one of her frequent visits, that her nerves were not up to finding a husband for Mary.

'No, Mary must stay here and be a comfort to me and Mr Bennet,' Mrs Bennet declared. 'And after we die you must take her in, Jane. She will be no bother. She loves only her piano and her sermons and she will do quite nicely and will be quite out of the way. She can help you with the children as you begin to have them, and so she will be able to pay her own way.'

Jane endeavoured to assure Mrs Bennet that she would be able to provide a home for Mary for many more years, and that Mary would find a higher place in Jane's home than governess when such an unhappy event as Mrs Bennet's passing on came about, but Mrs Bennet had already flitted on to another topic, in which Lady Lucas had offered up some slight and Mrs Bennet received the insult so eagerly as to make Jane suspect she enjoyed the opportunity to consider herself ill-used.

But what to do about Mary? Jane,

ensconced in the height of domestic happiness, began to suffer a niggling doubt. Could it be right that she should be so happy while her middle sister was not? Jane took up an accounting of the Bennet sisters' fortunes. Of the five, she and her next sister, Elizabeth, were married to men they loved and respected. Their youngest sister, Lydia, had become entangled with a disgraceful rake, in circumstances which had brought down a scandal upon the whole family. Then there was Kitty who, fortunately, was not yet attached. Rather than let her go the way of Lydia, towards which destiny Kitty's nature predisposed her, Jane and Elizabeth had each taken a firmer hand in her upbringing. For the sake of Kitty's future happiness and respectability they could not let her follow Lydia's example; it would not do to have *two* scandals in one family.

There was no need to have such a fear for Mary, who practised goodness with sober devotion and no little pride, and thus was less susceptible to the wiles of bad men. But even Mary, for all of her sermonizing against the evils of pleasant society, had expressed interest in a more fulfilling life than that of living on her sister's charity. Should not she have a chance of finding such happiness with a like-minded gentleman as Jane had found with her Bingley or Lizzy with her Darcy?

Jane worried, and when Jane worried, she acted. That evening she composed a letter to Lizzy.

Dearest Lizzy,

I hope this letter finds you well at Pemberley. Mama has just left after a long visit, and I confess that I am slightly weary of her nerves. But it was good to have her company, and it was rather like old times. My Bingley left us alone for much of her stay but he was perfectly amiable to her and her teases. Father was not able to come, and I believe him when he said that he preferred his library at Longbourn to ours, as we are not great readers, though we mean to improve! but I think we will see him in a fortnight or sooner.

Mama said something that gave me cause for concern regarding Mary. For all that we were terribly embarrassed when she pushed us towards eligible men, she seems to take no interest in Mary's prospects. She seems resigned — no, content — that Mary may not ever marry, and thinks more of Kitty's debut in London than of Mary's.

I am happy to be chaperone to Kitty in public and I see a vast improvement in her behaviour already, since she is no longer under Lydia's sway, poor misguided soul. I think, though, that we should not neglect Mary. She is as unformed in her way as Kitty is, and though her opinions are firm she holds them with little understanding of society and the world. I think we do a grave disservice to her if we do not offer her the same guidance that we give to Kitty, and I think it will be just as well received, if not better, by Mary.

I await your reply anxiously. Give my love to Darcy and Georgiana.

Jane

★ ★ ★

With this letter Jane hatched her plot and waited for Lizzy's reply.

★ ★ ★

Lizzy gave a fond smile when she received and read the missive. Always like Jane, to think of others as deserving of all good fortune that fell to her!

But if the world were as just as it claimed to be, all good fortune would be heaped upon Jane and those of like character, and there would be none for the rest of us, Lizzy said to herself. And that would not do at all. She stood and paced the small sitting room that she had claimed for her own when she became mistress of Pemberley. The great house was hardly a house at all and its inhabitants — Lizzy, her young sister-in-law Georgiana, and her husband Darcy — rattled about in it as loosely as buttons in an old hatbox. Elizabeth was used to cosier comforts. Longbourn was small, and old, and respectably shabby; this little room, which received the afternoon sun and looked out over a small bit of wilderness, reminded her of her childhood and her upbringing.

When her gaze fell on a miniature of her husband and all that it represented, she knew that Jane was right. Perhaps Mary would never find such happiness, but to withhold any opportunity from her by the simple expedient of assuming that she of all others would never fall in love, that she would never attract a respectable man, was as prejudiced a thought as any that Lizzy had been susceptible to.

For we all know how that turned out, she thought. *My prejudice almost cost me my love. How much more dangerous then, to hold such assumptions concerning my sister, and to wield such power by omission as to prevent her from ever discovering whether there is a man for her. Jane is right — we must do all we can for Mary.*

When she entered her husband's study and gave him a kiss as he bent over his letters, he smiled up at her, his expression lightening so much that it melted her heart.

'You have the look of mischief about you,' Mr Darcy said. 'Much as when we first met and exchanged words. Have I need to fear?'

'Not at all,' she said. 'I merely came to warn you that I am my mother's daughter after all. Jane and I are prepared to make a match for Mary.'

2

Oblivious of such plans being made for her by her elder sisters, Mary Bennet sat at the piano at Lucas Lodge and played her favourite airs as all around her young men and women of her acquaintance danced and laughed. She sat in the corner in the small ballroom, her face serious as she played, hardly looking up at the swirl of gowns around her. The dance was lively, for Sir William and Lady Lucas loved a party and enjoyed playing host to all the young people in the neighbourhood. And all the neighbourhood came to their assemblies, where conversation and laughter abounded. It was a merry time, and even Mrs Bennet, who had cause to look askance upon the Lucases, could be found sitting with the other mamas, all boasting of their offspring.

With the eldest two Bennet sisters married well and the youngest married but not spoken of, Longbourn was no longer at the centre of the small Meryton society. Now it was Lady Lucas's turn. Her eldest daughter Charlotte was comfortably settled, but Lady Lucas still had unmarried daughters to find husbands for, and she viewed Mrs Bennet's triumphs less with chagrin than with relief. Now there was a clear field for her other children.

For her part, Mrs Bennet only occasionally forgave Lady Lucas for her eldest daughter Charlotte's marriage to Mr Collins, a Bennet cousin and Mr Bennet's heir. To her credit, she did her best, but Mrs Bennet could not think kindly of Charlotte until her two eldest daughters had surpassed her marriage with their own. Even then it only took the word 'entail' to cause her nerves to dance with indignation.

When it came to the assemblies, though, she tried to put her feelings aside. To Mrs Philips, her sister, she said, 'It keeps Kitty happy to have a dance now and again, and as for Mary it gives her something to do. I think people whose daughters marry other people's cousins for the entail could be less happy, perhaps, but then again, my sensibility is extraordinary in that regard. None the less, I will not say a word to Lady Lucas but only smile and nod when she tells me of Charlotte and her new baby boy. No doubt Mr Collins had a son on purpose. However, I will not speak anything of it, though it is bad when a property is entailed away from its rightful owners.'

She finished giving this speech, just as

Mary brought a lively gavotte to an end with a flourish. The assembly broke into laughter and applause, then the dancers turned towards the punch bowl for refreshment, their faces flushed and their heads giddy. It was a cool summer night and the doors had been thrown open to the garden.

Mary sat back with her fingers folded, waiting to be called upon again. It was pleasant enough to have a position in the neighbourhood as the willing musician, but she felt a faint prick of disquiet as she looked out over the assembled guests. Almost all were young men and women with whom she had grown up. No, in many cases they were younger than she was. She had left the schoolroom some time since, and was now a full-grown woman of twenty years. She frowned, and then remembered her mother's strict admonitions not to scowl so, as it wrinkled her brow.

'Do you not get tired playing?' came a voice at her side. Mary started and looked up at the young man smiling pleasantly at her. She remembered that they had been introduced but she had already forgotten his name. His dress was unkempt and his hair overlong, but he had a good-natured smile and she smiled back at him.

'Music is the balm that comforts our souls,'

she said. 'It doesn't tire me to play.'

'Even music for dancing? I find it exhilarating, rather than peaceful. But I cannot sit and do one thing over and again. I must always be moving.'

Mary opened her mouth but had nothing to say. Young men didn't often talk to her. She felt heat rise in her cheeks and tried desperately to think of some aphorism or other. He didn't seem to notice her reticence. Instead, he suddenly smacked the top of the pianoforte, making her jump.

'I know. You should dance the next dance with me, and then we can compare whether dancing or music is the more tiring.'

He spoke as if it were the simplest thing in the world, that she should just rise and dance. With him.

Before she could say a word, Maria Lucas jumped in.

'Oh no!' she said. 'Mary doesn't dance — if she did we would have no one to play, for none of us has the patience. Go on, Mary — we're all ready. Play more for us. Mr Aikens, you are ready, I know, and you promised to dance another with me.'

The young man looked between them and his smile faltered. Mary felt her mouth move in a smile of her own, and she began another air. She kept her head down, concentrating on her fingers, until she sensed that the man had gone. When she looked up he was dancing with Maria Lucas.

★　★　★

The faint feeling of discontent pricked at Mary for days after that evening. The piano at Longbourn remained silent, its lid closed. Mary sometimes wandered towards it out of habit, but when she sat at the worn bench she felt a vague disgust. It no longer suited her fancy to sit and play. With the piano silent the house was quieter than ever, the liveliness that five daughters had brought to it muted. Kitty was full of chatter as usual, but only their mother answered her vivacity or querulousness with her own. Mrs Bennet never said a word about the unused piano — she only dozed in the afternoon in the parlour where the instrument stood. Mr Bennet was as silent as a father could be, spending his days on the farm and his afternoons in his library when he was not visiting Lizzy.

With the piano no longer bringing joy, Mary turned to her sermons, but the familiar words no longer brought the same comfort. She had read Fordyce's *Sermons for Young Women* so often that the pages had become smudged under her nimble fingers. Now, she read them with a less captivated eye. Where before she had found herself nodding in agreement with his admonitions concerning grace, charity, and humility, in which his opinions had so much become her own that she hardly knew where his left off and hers began, she began to grow uneasy. For instance, had her copy of the sermons *always* held this counsel?

It is very true, there are young ladies who, without any particular advantage of a natural ear or a good voice, have by means of circumstances peculiarly favourable, made great proficiency in music: But it is true that they have made it at a vast expense of time and application such as no woman ought to bestow upon an object to which she is not carried by the irresistible impulse of genius.

Mary was disturbed. What exactly had Fordyce meant? Surely he could not mean that a young lady could practise *too* much? It was as if he had aimed his words straight at her. She knew there was a vast chasm between what she wished to play and what she could play: her fingers, no matter how diligently she practised, did not run along the

13

keyboard as nimbly as did those of other women. And her voice was not pretty. Though she practised singing as often as she was able, she knew she had not the same pleasing tones as other women. None of the Bennet sisters could sing, but that was cold comfort. None of the others *wanted* to sing. Only Mary did.

And now here was Fordyce admonishing her for her application. That bolt shot uncomfortably close to home. She was so unsettled by the betrayal of a most well-loved and comforting book that she shut the volume violently, rousing her mother who woke from her nap with a small shriek.

'Mary!' Mrs Bennet said. 'Have some consideration for my nerves. You know I cannot stand sudden noises that sound as if your father were shooting pheasant in the kitchen.' She settled herself again, straightening her shawl and her cap rather like a ruffled hen.

'I'm sorry, Mama,' Mary managed, though the words choked her. She slipped out of the parlour and stood for a moment in the dim hall. I am as bad as Mama, she thought. I have the fidgets and cannot sit still. The sense of disquiet deepened at the realization that all of her comforts — piano, sermons and learned essays — had become as ashes to her.

Her father came out of his library and

seemed startled to see her in the hall. He looked astonished at her — she wondered if her face told of her agitation.

'Well, Mary,' he said in greeting. 'What meditations on the wickedness of men have you worked up for us today?'

She stopped to consider the question seriously, though she was no fool and knew he asked it only to laugh at her. 'Nothing yet, Papa,' she said at length. 'Perhaps, like Lydia, I should begin a thorough investigation of it myself.'

He did laugh — but it was a startled, appreciative one and Mary smiled back, somewhat shyly. She did not often make her father laugh, or at least, not as if he laughed with her.

The parlour door opened and Mrs Bennet peered out, her cap askew. 'For goodness' sake, Mr Bennet! What do you mean by laughing in such a fashion?'

'It was Mary, my dear. She has suddenly acquired a sense of humour.'

'Nonsense. Mary?'

'God wants us to laugh, I think,' Mary said, already a little ashamed of her previous remarks. 'It shows us that his creatures are happy and content, and so it cannot be deemed an unseemly thing.'

Mrs Bennet looked between them, lifted

her eyes to the ceiling, and disappeared back into the parlour. Mr Bennet raised a brow, then stumped off. Mary could hear him mutter, *Back to normal* and they left her alone in the dim hall.

★ ★ ★

The small village of Meryton was still a place of quiet amusements for Kitty and Mary. They walked there almost every day. Once Mary had gone unwillingly with her sisters, but ever since her strange discomfiture she was happy to walk with Kitty down the familiar lanes. Thrown together by the absence of their sisters they formed an alliance born of necessity. They could never be close in the way Kitty had been with Lydia, to be sure. The youngest two Bennet sisters had been thick as thieves from the time they were small children. Though the younger, always Lydia had led and Kitty followed. Mary sometimes thought of them as a single sister, *Lydiand-Kitty*. Now with Lydia gone, Kitty had no one to confide in save Mary.

Mary got used to Kitty's conversation on their walks on those early summer days. Their bonnets shaded them from the summer sun, and grasses swept along their skirts. It was not that she listened too closely to her sister's chatter — rather it rolled off her in the same way that a summer rain dripped off new leaves, barely noticeable.

'Jane said that she would bring me to Bath and London this year, and I will go to all of the balls, for I am already out. Mama has said that I can have as many new ballgowns as I like, for Bingley is so amiable he will surely pay for them. I only want to wait to buy them in London, for Meryton's dressmakers are nothing grand enough. I think a pink one and a yellow one to start, don't you think? I would love to have white lace for I know I will look just like a bride and everyone will look at me! but I am not sure Mama will approve — she will say that cream is best, perhaps. But perhaps Jane will — she is so happy she will say yes to anything! And Mama will listen to anything Jane tells her. Can you keep a secret, Mary?'

For a single moment Mary was startled into listening to her sister. Then she thought: whom could I tell, for you are the only one I have to talk to?

'It is a solemn charge to keep a confidence,' she assured her sister. Kitty grimaced in the way that she always did when Mary said something serious, and took a deep breath, as if to tell her her secret all at once.

'I wrote to Lydia to tell her I would be in

London and she wrote back and said that she would try to get Wickham to go there. And I am sure she has acquaintances that I would find most diverting, and she and Wickham would take me to private parties. I do so want to see Lydia, Mary. You are all right, and Jane and Lizzy being married are lovely, because they are so grand now and can pay for things, but I miss Lydia so much.'

Mary stopped on the path, in the dappled sunlight beneath a tree hanging over the old stone wall. She looked at Kitty, who looked back at her, the sudden tears in her voice appearing on her cheeks.

'You would do that?' Mary said at last, her voice low, and all thought of appearing wise vanished as she took in the impropriety of Kitty's confession. 'You would throw over every appearance of respectability, the opportunity of being with Jane and having the benefit of her good guidance, in favour of paying a visit to our sister?'

'La, Mary, you preach so.' Now Kitty sounded shaken and defiant.

'You know you mustn't see Lydia, ever. She is lost, Kitty, lost to all goodness and respectable society.'

'She knows you never loved her,' Kitty cried. 'You never cared for her, and only think of yourself.'

Of course Mary had loved her sister. Only, she hadn't liked her very much, and she knew that in her hesitation she had made that clear. Kitty's expression took on shades of malice.

'You of all people should not worry about Lydia's connections, as they cannot affect any prospects *you* might have.'

Mary grew warm and as a result she became speechless. It always happened in that way: she never could think of a response in time. All her sermons and essays could not help her when she argued with Kitty. 'You would be wise not to think of Lydia's connections except as a bad example, Kitty,' she managed at length. 'And don't grimace so. A lady should have a meek and mild expression.'

That made Kitty grimace even more. 'I knew you wouldn't understand. I should never have told you anything.' Her tone became bitter. 'Now I'm sure you will tell Mama and Papa and I will never be able to see Lydia.'

'I gave my word, Kitty,' Mary said, but she was suddenly unsure that it was the right thing to do. Fordyce spoke out against telling tales, to be sure, but if Kitty meant to visit Lydia on the sly, she did not think she should be silent about it. 'But you shouldn't see her, it's not right.'

'All right, all right, I won't,' Kitty said quickly. 'Pray let us talk no more about it.'

She continued down the path towards Meryton, and Mary followed in her wake, less and less sure about her promise. She knew better than to believe Kitty. Once she took to an idea, especially where Lydia was concerned, she held on to it. I promised not to tell Mama and Papa, Mary thought. But I didn't promise not to tell Jane. It was not quite right to split hairs in this way, but Fordyce would no doubt see the necessity of it.

3

Kitty's preparations for her stay with Jane took on an air of frenzy. She packed, and packed again, picked a quarrel with her mother over what she should take with her, and sobbed with such passion over not being able to buy a new bonnet for her journey that Mr Bennet locked himself in his library, determined not to come out until Kitty had gone and the house was at peace.

Mary sat out the fuss for the most part. She stayed out of the way in her favourite nook of the house, reading by the light in the large bow window that overlooked the best part of the small park. Although Fordyce had failed her in his support of her practice of music and singing — had he really meant that if one was not impelled by true genius one should not continue a well-regulated practice of improvement? — he and she were as one with regard to the improvement of the mind through reading.

The 'affection for knowledge', of which Fordyce wrote, and of which Mary read with great satisfaction, prevented idleness and dissipation. Other young ladies might fill their time with parties and amusements, but *she* would read.

Mary sat in comfortable self-praise that she was at that very moment earning Fordyce's highest commendation by reading good books and thus avoiding dreaded amusement and idleness, unlike Kitty, who was going joyfully forward to indulge in dissipation as was likely to leave her weakened, sorrowful and brokenhearted. She would come home to Longbourn a shadow of her former robust self, and she and Mary could have many comfortable talks about restoring her health and wit.

Then Mary became distracted by the view of the garden from her window seat. The diamond panes blurred the view and Mary occupied herself by looking out and finding where she could see clear spots in the glazing. She was suddenly shocked to see a familiar face outside the window, looking in. Mary dropped her book with an astonished cry.

'Mr Collins!' she exclaimed. He bowed and grimaced at the same time, giving a little sideways hop so as to give her a chance to view his self-deprecating expression. He mouthed something at her, though the glass was not thick. Mary lifted the hook and pushed open the window carefully — the frame tended to stick if one was not careful.

'Mr Collins,' she said again. 'Do forgive me — why have you come to the back of the house?'

'My dear cousin Mary,' he said, grimacing and bowing again. Mary bit her lip. 'Do forgive the intrusion, as I see that you are most diligently at your studies. Is that Fordyce's *Sermons* that I see? For a lady, certainly admirable, admirable. I am glad to see you are not spending time with unsuitable novels. As Lady Catherine de Bourgh always says — '

'Mary!' It was Mrs Bennet, come running round the side of the house. 'Mr Collins is here, but we cannot find him — oh, Mr Collins,' she said, breathing hard and holding her hand to the side of her gown. 'Whatever are you doing here?'

Where Mary's question had been simply one of surprise, Mrs Bennet's had a tinge of accusation about it.

'Mrs Bennet,' Mr Collins said, and he bowed and grimaced again. It wasn't quite a grimace but rather an attempt at a smile, Mary thought. 'I hope you forgive the intrusion. As I was explaining to Miss Bennet, I knocked on the front door but there was no answer; all your servants must be quite busy. I thought it would be no harm to come round to the back of the house and see for myself if anyone was at home. This garden is lovely and your little park befits your standing in society. I believe that grand vistas are inappropriately showy when they are flaunted by the truly humble. Yet a small park can have such proper form and function as is needful when it suits its owners' true position. It will do quite nicely.'

Having thoroughly insulted Mrs Bennet and simultaneously reminded her of the odious fact that he was to inherit Longbourn, Mr Collins bowed again.

Mrs Bennet swelled in indignation but a sudden dolorous lamentation from Kitty broke her concentration.

'Mama, this trunk is too small! Nothing fits and I shall have nothing to wear in London!'

Mrs Bennet took a deep breath and regained her temper in the same moment.

'Please forgive us for not being more hospitable, Mr Collins, but you have come at a very busy time. We are sending Kitty to visit her sister, Mrs Bingley, and there is much to do. However, you are welcome, and please do come round to the front of the house and we will let you in properly.' She looked at Mary and said sharply, 'Shut the window, Mary, you will let in the damp.' She then made an insistent face at her daughter, but Mary only frowned in puzzlement. Mrs Bennet made the face again and then Mary understood what her mother mouthed at her behind Mr Collins's back. *Make him leave.*

It took all of Mary's strength of will not to grimace back. Making Mr Collins leave was an impossible task, as he saw fit to visit them as frequently as fortnightly and to stay several days or more. To be sure he divided his time between Longbourn and Lucas Lodge, but he seemed to feel less compelled to spend time with his in-laws than he did to visit his future estate. It was almost as though he did not like to leave it in the hands of Mr Bennet where he had found it, now that he was settled with a wife and infant son.

Mary watched her mother and Mr Collins walk round to the front of the house. She heard Kitty cry out again. 'I cannot find my rose-sprigged muslin!'

Mary sighed, closed the window and went off to see about tea.

★ ★ ★

Once she had quite liked Mr Collins and thought that she could encourage herself to fall in love with him. He was serious, he was as studious as she, and he was as given to moralizing. A little flutter — her nerves, she supposed — had overtaken her when she met him on his first visit. She had thought, *at last, a man for me. The type of man whom I would suit very well.* Mary knew that men liked beauty first, but this man, this Mr Collins, was different. He spoke well, he read sermons, and he made of everything a little comment. She found herself at that first family dinner thinking of her best aphorisms and sayings in order to catch his attention. He would see that she was serious and a thinker, not like her younger sisters who giggled disgracefully every time he spoke.

Yet as she came to know her cousin, Mary started to realize several things. First, he never heard a word she said. He listened to Mr Bennet and Mrs Bennet and responded to them, but after the second or third time she spoke, he would merely look about and continue with whatever thought he was pursuing at the moment. Second, he never really looked at her — her conversation might have been coming out of thin air. He looked at Jane though. With little grimaces and winks and a ducking of his head, he made it clear that he saw Jane.

Mary had never begrudged Jane her beauty or her goodness or the attention she drew from any one, men or women. Jane was all goodness — even pert Lizzy, whose tongue could make one smart, knew it, and she softened under Jane's attentions. No, Mary knew that she could not match Jane for all those accomplishments a truly good person had. But she sometimes wished, though a little forlornly, that she could be the centre of so much attention with so little effort. And then had come Mr Collins! The man who, from the moment he walked into their house — *his* house — was clearly a match for Mary, was already half in love with Jane! Even the sober, dour, plain suitors, who should have known better, had known that Jane was marked for a grander sort of marriage than they could offer, even they could not see beyond her beauty to look about them for a better match.

And *then*. To discover that Mr Collins had transferred his attentions to Lizzy! That was an idea so ludicrous on the face of it that it was hard not to repeat 'Mr Collins and Lizzy!' in increasing tones of astonishment; that there seemed never to have been a thought for Mary was another unpleasant surprise.

When Mr Collins married Charlotte Lucas, Mary thought that she could at last understand her mother's nerves. To her it was as if someone had walloped her in the stomach.

She knew she had not loved him; far from

it. Mary was a Bennet, and she was not the stupidest one. That prize belonged to Lydia at present, though Kitty seemed likely to make a bid for it. No, Mary quickly discovered that Mr Collins was ridiculous and unsuitable for any one, even a one such as she. But was she so unnoticed, and so preposterous a marriage prospect that even *Charlotte Lucas* was a better match? As far as Mary knew, Charlotte never opened a book and her conversation centered on the doings at Meryton and her brothers and sisters, with never a thought about the wider world. What kind of rector's wife would she be?

He should have at least looked at me, she thought, as she sat in the drawing room with the tea, waiting for her mother and Mr Collins. He should have heard what I had to say. Why would he not listen?

A conversation caught her attention as her father met Mr Collins with a rumbling greeting. Before they all entered, with Mrs Bennet fluttering behind them, chattering about all the preparations for Kitty, Mary had one last small indulgence in self-pity.

It would have been fine if for once Mary Bennet had had the attention of even a most unsuitable suitor.

Mr Bennet and Mary entertained Mr Collins in the drawing room while Mrs

Bennet attended Kitty. At intervals they could hear from upstairs the sounds of much thumping and raised voices with occasional words, as mother and daughter enjoyed the kind of communication that is emphasized with many italics. Mr Collins pursed his lips as he sipped his tea, looking quite pleased that he could hold forth on the situation.

'I have observed in my little parish of Hunsford that many young females of good birth are easily excited by the idea of company in town. I have mentioned it many times to Lady Catherine, that young ladies, unlike Miss de Bourgh, seem to have a certain sensibility that would be better suited, not to town, where their passions are raised unduly by late nights, rich foods, and heady attentions, but to the quiet country life, where their emotions can be soothed by regular company and fresh air. As I told Lady Catherine, Anne does not have that feverish attack of sensibility, but rather is more calm and rational than many other women. Don't you agree, sir?'

'I think, Mr Collins, that you overestimate the power of the quiet country life on girls. I have not noticed it to any great effect, and I think I have had the benefit of quantity to go by.'

This, Mary thought, was where Mr Collins

would nod at Mary and point out that she, at least, was a quiet country girl unaffected by the desires and whimsical delights of the wicked city. Or, even more likely, would he not bring up Charlotte?

He would not. 'Perhaps the natural inclinations of your daughters have been more powerful than those of most others of their sex. As for my patroness's daughter, she seems to be more the type of female who finds dignity in quietness and patience. She would never dream of being so forward.'

Mr Bennet said something that sounded suspiciously like, 'Not with such a mother, she wouldn't.' He said it into his teacup and so the words were muffled, but Mary had to turn her own laugh into a cough. She had met Lady Catherine once and heard much more about her from Lizzy and even from Maria Lucas. She could put a picture together in her head. For the first time, she felt pity for the daughter. To have such a mother! Then she thought: Anne de Bourgh has suffered the oppressive effects of too much of a mother, while I have endured the permissive effect of not enough.

Her father's eyes twinkled at her over his teacup and for a moment he and she exchanged a silent understanding. In the sudden silence, they heard Kitty cry, 'It's not fair! It will make me look like a child!'

Mr Collins set down his cup hastily and stood, a blush coming over his complexion. 'I will leave you then to your day, sir. I hope that your plans to send this daughter into company will not go awry as they did the last time. Lady Catherine has expressly mentioned that she will be seriously displeased if another Bennet makes such a scandalous alliance, and this time I could not hope to restrain her anger.'

'Please tell your patroness that we would not dream of so disappointing her hopes,' Mr Bennet assured him.

'Thank you sir. And if you wish to ask her for advice in raising the remainder of your daughters I am sure that Lady Catherine will be happy to impart her wisdom to you, for she has most diligently raised the flower of nobility herself.'

'To be sure,' Mr Bennet said with great solemnity, 'Upon awakening every morning I ask myself, 'What would Lady Catherine do?''

With much bowing and grimacing and ducking Mr Collins took his leave. They saw him out and off he went to visit Lucas Lodge, where he had, no doubt, a vastly more welcoming audience, although, Mary thought, she had seen Sir William visibly gather himself when approached by his son-in-law.

Mr Bennet closed the front door behind him and turned to Mary. 'So what do you think, Mary? You know, he could have been yours, had you just been more nimble than Lizzy's best friend.'

She eyed him with great seriousness. 'Would you have permitted it, Papa?'

She expected a laugh; instead, in the dim hall, his face grew sombre.

'I hope I would not have allowed it, daughter.' He dropped a kiss on her forehead and stumped off to his study, leaving her to her astonishment.

★ ★ ★

Kitty was off in a final flurry of activity, the small carriage whisking her away to her sister Jane with several ill-packed trunks. Longbourn fell silent under the cool freshness of early summer, and Mary ventured to walk out by herself. The path to Meryton led Mary through verdant fields, though there was mud underfoot. She picked her way carefully to avoid wetting her slippers but still her hem was often deep in mud. It felt very odd, not having any of her sisters with her. She was not used to walking into the little village by herself. Her mother did not walk. Mrs Bennet said the exercise exacerbated her nerves.

Meryton lost its few charms when ventured into alone. Mary did not care overmuch for ribbons and bonnets, though the stationer's was a favoured stop for paper and pens, and also carried books and ladies' gazettes. After a few days of unhappy walking into town, Mary took to finding secret nooks in the fields and walks beyond Longbourn where she could read in the shade of trees and by the slow-running brook that ran into the pond by the house. Once, with great daring, she climbed the branch of an old tree that had a perfectly formed limb, just right for sitting, and she felt as if she were a child again. She tore her dress climbing down, though, and had to hide the tear from her mother until she could safely mend it in her bedroom at night.

That was different too. For the first time, she had the room to herself. It was her things on the nightstand and in the dressing-table drawers; her belongings were strewn exactly where she wanted them. At first it was hard to sleep at night without another body next to her and the warm breath and night movements of her sisters to comfort her. Then she grew to like it.

Perhaps Kitty will get married right away,

she thought. Then I would never have to share a bed again! Unless I married . . . the thought made her uncomfortable and she shied away from it. To settle her thoughts, she lit the candle to read a bit more, until her eyes grew tired and sleep came. The first page she came to, opened at random, was Fordyce's encouraging thought on marriage: *Establish it betimes as a certain maxim, that to be married is neither the one nor the chief thing needful.*

Certainly Mary had not thought of marriage as her one true aim. It is not that she did not wish to marry, she thought. It just didn't consume her every thought as it did those of her sisters and other girls she knew. Lydia, for one, had thought of nothing else but beaux, and look where it had led her, though Mary supposed that was because Lydia was easily led. When Mary thought of marriage, she often considered it as a state to be entered into rather by accident than by design, which she supposed was Fordyce's point. Striving to catch a gentleman was ill-behaved, to be sure. But there was a difficulty, once again, with Fordyce's opinion. If I *do* not marry, she thought, and I *may* not work, what will happen to me? Once again she grew cross with Fordyce. It was almost as if he didn't really understand young women and their position after all. One could be good and kind and not care about worldly things, and accept that an earthly beauty turned to dust after but a few years of youth and joy, but the fact remained that this world required one to be more practical. When her father died she would have to leave Longbourn, with her mother or without her. Mary knew not where she would go. Neither, she thought pointedly, did Fordyce. He didn't have all the answers. Happiness in the next world was indeed dependent upon forsaking the transient pleasures of this one; but still one had to eat and live.

There — if she kept thinking dark thoughts she would never sleep. It had happened before, when the night brought unhappiness banished only by dawn. Mary closed the book and blew out the candle and prayed to let herself be easy. As comfort warmed her and she drowsed, she had a curious thought. Perhaps she should not rest all of her hopes on Fordyce. He had been a good guide, but a narrow one, and she had begun, if not to walk a different path, then at least to question the mapmaker. I can still be good, she thought, sleepier now. But what price goodness if it comes too easily? Maybe she needed to put her goodness to the test.

4

Jane greeted Kitty with an affectionate kiss.

'How good it is to see you! Kitty, you've grown! Would you like to rest before we have tea?'

Her sister untied her bonnet, bubbling over with excitement from her journey. She turned and turned in the hall, so much grander than shabby Longbourn. Though she had been to Jane's on a few visits this was the first time she made the journey alone.

'Oh, I'm not tired at all. I am so glad to be here at last. Jane, I do so admire your house. So elegant. And it is so kind of you to have me! And Bingley too! Thank you so much! I can't wait — I want to do everything at once! And when can we go to London? I do so want to go there — and Mama said to tell you that I will do anything you ask of me and be very good, but — would it be all right if I had one gown made while I am here? It would be terribly hard to go to all the fine places with unfashionable country clothes.'

'Of course, Kitty,' Jane said, but she felt a small niggling alarm. She would have to stand firm, and she so disliked disappointing anyone. This concern had made her very apprehensive of Kitty's visit. She could not begrudge her little sister any thing, and she knew Bingley would be even more likely to shower Kitty with all the things her heart desired, for he wanted only to make his wife happy. It would be up to Jane herself to curb Kitty's natural greediness. She almost wished Bingley were not so amiable in this matter.

Unaware of her sister's misgivings, Kitty chattered on as she let the servant take her bonnet and shawl and followed Jane into the parlour with a happy sigh and lightness of foot.

'How are Mama and Papa? And Mary?' Despite her effort to keep the question light, Jane could hear the significance she herself put into it. Kitty did not notice.

'Oh, they are well, as can be expected. Papa reads, Mama fidgets — she was so amusing when she told me I could make this visit by myself! She said that it would be most enjoyable and she wished she were sixteen again to be able to go to London with only her sister as chaperone!'

Jane winced. She took her duties more seriously than her Aunt Philips would have done; she could only imagine the mischief her mother could have got into under so light a hand. She took a sip of tea. 'And . . . Mary?

Still playing the piano and reading sermons?'

Kitty responded with an airy wave but then frowned. 'Oh, but you know, she hasn't played the piano much at all. No, I don't believe she has.' She brightened. 'She had better keep it up because who will play for us at Lucas Lodge, I can't think! Did you know — at the last assembly a young man went up to Mary and asked her to dance! I laughed like anything and Maria Lucas had to tell him that Mary doesn't dance because no one else will play the piano!'

Jane composed her thoughts, her heart sinking. 'I see. And what did Mary tell the young man?'

Kitty shrugged. 'I don't know. Oh, what a pretty brooch you are wearing, Jane. Is it a gift from Bingley?'

So Kitty thought nothing of her sister's plight. Well then, Jane thought, as she gave in to Kitty's teasing and let her put on the brooch. She watched her little sister admire herself in a small mirror, turning this way and that to make the brooch sparkle in the sunlight coming in from the large window. It was not a moment too soon to do something about Mary.

★ ★ ★

As Kitty chattered on and she and Jane enjoyed each other's company, Lizzy was writing to her parents, asking them to allow Mary to come and visit her and Darcy at Pemberley.

'What do you think of this, Mr Bennet?' Mrs Bennet asked her husband, peering over his shoulder as he read Lizzy's letter. 'Asking Mary to come and visit Pemberley when she has scarcely ever asked me to visit! I must say, I wonder what she is about! What can she possibly mean by asking Mary to visit Pemberley!'

Mr Bennet, after his short and rather odd conversation with his daughter regarding Mr Collins, began to have an inkling. He scanned the letter's contents again, his brow wrinkling over his daughter's precise handwriting. He kept back a smile out of consideration for his wife's feelings.

'I think it would be a fine thing for Mary to go and visit her sister, my dear. And look, Lizzy writes that when we come to fetch her we can all be together as a family at Christmastide. Kitty will come with Jane and Bingley and we will all celebrate at Pemberley.'

Neither mentioned Lydia and her husband, Mr Wickham, though their presence could be felt in the pause that followed this remark.

After a moment Mrs Bennet went on, hardly mollified, 'Yes, of course, that will be very well. But Mary! Lizzy knows she doesn't like company. What will she do with herself in that grand house? I know that she will make Darcy tired of her long words and talking of things that matter to no one. And then Lizzy will never be able to have any one of us visit her, for Darcy will put his foot down. And oh, if Lizzy takes her to town! What will Mary do in town, I wonder? Mr Bennet, you must write to Lizzy at once and tell her Mary does not want to visit her. Oh, what are things coming to? My poor nerves. Just thinking about Kitty going away and now we have to think about Mary too? How will we pack for her? I am thoroughly exhausted by my efforts with Kitty.'

Mr Bennet simply nodded and let her continue on, as he read the letter once more, then tucked it into his pocket. Mrs Bennet soon took herself off, still bewailing of all these sudden comings and goings of her daughters and the trouble it gave, while he went to find Mary.

He found her crossing the fields from Meryton, hurrying a little for the sky was greying and a menacing low cloud came down behind her. The wind had whipped up and the weather had turned chilly. Mary was too far away for him to see her clearly; as he stood in the doorway looking out at the sudden change in weather, she picked up her skirts and ran. She arrived over the threshold inside just as a scattering of drops drove in behind her.

'Quick, Papa!' she cried as she hurried inside, and he closed the door behind her just as a gust of wind and rain followed.

The weather was cut off but Mr Bennet remained astonished. Mary was *laughing*. The exercise had brought colour to her cheeks and her lips, usually pale from staying indoors. Her dark hair had loosened from its prim knot and her bonnet had fallen askew. Still laughing, Mary unknotted it. She used a slightly damp handkerchief to clean the raindrops from her face.

'The wind was most uncommon today,' she said, shaking out her skirts. 'I thought it was almost playful at first, with the clouds scudding along like ships at sea, but once the sun was obscured, I knew I had to hurry. I almost got drenched.'

As if to emphasize her words a gust of rain spattered on the door.

'Well, come along, come along,' he said gruffly. 'Call for tea and change into dry clothes and then come to see me in my library — no need to take cold on account of a romantic fancy about the wind.'

She bobbed and gave him a smile and continued up the stairs with a light step quite unlike her usual measured tread. Mr Bennet rubbed his ear and continued to his sanctuary. He was settled at his desk with a book, waiting for his daughter, when it occurred to him that he had never seen Mary look quite so lively before. She had always been a dark, prim little thing, even as a child, her temper easily roused and her first expression a scowl, not a smile, her first reaction to disapprove.

This Mary looked almost mischievous.

A knock came at his door.

'Come in,' he called. Mary came in, her hair smoothed back and her dress shaken out and hastily towelled dry. She wore a shawl around her shoulders.

'Well, Mary,' Mr Bennet said gruffly. 'Your sister Lizzy has written and wants you to come to visit her at Pemberley. You would stay the summer, and go to town with her, and at Christmas we would come to fetch you and celebrate the season with her and Darcy. Tell me, you and Lizzy have never been close — would you go to her out of a desire to increase your sisterly bond or would you go because of a desire to be in the orbit of Darcy's wealth and influence?'

Mary thought for a moment. To be sure, she was intimidated by Darcy, but she also liked him — he conversed with her gravely and heard her opinions. She thought that even if he didn't agree with her, he would still hear what she had to say. And Lizzy — it wasn't that she didn't like her sister. But sometimes it was very tiring to be in company with Lizzy, who could have a sharp tongue and liked to make fun of everyone. Mary wondered sometimes why Lizzy could say the most shocking things, but when *she* observed some facet of human nature, everyone chorused, 'Oh *Mary.*'

She had been to Pemberley once before, and was astonished by the grandeur of the estate. She had remarked to Lizzy that one could not consider it a home, but rather a responsibility to live up to, and to her amazement, Lizzy had sighed and nodded.

She's lonely and wants her family. It was an astonishing thought, but it carried with it a kind of sense. Jane had her own household, and Kitty now was off to visit her. Even Lizzy's best friend Charlotte had a new baby to care for.

'I would like to go, Papa, for the first reason, and not the second, though I think Darcy is a fine kind of person and he and Bingley are my brothers now so I must like them. But I think you are right — Lizzy needs her family and I would like to go.' Another thought struck her. 'If you and Mama can spare me, of course.'

Her father laughed. 'I can, my dear, though you have become surprising to me in the last few weeks. I cannot imagine what changes a few months under the influence of your sister can bring. As for your mother, she can spare you though she will tell you she cannot — that is jealousy, so pay it no attention.'

Before Mary could ask him what he meant, he stood up. 'Then it is decided. You will go to visit your sister, and we will all be together again at Christmas. And we will see if being surrounded by ten thousand a year will turn your head as easily it has done everyone else's in this family.'

'Great wealth is as much a curse as it is a blessing, but I think that if one prepares oneself, one can resist temptation,' Mary said. She was already looking forward to the challenge. Her father looked doubtful.

'What? Not a ribbon or a silk stocking or a pretty bonnet to change your mind? We will see, Mary, if your great resolve is enough to keep you out of the gravest danger of greed and gluttony. But there — I send you to your sister, not to Brighton, so maybe you will manage to withstand the forces that all the fripperies in London will bring to bear.'

'You will see, Papa, I will not fail.'

At that he laughed and waved a hand at her to go. 'You go to visit your sister, not minister to heathens in the East, Mary. You are allowed a ribbon or two.'

5

It was decided that Mary would travel to Pemberley with her Uncle and Aunt Gardiner who often journeyed to Derbyshire to visit Lizzy. The Gardiners were special favourites of Darcy and Elizabeth, as they had been instrumental in overcoming the barriers the two young people had put up against each other. Both uncle and aunt dismissed the assertion as preposterous, but were secretly pleased that their niece and her husband thought, or pretended to think, that they had had a hand in their current happiness.

When they stopped at Longbourn, Mary gave her aunt and uncle a kiss and all her little cousins in turn, two lively girls of eight and ten, and two small boys. They were very happy to see her, for though she was not Jane, Mary was kind to her young cousins in a grave, solemn way. The children had never liked Lydia and Kitty, for they would often tease them and laugh at them.

'Why Mary, you look very well,' Mrs Gardiner exclaimed, giving her another kiss. Mary's complexion was clear and pink and her brown eyes bright. Mrs Gardiner noticed that her middle niece had lost the scowl that perpetually drew her mouth into a down-turned line, and the plain blue frock she wore gave an added brightness to her expression.

'It is so good to see you, Aunt,' Mary replied. Her uncle crushed her into a hug.

'Good to see you, my dear girl,' he said in his bluff and hearty way. 'It's about time you got out from behind a book. How are you? Enjoying your solitude, I hear?'

'Somewhat,' she replied judiciously, for she had been thinking lately about her current aloneness. So often before her sisters had gone away had she wished for solitude. 'I had not realized how much I would miss my sisters now they are gone. Family are so important to one, but we don't ever know how much until we are separated.'

'No, we don't,' Mr Gardiner said, smiling, well used to Mary's ways. 'Well, now you go off to enjoy the delights of Pemberley and Lambton, and I am sure you will have much to tell us when we see you again at Christmas.'

At the mention of Christmas the little cousins all put up a clamour about their favourite Christmas puddings and songs, games and gifts, until Mr Gardiner had laughingly to threaten them with no puddings and no games unless they could refrain from deafening them all. In the hubbub Mr Bennet greeted his wife's brother and they conversed while helping to transfer Mary's trunk and cases into the carriage. In the meantime Mary and Mrs Gardiner and Mrs Bennet let the children run to give themselves the patience to withstand the rest of the journey. As they walked they chatted, with Mrs Bennet giving Mrs Gardiner the news of Longbourn and Meryton, unaware perhaps that Mrs Gardiner could take little interest in such news as she did not know any characters in the drama as Mrs Bennet recounted it. At her first opportunity, Mrs Gardiner turned to Mary and asked her if she looked forward to her journey.

'Mama was not happy at first that I was to go,' Mary admitted. 'And I do feel some guilt, but I think it might be better for us to separate now, for we can only feel our reunion that much more strongly.'

'Nonsense, Mary!' Mrs Bennet said. 'You will not miss me, for what is Longbourn compared to Pemberley?'

'It will be a lovely holiday,' Mrs Gardiner agreed. She raised her voice. 'No! Not in the farmyard!' The exuberance of the children proved too much for Mrs Bennet. She admonished Mary to not bore her aunt with her sermons, and hurried thankfully back to the house to see about luncheon.

'Now tell me dear, what of Lydia? Have you heard from her?'

Should I tell her? Mary wondered. She hesitated, then said, 'Kitty writes to her, but Lydia writes hardly ever in return, and when she does her notes are short and ill-presented. Lydia writes to Jane much oftener, but I think it is only to ask for money.'

Mrs Gardiner shook her head. 'Does Jane send any?' Mary just looked at her, and Mrs Gardiner sighed. 'Of course she does.' They both laughed a little, an unspoken *Dear Jane* between them. Mary felt a shade of pride that she and her aunt were sharing a conversation as between two grown women, not as between aunt and niece. Then Mrs Gardiner said, 'She shouldn't, though I fear that I don't know what is worse, that Jane supports them or that she does not.'

Mary puzzled over that for a moment, then she said, 'Do you mean . . . if Lydia does not get money from Jane, she and Wickham will do something . . . dishonourable?'

Mrs Gardiner nodded. 'We all feared, you know, that Lydia had gone on the town when she first disappeared from the Forsters. Her marriage is ill indeed, but at least we can be relieved that at least for now she is saved from that fate. Unless — I do not know what would make Mr Wickham honour his marriage vows once the money runs out.'

Mary felt a chill for her sister. 'How easily a woman falls,' she whispered. 'How narrow a path she must tread.'

Mrs Gardiner instantly felt a pang for talking so forthrightly to a young woman. 'Well,' she said awkwardly. 'Yes, to be sure, but Mary, remember, that goodness is in part chosen. Lydia was given all the advantages of respectable breeding and upbringing, and she chose to throw that all away for an irredeemable wastrel. *You* have nothing to fear. You have too much sense to lose your self-respect in a bad alliance.'

I don't know what I fear more, Mary thought, but could not say as much to her aunt. Losing my respectability . . .

Or never having the opportunity to prove myself.

★   ★   ★

With the carriages loaded, they all went back to the house and enjoyed a leisurely luncheon. A gentle rain had fallen that morning, but the afternoon was clear and bright, a little breeze sweeping in through the open windows. The children chattered, the men talked over business in their bass

50

voices, and Mary found herself taking part in all the conversations about her with an ease and joy. With the children she discussed kites and hoops, ponies and favourite trees to climb. With Mrs Gardiner she listened as the older woman discussed her roses and her favourite flowers in her garden. She listened to her father and uncle as they easily conversed on the business of town and country and ventured once or twice to make a small comment. They listened in turn and she felt gratified at their attention. Even her mother was less impatient than usual. It was somehow easier to converse when one didn't have to wait for a chance to impress. Here were only her father, her mother, her aunt and uncle, and their children. With what ease Mary was able to carry on a sensible conversation without attempting to over-awe her companions. In the first place, the children would be insensible to it, and in the second, as she had become acutely aware, her elders would not be insensible enough.

At last they finished their meal and took their leave. Mary gave her mother and father a hug and a kiss before climbing into the carriage with the Gardiners.

'Be good, daughter,' came Mr Bennet's gruff good-bye. 'Remember, you may have as many ribbons as you want, for I know you of all my daughters will not let it go to your head.'

Mary tucked herself inside and waved to him as they rattled on their way. When at last she pulled her head back inside the carriage, tightly packed as they were, she thought to herself scornfully, ribbons! Her father certainly seemed preoccupied with them.

She pulled herself together and settled in for the long journey.

★　★　★

Their welcome at Pemberley was everything the travellers could wish for. Lizzy and Darcy and Georgiana waited to meet them at the top of the drive where their tired horses pulled up in front of the great house. The children tumbled out of the coach; Mr and Mrs Gardiner and Mary followed more sedately.

Mary threw back her head to look up at the house, tilting up the brim of her modest bonnet. It was not the first time that the Bennets had been to visit Pemberley, but the beauty of the house never failed to strike Mary, who found herself conscious of its age and dignity. This house is almost human, with a great character, rather as if it were a statesman, or a king, she thought. She resolved to write down all of her flights of fancy during her visit, for she was sure that she would be inspired by her surroundings.

The children and her aunt and uncle were still greeting Lizzy and Darcy, but Georgiana caught her eye. The young girl smiled and bowed, and Mary bowed in return. Georgiana was the same age as Lydia and Kitty, but she was so shy and stiff that Mary had barely exchanged a few words with her.

'Hello,' Mary said awkwardly, wondering whether they would exchange a sisterly kiss. Georgiana blushed but she held out her hand. 'I am so pleased that you've come,' she said, as if she had to force the words past her lips.

'Thank you. I am happy to be here,' Mary said. This was so hard! She could not think of anything else to say. *Your house is lovely?* Mary thought that everyone must tell Georgiana that. Desperately she cast about for some conversation, when Darcy came over to stand by his sister. His smile was not forced but grave, as he always was. Mary was intimidated by her new brother. How she remembered with sharp embarrassment her own attempt to attract him when he first came to their little town with Mr Bingley. She had no charms except for the piano and her voice, which even then she knew were inadequate to the task. She remembered hoping that he would be impressed by her knowledge of music and its delights. Now she hoped his memory was not as keen as her own.

'Miss Mary, I trust your journey was not too fatiguing.' Still solemn, he bowed.

'Not any more than can be helped,' she said.

Lizzy broke away at last from the little cousins and came and took Mary's hand.

'Oh Mary, do not try to converse with him, the two of you will be miserable exchanging small talk.' She gave Mary a hug, held her tight, and Mary held her back. They were not often affectionate, but this time Mary felt certain that her sister had been missing her. 'Come, you can rest after your travels, for I know how cramped a carriage can be. Come, all of you, into the house, and we can talk to our heart's content in more comfort than on the drive!'

Mary watched her sister as they all trooped in, still a chattering, conversing group. Lizzy looked much the same — after all she had been married scarcely a year. But her conversation had lightened, become less teasing, less likely to draw blood, she thought. Perhaps marriage had softened her edges. The thought unnerved her — was the old Lizzy gone?

She felt someone looking at her and looked

over at Georgiana, who by virtue of the large group now walked next to her. Fortunately she remembered something about the girl from the last time they met.

'Do you still play piano?' Mary ventured. Georgiana smiled with relief.

'Yes, as often as I can. Your sister is very kind — she says she enjoys listening to me play.'

At that Mary felt a pang of jealousy — how often had Lizzy impatiently said to her, 'For goodness' sake, Mary, leave off!'

Georgiana went on, 'But you play, too, and sing. We must play together. It will be so much fun.'

Mary opened her mouth but could not speak under a rush of so many memories and new feelings. How could she claim to play when she hadn't touched a piano for weeks? And she remembered the last time she had sung in front of Darcy and Bingley and the rest. Would that she had never become so self-aware!

'I — I don't,' she said awkwardly. Georgiana looked at her and, with the idea that she had been mistaken, her colour stained her cheeks in another blush. Mary tried to explain but she couldn't. 'I stopped,' she concluded lamely, just as they reached the doors.

'Oh,' said Georgiana. The two of them

turned away from one another, discomfited.

Their conversation had involved only each other and had been conducted under the guise of the general chatter, but somehow in all the confusion, Lizzy must have heard. She turned and looked at Mary, her expression one of surprise and confusion. Mary ducked her head and hurried past. She would rather not explain that she thought she could not bear to play and be compared to Georgiana Darcy, due to inherit £30,000 and the adulation of society. Georgiana was judged to be quite accomplished, she knew, and she, Mary Bennet, had only small accomplishments to her name, and those were of little consequence, even to her family and her circle of acquaintance. She could not let herself be compared to Georgiana Darcy for she would only come up wanting.

She knew what Fordyce would say. He would write that she should accept with humility her limitations and be a true lady, meek and mild. Something within Mary rebelled. I don't want to be humble, she thought. I want to be known as accomplished. I want to be known for doing something no one has ever done before. If I am not supposed to have these feelings and these ambitions, why was I given them?

As she followed the others into the house, Fordyce was silent on the matter.

6

Mary's feelings of discontent waned gradually over her stay. Lizzy, Darcy, and Georgiana made her feel very welcome, and the house was so grand that it was like living in a palace. Mary's room was larger than all the bedrooms at Longbourn combined, and she had her own sitting room if she wanted.

'We have no shortage of rooms here — sometimes I wonder at the architect,' Lizzy said tartly as they took tea with Georgiana in Lizzy's own parlour. It was a little smaller than the others and more welcoming, and Mary smiled when she saw some bits of furniture and old things from Longbourn that Lizzy had brought for her own use. A faded footstool, upon which Mary now had her slippered feet, a vase in the shape of a somewhat chipped and battered dryad, and some little boxes and pillows now adorned the room.

'I did not know that they had been removed from home until I saw them here,' she murmured. 'What did Mama say?'

Lizzy smiled and did her best to imitate their mother's flustered tones. 'Lizzy! You surely do not intend to take all these old things to Pemberley!'

'I like them,' Georgiana said stoutly. 'I am very glad you brought them because they are very sweet.' She wrinkled her nose, looking much younger than her seventeen years. 'They remind me of you, Lizzy.'

'What, old and faded and chipped?' Lizzy laughed and, after a moment of shock, so did Georgiana. Mary could see that she was still not used to her new sister.

'It is good to be reminded of home, I think, but also not to dwell too much on it,' Mary said. 'One must get used to one's new situation.'

Lizzy looked at her again with that same half-puzzled expression, but she let Mary's comment pass, and the women discussed other things. But later, when Lizzy took her for a walk outside in the grounds, she said to Mary.

'Do you think that I am unhappy here?'

They faced one another at the end of a long greensward, the wind whipping at the tendrils of hair peeking out beneath their bonnets. Mary took a long time to reply, wondering what to say.

'You seem different,' she said at last. 'You used to be more light-hearted.'

'Oh Mary,' Lizzy said, but it was not with

the usual tones that Mary was used to. Lizzy was almost crying. 'I am not unhappy. I am so happy with Darcy that sometimes I cannot sleep at night for fear I will wake up and it will be all a dream. I do miss my family, though and I do miss Longbourn. That is why I brought those little ornaments with me, not to remind me of home because I hate Pemberley, but because I *am* Longbourn, just as those things are, and they, and I, have become Pemberley, and so does Pemberley become Longbourn.'

Mary had been holding her breath. At the end of Lizzy's speech she expelled it with a small gasp. 'Oh Lizzy,' she said. 'I thought — what if you were not happy here? I didn't know what to think. I came because I thought you missed Longbourn so much and I was the only sister who could comfort you.'

This time Lizzy was speechless. 'Oh,' she said at last, softly, and in that word Mary knew she had been mistaken.

'Then, why did you want me to come?' If it was not for Lizzy's sake what had been the reason?

Lizzy took her hand. 'I feel I may have behaved very badly,' she said, and her expression was merry again. 'Please do not hate me, Mary, for it is Jane's fault.'

'Jane?' This was becoming stranger and

stranger. What had Jane to do with Mary coming to Pemberley?

'We felt you needed a respite from Longbourn. Kitty and Mama let drop some small hints without knowing it that you were at a loose end, so we conspired to bring you here.'

No small bit of outrage stiffened Mary's back. 'What did they say?!'

'Nothing ill, just that you seemed at odds with yourself. And then, when you arrived, you told Georgiana that you didn't play any more. Mary, music was your solace. What has happened?'

Lizzy looked at her intently. Mary found tears coming into her eyes and she forced them back; then, impatiently, she wiped them furiously with a small scrap of handkerchief.

'Sometimes, Lizzy, one can practise and practise and still not become accomplished. And even if one is pronounced accomplished in a very small society, it is not much compared to a grander set. So there. I don't miss it one bit, you know.'

Lizzy let her sister compose herself, knowing that any expression of sympathy would only cause Mary to become quite overset. When she felt that enough time had passed she glanced over at the younger woman. Mary's nose was red but otherwise she had calmed herself. Lizzy said gravely, 'Society — true society — doesn't vary, whether it is small or grand. You should not let imagined censure close you off from something you love and that gives the world a little pleasure.'

Mary sniffed and smiled a watery smile. 'It doesn't give me pleasure any more. So I will refrain from playing.'

'Of course,' Lizzy said. She knew that was the end of it for now. She patted her sister's arm, and they continued their walk in silence.

★ ★ ★

The days at Pemberley drifted through the summer. Darcy often had business in town or on the estate, but Lizzy made sure that she and he had time together alone, either walking or taking the carriage about. Lizzy did not ride but would drive a little phaeton and pony as Darcy rode his favourite horse in the grounds. Once Mary watched them as they came back from one such time together, Lizzy with her hand on Darcy's arm, and Darcy bent protectively over Lizzy as they walked and conversed. She wondered then how she could have thought Lizzy was unhappy. Darcy, too, was as grave as ever, but all he had to do was look upon Lizzy and his face lightened with joy.

Georgiana and Mary drew close, although as Mary already had four sisters she was not sure she was ready for another. Still, Georgiana was a good girl who at first was quiet and then, when Mary grew more acquainted, showed a mischievous streak. Georgiana tried to hide this from her brother, who looked upon her with a kind of grim foreboding, as if he expected his sister to perform some extraordinary frisk. Georgiana was quite different with Mary from what she was with her brother or Lizzy, and Mary rather liked her vivacity.

Though Georgiana was accounted most accomplished, she also liked reading, though her taste tended towards the wilder sort of poetry and novels. She pressed her favourite volume in Mary's hands, and dubiously, Mary began it. Half-scandalized and half-enraptured, she read it quickly, lest she be found with it by Lizzy or Darcy. She wondered what Mr Collins would think, and then she thought, Fie on Mr Collins! She laughed to think of his shocked expression and his expressions of dour censure. What would he think, of her having received a novel from Georgiana Darcy, of all people? Still, she hastened to finish the book and give it back to Georgiana.

Then they discussed it for hours, Mary's dark head and Georgiana's fair one close together as they reread their favourite parts. What adventures young Catherine had in *Northanger Abbey*! And for the first time, Mary thought it might be fine to meet a young man in the assembly rooms in Bath, even if he didn't have a stern father or a scandalous elder brother.

'I like this one better than *The Mysteries of Udolpho*,' Georgiana said. 'Catherine seems more like us, as if the author knows what a girl really was like. But Udolpho is quite frightening. I couldn't shut my eyes for several nights after I read it.' She trembled with the memory of the delicious fright.

Novels, Fordyce said, were unfit for expanding a young woman's horizons. They turned a female away from her true study and excited emotions unacceptable in a genteel lady.

'*The Mysteries of Udolpho*,' Mary said. 'I have heard of it. I'd like to read that one next.'

★ ★ ★

Pemberley was not as lively a household as Bingley's could be. There, Jane and Bingley entertained often, and it seemed sometimes as if all the young people of the neighbour-hood gathered at the house nightly for an informal assembly. No, at Pemberley, Lizzy and Darcy kept a quieter household, though they enjoyed entertaining guests and visiting in their turn.

One morning Darcy took Lizzy's hand, a gesture that Mary often found both puzzling and disquieting — it was such a proper display of affection yet it held such a private meaning.

'Lizzy,' he said, 'Do you remember meeting Tom Aikens? He has written to me saying he is coming to stay in the village on business, but has expressed a wish to visit us.'

'I do remember,' Lizzy said. 'He is from ——shire, is that not so? A fine horseman?'

Georgiana gave a sudden laugh. 'I remember! He was such a funny young man! How he made me laugh! I scarce could keep up with him, he would talk and talk on all manner of topics.'

Tom Aikens was a young man of not more than two-and-twenty, of respectable family. The recent death of his father had left him the inheritor of a small estate, which he was ambitious enough to expand in all ways possible, instead of merely squandering its wealth, as many young men with lesser drive were wont to do. He had a great interest in horses and would talk of almost nothing else to anyone who would listen.

'Be prepared, Mary,' Georgiana said to her. 'For he will talk to you of nothing but horses, hunting, and racing. He cannot sit still but must always be moving. It is a wonder he can sit still in the saddle.'

'Oh,' Mary said. 'He sounds alarming.' To herself she thought he was precisely the sort of young man who was rowdy and boisterous and had nothing to do with quiet young women such as herself. Therefore she would not care to meet him, for he would not care to meet *her*.

Mr Aikens was true to his reputation, for soon all of the little village at the foot of Pemberley's estate were talking of the young gentleman who rode a fine black horse and thought nothing of jumping over all the hedges all across the country. It was as if a wind blew behind him at all moments. There was talk of nothing but Mr Aikens at all the social gatherings in the county and though Mary had yet to meet him, she found herself already tired of him.

'For goodness' sake, Lizzy,' she remarked with some exasperation one morning as they made their way through the village's crowded little high street, 'It is as if no one like Mr

Aikens has ever visited us before. What will become of us when he leaves?'

'I almost wish he would,' said Lizzy, half under her breath, nodding cordially to a neighbour. 'Then we might have some peace. But you know how it is to live in such a small town. When there is little that happens, everything becomes such a to-do. At least it is just one Mr Aikens and his black horse and not a regiment of officers.'

Mary surprised herself by giving a laugh. 'He is likely to cause less trouble, even if he gallops about so intemperately on horse-back.'

Lizzy gave her a smile in return. 'I wonder why we ladies of Longbourn never learned to love horses. I never was a good enough horsewoman to enjoy the exercise, and I think Jane learned only enough to stay on.'

'I remember our dear little pony,' Mary said. She had never forgotten the small brown horse, with his black mane and tail and mischievous temper. He would bite if one wasn't careful, but he smelled of oats and was fat and comfortable when one of the girls begged a ride from the grooms on the farm.

'Yes, but I also remember that he mistook my straw bonnet for his luncheon. Do you remember how Mama screamed when she saw that he had chewed his way through my ribbons and was fairly on his way to my hair?'

'Is that why he was banished to the Lucases? You traitor! I liked him. Once Leigh let me ride him by myself through the fields.'

'Yes, and he abandoned you halfway through a wet swale after being frightened by a covey of grouse.'

Mary wiped tears of laughter from her eyes. 'Oh dear. Mr Aikens will find us wanting, I think.'

Lizzy suddenly tightened her hand on Mary's arm. 'Sooner than you think, Mary. Look.' She nodded up ahead at them. There was a crowd of men and horses, and a hubbub of conversation. One young man sat on his black horse speaking to the rest, his pose casual as his horse danced nervously in the street. He wore a tall hat on his curly brown hair, and his coat was grey with a considerable amount of dirt upon it. The effect was compounded by muddy boots, as if he had been trampling about in wet fields, but there was no denying that he was a horseman of great prowess. He never moved, and controlled his horse with almost imperceptible effort.

'Oh,' Mary said with some surprise. It was not only the sight that he presented that was engaging. She knew him. He had been the young man at the Lucases who had asked her to dance, only to have Maria Lucas claim him instead.

She became overwhelmed with nervousness. She wondered whether he would remember her, told herself that he could not possibly; she was surprised at herself that she even remembered him, she had such a small glimpse of him and their conversation had been so brief. Is it he? she thought. It hardly seems likely. To be sure, she made a little moue, just as he looked at them over the crowd. Mary had the self-knowledge to realize that he would think she was scowling at him and felt her colour rise. She wanted to turn away, but he lifted his hat and Lizzy curtsied. Mary followed suit hastily. Lizzy threw her a quick glance, wanting to see what made her act so strangely. She had no time to explain. Mr Aikens dismounted and led his horse over to them, the crowd parting to let him pass.

'Mrs Darcy,' he said. 'A pleasure to see you again, ma'am.' He shook Lizzy's hand and then bowed to Mary.

'Mr Aikens, it is indeed a pleasure to see *you*. May I introduce my sister, Miss Mary Bennet?' Lizzy said. Mary curtsied again as he bowed. When he looked at her he narrowed his eyes for a moment, his expression at once aloof and searching. It unnerved her, so she spoke quickly.

'Mr Aikens, you may not remember, but we have met.'

With Lizzy staring at her as if she had lost her mind, Mary was about to remind him of their first meeting, when he broke into a smile.

'I knew it!' he cried. 'At Lucas Lodge! I thought I remembered you. I could not for the life of me remember where I had seen you, though.'

Mary was conscious of a great relief and pleasure. He had remembered her, and it appeared that the memory was not at all painful. 'Capital!' he went on, 'for the Greys have said they are planning a private ball and are inviting all the neighbourhood. You will be able to play for the assembly!'

Mary's smile froze. Mr Aikens went on, oblivious to her dismay. 'What do you think of my horse? I've named him Hyperion. All of my horses are named after the gods. It suits them, don't you think?'

With Lizzy cautiously patting the horse's gleaming neck, Mary took a breath and tried to regain her calm. He could not have known how his words had stung, but she could not help but feel the pain. She felt an unhappy fluttering in her stomach. She wondered why her mother seemed to enjoy feeling like this.

As Mr Aikens and Lizzy discussed the merits of his horse, or rather, Mr Aikens talked and Lizzy nodded and tried to put a word in edgeways, Mary took the opportunity to pet the animal's mane. The horse, so much bigger than the pony of her childhood, turned his head to look at her. He breathed with a snort out of large nostrils, and his ears cocked forward at her. She knew little of horses except that this one seemed calm and happy to see her. She held out her hand to him and he blew on it.

'He likes you,' Mr Aikens said, breaking off his conversation with Lizzy in mid-sentence. 'He is a great judge of character. I turn to him for his opinion on all of my acquaintance.'

'You rely on his judgement? What if he is easily swayed by oats and apples?' Lizzy said, smiling.

Mr Aikens scoffed. 'A man would be more easily led. No, Hyperion recognizes breeding and true gentleness and is not to be bribed. His good opinion is absolute.'

Lizzy laughed, delight in her eyes. 'Does he ever change his mind?'

Mr Aikens pretended to consider that. 'No, I believe he is right the first time. It makes it much easier for me, you see. I simply observe to whom he gives his approval and follow suit.'

70

Mary said, 'No human fallibility then, can mar his judgement. How happy men would be could they always be so right.'

'No offence to Hyperion's excellent judgement,' Lizzy said, 'But I have it on good authority that at least one man is relieved that his first opinion was trumped by a second.'

'But horses can have no such regrets,' Mr Aikens said. He smiled. 'At least I think they do not, and on that point, Hyperion has not been able to enlighten me.'

'If God had given them the gift of speech, they would not be animals,' Mary said.

'And perhaps it is just as well,' Mr Aikens said. 'I fear God's judgement but I think that animals would have more to say about man's perfidy against them.'

Mary was shocked by this blasphemy and said no more as Mr Aikens and Lizzy conversed. In the end, Lizzy invited him to dinner that night, and Mr Aikens accepted. They parted company, continuing their little excursion down the village high street while Mr Aikens remounted his horse and rode off on the rest of his errands.

'A most unusual man,' Mary said at last. 'I hardly know what to make of him.'

'But you met him before,' Lizzy said. 'How was it you did not tell us?'

'I had not ever learned his name,' Mary

admitted. 'You know how it is at the Lucases. One scarcely has time for introductions before all are off in a frenzy of activity, whether it is dancing or cards or some other game.'

'He remembered you,' Lizzy said, and there was a mischievous light in her eye.

Mary blushed. What was Lizzy scheming? 'As I was the only girl at the piano, I was easy to remember.'

She rather liked the idea but had to hide a pinch of disappointment when Lizzy said, 'Ah, that must be it.'

Mary turned away, pretending to adjust her glove. 'He is a fine young man, to be sure. But I would be surprised if he opened a book, and the way he spoke about his horse! One must not give to animals the attributes of mankind — it is blasphemous, Lizzy.'

'He was funning, Mary.'

Was he? Mary knew she had little experience with men, and even less with men of Mr Aikens' stripe. Had she misunderstood? She stared after the departing Mr Aikens, still in sight for, though there was much traffic along the street, he sat so high.

'Anyway,' she said, mostly to herself, 'Mr Aikens and myself are as ill-suited as you and Mr Collins would be.' Then Mary heard what she had just spoken out loud and wished she could take the words back. Now Lizzy would think that she thought of Mr Aikens *in those terms*. But Lizzy said only,

'No couple can be as ill-suited as that,' Lizzy said. 'I won't allow the possibility.' She took Mary's arm and they continued their slow promenade down the village street.

7

Mary was not required to play the piano for the Greys' party after all, as they had engaged a small ensemble of musicians to provide music for dancing. For the first time in years, Mary would be required to dance. She steeled herself, laid out her best gown on her bed and sat and stared at it. No matter what she did, she could not make herself handsome. She was thin, her complexion plain, her features unremarkable. Her eyes had not that beauty that other unremarkable young women could claim, and her hair was thin and could not hold a curl. And where Jane was accounted a great beauty, Lizzy noticed for her vivacious character and fine eyes, and Kitty and Lydia for their youth and good humour, Mary had no saving grace by which to distinguish herself. Society looks for attributes in others with which to please itself and rewards the owners thereby; Mary neither smiled nor spoke prettily and was judged accordingly.

Perhaps I am unwell, she thought hopefully, but she had nothing, not even a headache. Still, she thought of crying off but she knew that it was likely that Lizzy would want to stay at home with her. Mary sighed.

'It is my trial,' she said to her pretty room. 'I must meet it with all the strength and courage I can muster. I will simply say that I do not dance.'

She summoned up her severest expression. If she took her little book of sermons, perhaps she could make it clear that Mrs Darcy's younger sister was to be taken quite seriously.

For a few moments Mary indulged in a little daydream, one that had given her solace before. She is at a ball, and all are dancing, she alone reads from her little book. A young man, serious as she, perhaps a curate who had just got a living, sees her and asks what she is reading . . .

A rap at the door caught her attention and she sat up.

'Come in!' she called out, her voice wavering with a bit of fright that she had been caught out in her little dream.

It was only Lizzy; her sister peeped round the corner and came in.

'I came to see if you needed help to dress. Oh, that is a lovely colour,' she said of Mary's blue gown. 'It will suit you quite well.'

'It is very plain,' Mary agreed.

Lizzy cocked her head. 'Yes, it is, but it suits you, and we can ornament it with a few small pearls. Would you like me to help you with your hair?'

'I can manage a simple plait,' Mary said stiffly. She wanted to scream. *Don't turn me into a peacock!*

Lizzy looked as if she would protest, then nodded. 'Still, I will send in my maid. She can make a very pretty plait for you and you will see — it will suit you as well as the gown. I promise.' She smiled and closed the door behind her, and Mary turned back to her gown.

She rarely went to balls outside Meryton; that society had been all she had known prior to that summer. She could not make herself handsome, and her best blue gown would look nothing like the gowns of her sister and Georgiana. *I am poor Mary Bennet, a country relation,* she thought. *If there is any consolation, it is that none will pay any attention to me.*

True to her word, Lizzy sent in her maid. The girl braided Mary's hair, chattering on about how pretty her nut-brown tresses were, and pinned them up like a crown on her head.

'Ooh, that looks lovely, miss,' she said. 'Let me make it fancy for you, now. Just you wait.' She fashioned small curls around Mary's forehead and her temple to frame her face.

Then she handed her the looking-glass. Mary was pleased. She did not look like a peacock. Somehow in the light and with the curls her face was rounder and softer, but she still looked like herself.

'Those are pretty ear-bobs, miss,' the maid said.

'Thank you,' Mary said. The small pearl earrings had belonged to Mr Bennet's mother and were old-fashioned and simple. Just like me, Mary thought. She stood. Her blue gown was plain, but it had lace at the collar and a satin ribbon at the high waist, and little flowers embroidered along the sides and the hem. Her slippers matched her gown, and their little heels and buckles gleamed. She gathered her light wrap over her arms and pulled on her long gloves, borrowed from her sister.

The maid curtsied, and Mary took a deep breath and went off to meet her fate.

★   ★   ★

The Greys welcomed Mr and Mrs Darcy and Georgiana as befitted the leading family of the neighbourhood, and they were kindly to Mary as well. She thought once, longingly, of her little book of sermons, waiting for her on her dressing-table, and then resolutely turned her thoughts to what lay before her.

When they found seats Lizzy leaned toward her and under cover of the noise of music and dancing she said,

'There. You see? There is nothing to it.'

'Indeed,' Mary said. 'The society at Pemberley is much the same as at Meryton. People are gay or not as their nature dictates, and are as fond of dancing as anywhere. I think it would be strange if it were otherwise.'

'Oh, perhaps in India or China, or even in the colonies you might find different customs, but not more than thirty miles from home, I imagine not,' Lizzy said.

They did not sit quietly for long. Georgiana was much in demand among the younger set. Mary watched her sister and Darcy as Georgiana amused herself. Every time his sister changed partners, Darcy stiffened and his face hardened. Lizzy glanced up at him and touched his arm as if to tell him, *I am here, there is no worry,* but he scarcely seemed to notice.

He does not like his sister to dance, Mary thought, and she wondered why. The young men all seemed perfectly amiable, rather like the young men of Meryton. And there is not an officer to be found, she thought, lowering her gaze to hide a smile behind the pretence of adjusting her wrap. She stayed her hand at the thought. Was *that* what Darcy feared?

That his beloved sister would follow the wayward example of his sister-in-law? Mary bit back anger. Are the Bennets made to answer for all of woman's folly? she thought. She wondered how Lizzy could stand such censure if that were the case.

'There you are,' said Mr Aikens. He bowed, and Mary and Lizzy rose and curtsied to him. He wore an evening coat on this occasion, and his boots had had the mud knocked off them, but they were the same boots. Out of the corner of her eye Mary saw Lizzy hide a smile, and hoped the young man did not see. He would think she was mocking him, but Mary knew Lizzy and recognized her appraisal of his easy manner.

'How do you do, Mr Aikens?' Lizzy said. 'How is your business in town?'

'Very well, thank you,' he said. 'I cannot think a day better spent than in riding about the countryside and then attending a ball in the evening.'

'To many it would be rather tiring,' Mary put in, meaning to add that she approved of such activity when so many others would choose indolence, but she could not finish the rest of her thought before he interrupted.

'Not at all! I find it invigorating. A fellow would rather fall asleep after a day inside at cards or conversation. It makes me very low to have nothing to do and only to sit about with only a modicum of exercise.'

As that had been the pattern of much of the ladies' day there was an awkward pause. Mary was struck by the thought, not previously entertained, that perhaps her unquietness of spirit came about because she had too little to do. Before she could explore the idea further, Mr Aikens turned to Lizzy.

'Mrs Darcy, would you think me very forward if I asked you to dance?'

Lizzy looked at first surprised, then she smiled. 'I would not think you forward at all, but you see, I am keeping my sister company, and I am waiting to stand up with Mr Darcy when he is finished dancing with his sister.'

'Of course. I had heard you were a capital dancer, and I thought it would be great fun to have one dance.'

Lizzy thanked him for the compliment. Mary kept her attention out at the swirl of dancers, the women's gowns intermingling with the sombre black coats of the men in a most mesmerizing fashion. It doesn't matter, she thought. I do not like him and he does not like me. If Jane were here he would fall in love with her. As it is, he is in love with Lizzy, of course. And if she dares to mention that he could dance with me as second best I shall . . . I shall . . .

She didn't finish the thought.

'Miss Bennet?' he said. 'Then perhaps you will do me the pleasure?'

Mary's mouth opened and she was conscious of heat rising into her cheeks. 'I — ' she began faintly, but once again he did not let her finish.

'I know that you don't usually dance, but that is because you play,' he said. 'Except here you are not playing, and not dancing, and so . . . ?'

He looked at her very earnestly. Mary looked at Lizzy for help. Her sister nodded the tiniest bit. Mary grabbed on to all of her courage and mumbled an assent.

'Good!' He took her hand. 'Just in time, for this dance is ending and we have time to find our positions for the next.'

It had been so long since she had danced that she was a bit stiff at first, but she soon felt at ease with the familiar music. She was not permitted to manage the figures with more comfort for long. Mr Aikens danced much as he did anything, without stopping and with a great enthusiasm. Mary found herself alternately laughing and scandalized at his performance. Everyone would be looking at them! Soon others in their set were laughing as well, and all of the couples swung their partners with abandon. Mary could almost not keep up but the fun was infectious. Years of reserve were broken down in minutes of lively music. Mary breathed hard at the end of the dance, and she curtsied to his bow with a happy smile as the musicians ended with a flourish. Mr Aikens clapped happily, and all of the couples laughed and clapped as well. One young lady opposite Mary, her complexion roses on milk and her brown curls dishevelled, said to Mary, 'La! I have such a stitch in my side! What fun!'

Mary could only agree while at the same time marvelling. Dancing with a young man, and conversing with another young lady! Perhaps this was why people enjoyed rather than endured assemblies and balls.

Mr Aikens took her by the hand. 'Capital!' he said. He smiled at her. 'Hyperion didn't lie, you see.'

'Hyperion! Your horse tells you whom to dance with?'

Mr Aikens grinned. 'Oh, remember, he is just a dumb animal to whom God has not granted speech. But he whispers it to me, like this.' The last two words were spoken straight into her ear in a whisper, as Mr Aikens dropped his head and put his lips close to her ear. Mary stood straight, rigid with shock at the feel of his warm breath. She could scarcely look at him, as the next dance started straight away, the warmth of the exercise not accounting for the colour in her cheeks.

She hardly knew what to do with herself then. The dancing began again and she took his hand, conscious of his strong fingers around her hand. He tightened his grip as they swung through the steps and a little bit of the abandon she had sought came to her. Mary was conscious of her hair flying free around her face and her gown making each turn a small dance in itself. At the end of that dance she curtsied hurriedly and almost ran back to Lizzy before he could make her dance another.

Lizzy had gone. Their seats had been taken by another couple and she stopped in bemusement as they looked up at her with surprise, and, she thought, some disfavour. Mary curtsied again, stiffly, and made her way to a small anteroom with as much decorum as she could muster.

She sat at the pretty little window seat, telling herself she needed some air. Where had Lizzy gone? She craned her neck to see her in the narrow view she had of dancing in the ballroom. Couples swirled by the doorway, but none of them revealed Lizzy. She calmed a little, wondering why she had reacted so strongly to Mr Aikens's partnering.

It was hardly a liberty, to whisper something in a friend's ear — except that they were not friends, only acquaintances, having just been introduced. He was certainly lively, but not indecorous. She shivered a little at the memory of his whisper at her ear. She stood and took a deep breath. She resolved to go back into the ballroom and when they crossed paths again she would simply say nothing about it. It's not a lie of commission, she thought. It will do us both a favour, just to say nothing of it ever again, for he would be embarrassed to find out how much he embarrassed me, and I would not want to make him think ill of himself.

Mary ventured back into the ballroom and was enveloped in heat and light and music all at once. Someone came up and grabbed her sleeve, laughing. It was Georgiana.

'Mary! I saw you dancing with the alarming Mr Aikens,' she said, her expression bright. 'He dances as if he were riding to hounds. I thought I would have a fall at the fence.'

So he had danced with Georgiana too. Mary hid her pang.

'He was most energetic,' she agreed. 'Where is my sister?'

'Oh, they are in conversation with Mr Grey.' She nodded in their direction. 'This is such a wonderful night. I have danced almost all the dances so far, and this time my brother has not hovered over me. I think it is Lizzy's doing — she has made him forget his fears.'

Or at the least not act on them, Mary thought, remembering Darcy's still expression. She was almost about to ask Georgiana what Darcy had to fear about her dancing with a young man when a shadow passed over the young girl's face. 'I should not be exasperated with him,' she said. 'He is worried, and he has reason to be. It's just — he doesn't have to fear for me any more. Mary, sometimes I think he doesn't know how much I've grown up.'

Mary was about to venture the opinion that brothers rarely do know about their sisters, when she remembered that she had no brothers of her own to compare. At the Lucases, she knew that Maria and Charlotte's brothers took no more notice of their sisters than they did of their mother. Yet Darcy did not seem so careless. It was all confusing. Men were brothers, gentlemen, fathers — all so commonplace, yet one knew very little of them at all.

She heard a familiar voice rise up in indistinct conversation over the general commotion of dancing, music, and laughter. Both she and Georgiana looked over at Mr

Aikens, standing with a group of young men, laughing in rowdy tones.

The music finished with a flourish and there was much clapping and general cheer. Then in the din a small bell chimed, and the company began to file in to supper. Mary found a seat at a table next to her sister and family, but was conscious again of Mr Aikens at a table near them, deep in conversation with the others. As luck would have it they sat with their backs to each other, and Mary found it highly distracting to be so near him.

'So have you come to an opinion about this ball and its merits compared to those at Meryton?' Lizzy asked Mary.

'I think a ball is very like a ball anywhere,' she replied. Lizzy's expression was merry.

'Come now, Mary, I cannot believe you. You danced the liveliest set of them all. Surely this ball is better than any of those in Meryton?'

'But they are the same,' Mary insisted. *It is I who am different.* She went on, 'But I don't think we look for variety in our entertainment. If that is the sole purpose we quickly become jaded.' Mary paused, trying to collect her thoughts. 'I wonder whether balls should not always be the same, so that they become as comfortable and familiar as anything else.' Then a person would not have to build them up so, whether in anticipation or dread. It would just be a ball, and one could enjoy the dancing and the company.

'Well, I think they are great fun,' Georgiana declared. 'And if this one seems no different from the others in your experience, it is different in mine, if only because my brother has decided to let me dance.' She gave him a look full of impudence.

Darcy raised a brow at his sister. 'You have Lizzy to thank for that, Georgiana. She persuaded me that locking you up in the tower as you deserve would only give you delusions of persecution. Henceforth I ignore you for your own good.'

The whole table laughed at their teasing, and Mary felt a nudge at her back.

'I beg your pardon,' Mr Aikens said. He turned around and put his arm over the back of his chair most familiarly. 'But I could not let your opinion of this ball colour your opinion of all of them.' His eyes crinkled in a smile. 'This is the best one, for that is the way of it — they are always the best, until the next time.' He paused for effect. 'But no ball, no matter the music or the dancing or the pretty girls — ' he made sure to look at all of them each in turn, Mary too — 'can compare to riding to hounds on Christmas morning!'

He was booed good-naturedly by all who

heard him, and even Darcy took part in the teasing. Mary found herself laughing with the others.

★ ★ ★

It was late when they made their way back home to Pemberley. A ghostly half-moon was shrouded by thin clouds as the tired horses carried them back at a solid trot. When they reached the door and the footmen handed them out, one by one, Mary was so tired that she stumbled down a step. But with a strong hand the footman helped her up and she thanked him in a small voice.

It was hard to resist the urge simply to tumble into bed. Instead, Mary unpinned her hair and undressed, letting the maid help her as she sleepily pulled on her long comfortable nightdress. As she fell into bed, she thought that Mr Aikens was wrong. This ball was the best and no other party to follow would ever surpass it. She fell asleep to the memory of his hand holding hers, his warm breath, and the way he smiled at her at dinner.

For once, Mary Bennet had the attention of a most unsuitable suitor.

8

Dear Jane, Lizzy wrote. What do you think has happened? Mary danced at a ball. I could not have believed it myself had I not seen it. Even more surprising — she enjoyed herself, or I think she did. One young man paid her particular attention. I think he is quite kind, and means nothing by it, and I don't think Mary is the sort of girl who will break her heart over a young man who is rough around the edges, but the compliments will be good for her . . .

The letter went on with the usual discussion of the little news and doings of Pemberley, but concluded with Lizzy sending her love to Jane and Bingley, her attentions to Bingley's sister Caroline, and a last post-script:

PS. Oh. Mary has given up playing the piano. I don't know whether we should be concerned and I am not quite sure what has happened. But she seems quite comfortable and happy and so I must conclude that it is her choice and nothing dangerous. PPS. The young man is Mr Aikens. He is quite an original person with very high spirits and a great deal of vigour. Darcy speaks highly of him, and Mary even met him at the Lucases where she did play the piano.

Lizzy looked down at her letter, frowning over what she had written. All of it was simple enough. Mary had danced at a ball. She no longer played the piano. She had met a young man.

'There is a puzzle here,' she said out loud, as she folded the letter and addressed the outer sheet in her careful hand. 'But I cannot make it out.'

★　★　★

Unaware that she posed such a puzzle to her sister, that same morning Mary went out and about on a ramble over the grounds of Pemberley, *The Mysteries of Udolpho* in her hand for when she found the right place to stop and read. The day was fine and clear, but a light breeze made her glad of her little spencer jacket and her bonnet. She had grown used to walking about the park by herself, and two of the hunting dogs that lived in the stables attached themselves to her for the adventure. Pemberley had a fine expanse of parkland overlooking a rather small lake, from which drained a pretty little stream. Mary liked to walk along the lake, across the stone footbridge, and watch the swans and the ducks. Accordingly, she took herself that way, the dogs coursing in front of her with their noses to the dewy grass.

The sound of hoofbeats made her turn. Behind her galloped a horseman on a black horse. Mary's heartbeats quickened. It was Mr Aikens on Hyperion. He saw Mary and changed direction, coming towards her. The dogs all frisked and gambolled, for they knew that a horseman meant a fine ramble. When they got close enough, Hyperion half-reared at their antics. Mr Aikens simply sat in the saddle as if the horse stood still.

'Miss Bennet! How do you do?'

'Quite well,' she called back. 'But I fear that the dogs are too alarming for Hyperion's taste. And I don't know how to draw them off.'

'Nonsense. Hyperion is only being dramatic. He enjoys dogs, likes them as if they were brothers.'

With that, Mr Aikens jumped from the saddle, threw the reins over Hyperion's head and led the horse towards them. The dogs settled in behind.

Mary smiled, trying to control her nerves. 'How do you do, Mr Aikens?'

'Never better! I enjoy a fast ride over good ground. Darcy has some of the best turf in the country. Have to watch out for rabbit holes but I daresay he wouldn't allow a rabbit on his land. Hyperion jumped straight across country, not missing his stride.'

As he talked, he kept up a fast pace. The horse steamed wet at his side. Mary was hard put to keep up with him. She managed to look at him as they swept across the lawn towards the little bridge.

Mr Aikens wore an ill-fitting coat, and his face was ruddy from his exercise. His hair curled up around his ears, and he had not shaved that morning. He glanced down at the book in her hand.

'Oh! Do you like reading?'

The old Mary would have expounded at length on the virtues of a good book, one in which the liveliest plot was married to the most virtuous of morals. However, this book was one of Georgiana's novels. There was little about it that was virtuous, though it was lively. So she blushed and said only, 'Yes. I find it an amusing pastime.'

'Do you?' he said, as if thunderstruck. 'Do you? Why, that is the most unusual thing. I cannot sit still long enough, but must always be up and about. Can't read a book on the back of a horse.'

'No, I could not imagine doing so,' Mary agreed.

'Extraordinary, that some people like books so much they read them anywhere.'

Mary's embarrassment began to turn towards irritation. What on earth was so remarkable about a liking for books?

'I do like to read, Mr Aikens. I find it exercises the mind and can even enrich the soul, if it's the right book.' She thought of Fordyce's *Sermons* and how often she took comfort in the familiarity of its passages, the way it informed and reinforced her most decided opinions. He nodded at the book in her hand.

'So what is that one about?'

Oh dear. He had to ask. 'Oh,' she said, stumbling over the narrative. 'This one is rather more exciting than uplifting.' He waited with a keen expression, so she began to narrate the plot as best she could.

'It is about a girl who is beset on many sides by terrors both real and imagined. She is orphaned and sent to live with a relative who treats her with disdain and forces her to give up her inheritance. She has many adventures,' she concluded lamely.

'By Jove! How does she fare?'

'Oh, Mr Aikens, it's just a pretty little fiction. Emily St. Aubert doesn't exist at all.'

He looked thunderstruck. Mary was mortified. Had her correction insulted him? She was so unused to men!

She looked at him from the corner of her eye. He did not look angry, but pensive.

'So it is like a play,' he said at last. 'I like the theatre better than books, I own. Some actors are just splendid fellows and I like the plays with plenty of good swordfights, though you can tell that if those fellows really fought like that, well, they would be dead in a minute. Have you ever seen the play *Hamlet*?' At her quiet head-shake, he went on, 'Lots of thee-ing and thou-ing and I can't always understand it. But it ends with a capital swordfight, and that makes up for the rest.'

While Mary was made envious by his having seen one of the great tragedies, Mr Aikens went on in a more thoughtful tone. 'I sometimes try to read,' he admitted. 'But I must always be up and about. If I could just get past the first five minutes, I always think I will like the story, but the letters jump around so.'

'Perhaps I could read to you,' Mary suggested. She almost clapped her hand over her mouth. What was she thinking? Had she proposed reading from a romantic novel to a strange man?

Mr Aikens beamed. 'Read to me! Read to me! Why, who would have thought of such an idea! Capital idea! But first I must finish walking Hyperion out so that he's dry, you know. Can't leave him standing.'

When Mr Aikens had deemed that Hyperion was safe to let stand, after checking the horse's chest, they settled into a small shady spot under a tree at the edge of the field. Mr Aikens took off his coat to let her sit on it, and the dogs settled down, panting and smiling, waiting for the fun. Mr Aikens sat down with a most intent expression on his face so that Mary was a little alarmed. Since Mr Aikens had not read the book before, she started from the beginning.

On the pleasant banks of the Garonne, in the province of Gascony, stood, in the year 1584, the chateau of Monsieur St. Aubert . . .

She read with all the expressiveness she could muster, falling into the story with great anticipation. She almost felt as if they sat on the bank of the French river in Mrs Radcliffe's book, and Mary was very conscious of the young man sitting next to her on his coat. They were so close that their shoulders brushed against one another and she was highly sensible of his presence, sometimes so that she lost her place.

He managed to sit still for a page and a half before jumping to his feet, startling the dogs.

'There! That is all I am capable of, Miss Bennet! There were so many words, I just couldn't keep track of 'em. They jump about in my head just as much as they do on the page, and there you go, I must be off.'

Startled by his sudden action, Mary stared up at him. His expression showed distress, and he went on. 'Now I've disgusted you, just as I have my tutors and teachers.'

Mary endeavoured to assure him that she was not disgusted, but he shook his head. She remembered that she sat on his coat and got to her feet with haste. She picked it up and handed it to him. Dampness from the grass had penetrated through it to the skirt back of her gown though she had not felt it. She felt uneasy about walking home with a damp skirt, and hoped it would dry by the time she returned to the house.

Mr Aikens still looked downcast.

'I think it is a matter of practice,' she told him. For a moment both held on to the coat. 'Oh, do not put your coat back on, Mr Aikens, it's still quite damp. But I think that you cannot be expected to sit still all at once, just as I could not be expected to ride a horse without first being led about on a fat pony.'

Heedless of her warning about his coat, he shrugged into it anyway. 'But everyone else can learn to read and sit and listen,' said he. 'Why not I?'

Mary cast about through all of her learning but could not come up with an answer for him. 'I think,' she said at last, 'that we are what we are meant to be. And so long as we are good and kind to others, we should not allow our shortcomings in some areas to poison our enjoyment of others. I have often wished . . . ' she stopped, for she had come dangerously close to telling him what had been her heart's desire.

He looked at her, having forgotten his own frustration now that she had started telling him of hers.

'What?' he said with keen interest.

Mary blushed, and shook her head. 'It doesn't matter,' she told him. And though he teased her about it, she refused to say, and she even enjoyed the battle between them, because it wasn't often that a young man paid her so much attention that he would care about something she said, let alone did not say.

He gave up after a while, or perhaps grew tired of the game. Mary felt a pang. Had she proved too hard a challenge? And on the heels of that thought came another: had she been *flirting*?

Mr Aikens did not seem upset, just distracted, as he often was when he talked of many topics all in the same breath.

'Well, well, I see you will not tell me,' he said at last. 'You stand firm, Miss Bennet, you do indeed. I could not do it. I have no sense of constancy, except toward my beasts.' He gave her a look then, as if considering her in a new light. 'I hope you get your wish,' he said at last. 'You deserve it.'

They walked back to the house in silence then. He shook her hand when they arrived at the drive, and Mary curtsied and watched him mount up and ride off. The dogs set up barking and Hyperion shied sideways, but kept on going.

'Oh hush,' she told them crossly, and they wagged their tails apologetically. She sighed and went into the house.

It was good of Mr Aikens, but she would never get her wish, to be known as the accomplished, scholarly Miss Bennet. It would no more happen than it would that Mr Aikens could sit still. She would have to take her own advice. We are what we are meant to be, and if we are kind and good, then we should not let our shortcomings poison our accomplishments.

9

While the Darcys spent a quiet summer at Pemberley, it was not to be supposed that they were to be left in peace. For there was one person who had a particular interest in Pemberley and Longbourn, and a connection to both: Lady Catherine de Bourgh. An aunt of Darcy's, she had been used to having him at her beck and call. As the patroness of Mr Collins, she also took a great interest in the Bennets, and she was not sanguine about how one Bennet in particular had thwarted her hopes for her own daughter, Anne, who from birth had been destined for Pemberley. To Lady Catherine, Elizabeth Bennet had stolen Darcy from his rightful wife.

With Mr Collins as her go-between, she kept abreast of all the doings of the Bennets and the Darcys and even of the Bingleys, though that household meant little to her except in relation to her own sense of importance. She did not scruple to continue to demand Darcy's presence, sending letters by post and by the hand of her own footman in her own livery.

Darcy turned down her demands for a visit with the same demeanour that he presented to the world: a calm, measured one. After the fifth such letter, however, he turned to Lizzy. Silently he handed her Lady Catherine's demands, written in the lady's stilted, angular hand, and waited for her to read it. She did and passed it back to him.

'I feel a sort of frightening shiver,' she said, her small smile belying her words. 'Do you think she will do as she threatens?'

'I think she is entirely capable of doing so,' he said. 'She has always felt as if she owned Pemberley herself and has no qualms about arriving here unannounced. I think it is better to do as she requests — visit her at Rosings, rather than risk a visit here.'

Lizzy nodded. 'As for that, it will be easier to devise a reason to break off our visit than one to break off hers,' she said, her voice breaking into a laugh.' Her smile changed from mischievous to happy. 'And it will be very good to see Charlotte and her new baby. I will write to Charlotte to let her know we are coming, but you, my dear Mr Darcy, must write to Lady Catherine, as I know she will not receive a letter from me.'

★   ★   ★

Mary had only ever heard about Rosings from Mr Collins, Lizzy and Maria Lucas,

Charlotte's younger sister, but its charms had been so well described that she thought she was prepared for the magnificence of the estate. However, nothing could prepare her for the opulence in the very air about it. Every column, every bit of glazing in the windows, even the way the gravel in the drive gleamed as if it were made of crushed diamonds, all of it proclaimed an exalted self-regard. As their horses trotted up the drive in the afternoon sun, Mary wondered whether Rosings were the cause of Lady Catherine's puffed-up nature or a reflection of it.

Growing up here, how could one not become insufferable? She caught Lizzy's eye across the carriage and her sister gave her one of her bright smiles.

'So what do you think?' Lizzy asked.

'I think I understand everything a great deal more now,' Mary said, still too astonished by the vista to curb her tongue or try to express her emotions in grand terms.

To her surprise Darcy laughed. 'Well put, Mary. Well put.'

They were ushered into the house by an army of footmen, the doors opening for the party as if invisibly, the servants hidden behind the massive carved wooden panels. Though Darcy was a tall man, he was dwarfed by the walls and high ceilings, though this did not seem to affect him. Mary looked around at the frescos and the gilding and almost laughed. It was preposterous. Utterly preposterous. One could not imagine taking tea in such a house, or really doing anything human at all. She indulged a small whimsy, imagining Lady Catherine and Anne living in a small house behind this grand one, staying here by day but whisking themselves home with relief at night when they could let slip the pretence.

It was the thought of Lady Catherine in ragged slippers and a floppy cap that made Mary laugh just as the last door opened and they were in her ladyship's presence at last.

The butler announcing them never quite overrode the echo her laughter made, and Lady Catherine, in a large ornate chair, looked at her with a piercing glare. Mary bit her lip and swallowed the rest of her laughter. Darcy bowed; the ladies curtsied. Lady Catherine gestured with a magnanimous hand. She was alone except for her servants. Mary wondered where Miss de Bourgh could be.

The butler finished his recitation.

'So,' Lady Catherine snapped. 'You're here. Well, if you must come to overwhelm me, I suppose you must. Darcy, you know that I asked for you alone, or you and your sister. Instead, I see you've not only brought your wife, as I suppose you must, but also the plain Bennet.'

'I thought you would enjoy a party of young people, Aunt,' Darcy said.

'Nonsense! You are not young, nor is your wife. As for your sister, Georgiana, why have you not come and given me a kiss?'

Georgiana ran forward dutifully and kissed her aunt on the cheek. Lady Catherine waved her away impatiently. 'Yes, yes, you are a foolish girl. Are you over all that nonsense now?'

Again Darcy and Lizzy looked askance and a little angered as Georgiana blushed and mumbled something. Mary wondered with sharp curiosity what it was that they all seemed to know. What had Lady Catherine meant?

'You've come at a most inconvenient time,' Lady Catherine said. 'Anne is ill. She has a very sensitive constitution. I expect her down for dinner but not an instant sooner. I shall have the Collinses come to dine with us. I shall send the housekeeper's daughter to sit with the baby.'

'Is that wise for Charlotte to leave her baby?' Lizzy said with some astonishment. The boy was but a few months old. Lady

Catherine fixed her with a glare.

'Miss Bennet — rather, Mrs Darcy. *You* can hardly be an expert on children. Mrs Collins knows to defer to my judgement and that of her husband when it comes to raising a child. Such a boy will be ruined if his mother coddles him with attention and affection, especially a child in such a circumstance. He must learn from the youngest age to curb his own needs in accordance with those of his parents.'

Lizzy kept her composure and Mary knew that it required the greatest effort her sister could give.

Lady Catherine fixed her eye on Mary.

'So,' she said. 'You are the middle Bennet, are you not?'

Mary curtsied most awkwardly. Lady Catherine harrumphed. 'I told you, Darcy, that you were only to come yourself. There is not enough room at Rosings for such a large party. For I expect that you will wish to share your apartment with your wife, while Georgiana must have her own room, and Mrs Jenkinson cannot be removed from her room, as it is the one next to Anne. There is not another such room for Miss Bennet. She will have to stay at the Collinses. I shall direct a footman over there with her bags.'

Mr Darcy made as if to protest but Mary

looked at him with a pleading eye. She did not much engage in conversation with her brother-in-law, for he was so stiff and formal that it was hard to come to any meeting of the minds with him. This time, though, she cast her unease aside and begged him silently not to counter Lady Catherine's will. She would much rather stay at Charlotte's, even though that could only be awkward too.

Mr Darcy coughed slightly to cover his false start. He gave Mary a mere nod and turned and bowed to his aunt. 'As you wish,' he said. 'We do not mean to presume too far upon your hospitality.'

As Lady Catherine dismissed them and told them not to bother her until dinnertime, Mary could hear Lizzy conversing with Darcy in a low, angry voice. Her words she could not hear but she could easily hear Darcy's reply:

'I give her only the respect she deserves as my relative and as a person of great countenance. That does not mean I agree with her, my love.'

★ ★ ★

As they were all at loose ends until dinnertime, they resolved to visit Charlotte and Mr Collins and follow Mary's trunk to the parsonage. The small company walked over to the modest house given the Collinses as part of Mr Collins's living.

Mr Collins answered them at his door, and was full of astonishment and gratitude, but it did not escape Mary's notice that he did not seem to notice Lizzy or herself but was entirely attentive on Mr Darcy. It was many minutes before they were allowed in as they had to wait on his exclamations.

'Mr Darcy! Mr Darcy! What an honour, sir! I am your humble servant.' Here he made an awkward attempt at a bow, but he was winking and nodding so much that it was more as if his back were hunched with rheumatism than with civility. Mary tried to keep back her smiles and could not dare look at Lizzy lest they both break into peals of laughter. Mr Darcy bore it all with a severe demeanour, but even Mary, without a wife's familiarity, could see he was losing his patience and regaining all his contempt.

At last Mr Collins turned to Lizzy, the woman to whom he had once professed undying, raptured love. 'My dear cousin,' he said. 'May I congratulate you once again on allying yourself with one of the greatest families in all of England?' He winked at her with a familiarity that almost sickened Mary. 'I can see now why you had to turn down a humble cleric when such a grand connection awaited you. And this must be Miss Darcy! A relation of my patroness is always a friend here.'

Georgiana curtsied, confused but mindful of her manners, and Mr Collins went into raptures once again. He hardly noticed Mary, but by then she was so used to it that she barely heard him as she waited for him to stop talking.

'But come in, come in! You must all come in. Charlotte is no longer quite indisposed, and the child — a boy, he is a boy, my dear son — grows fat and well. Come in, come in, and grace my humble abode!'

Mr Collins ushered them in with his nods and bows and scrapes, stuttering all over his words as he looked towards Darcy and Georgiana and back again. If he had his way, Darcy and then Georgiana would have led, but Georgiana stepped back out of normal deference and so first Lizzy, then Darcy, and then Georgiana walked into the house at last. Mr Collins bowed them all in, but his eye fell upon Mary as she passed over his threshold and into his home. She smiled and gave him a small curtsy, then she saw something in his eye that she did not at first understand. His gaze shifted behind her and he saw the footman with the trunk.

'My word,' he said. 'Whose belongings are those?'

Now Mary felt all the awkwardness of her situation. If only the footman had arrived before them and had been able to deliver Lady Catherine's message. It would have been more acceptable then. Now she had to tell him that she was a house guest, whether he would or no. Oh, if only Charlotte had greeted them!

'It is mine, Mr Collins,' she said as forthrightly as she could. 'Lady Catherine said there was no room at Rosings.'

His expression was all astonishment, and Mary felt as if she could sink into the small gravelled path. She had barely set foot inside the house.

With great relief she heard Charlotte's voice from within. 'Mr Collins! What do you mean, by keeping Mary Bennet from coming inside! We're all here, waiting on you! Lizzy says Mary is to stay, so let the man bring in her trunk!'

At the bidding of his wife, but still uncertain and unspeaking, Mr Collins stepped aside and let Mary in. She bowed and hurried past him. The footman followed and she could hear Mr Collins give orders to bring the trunk upstairs with at least ten words to every one he needed to get his point across. Gratefully

Mary left him behind and entered the parlour where the rest of her party were gathered.

Charlotte waited on the stairs, her hair dishevelled. 'Oh good, Mary, there you are. I am all undone, and will be down in a moment. Please forgive — well, all the uproar. Mary, I am so glad you are to stay.' She whisked herself back upstairs.

Mary could have kissed Charlotte for her kindness, but she was slightly alarmed at her appearance. She was not even in half-dress but looked as if she were still wearing her morning wrap. Her entire party had the same uneasy expressions, as if they too were not quite sure of what had just happened. Awkwardly, she looked around her. The comfortable house reminded Mary of Longbourn. Charlotte's touches were everywhere, although the house itself was somewhat untidy, with clothes scattered here and there and dust in the corners.

A baby's wail could be heard at the back of the house. Mr Collins started.

'Please sit and make yourselves at home in my humble abode,' he said. 'Such good fortune that brings you here for our blessed event — a blessed event it is! Though loud, and we haven't been able to sleep. But I hope for you to be equally blessed, for marriage and children are God's natural order of things, and I cannot conceive of marriage without the blessing of children.'

'Perhaps we may be forgiven for starting out childless,' Lizzy said, 'If we take care not to continue in that state.'

She twined her fingers with Darcy's and gave him such a smile that Mr Collins's mouth dropped and he merely gasped like a fish a few times. Mary turned on her heel and pretended interest in a pretty plate over the mantel, trying to control her expression. Lizzy was most impertinent! How could she say such things? That was something Lydia would say or do, not a proper married woman. What had come over Lizzy? For once almost wordless, Mr Collins bowed again and muttered a few words about Charlotte. He rushed off with such speed that he almost bumped into the door.

They all sat in silence. Charlotte's parlour was bright and cheerful, with the sun from the garden coming in, but there were still tea things and crumbs on the small table and the pillows were askew. There were more clothes in the corner, some half-finished knitting, and other small unfinished tasks lying about. They all looked around awkwardly.

The baby's crying got louder, then stopped abruptly. The door opened. They all stood, but only Mr Collins appeared. He looked at them, still as flustered as before. Then he bowed awkwardly to Lizzy. 'Dear cousin, my wife asks for you at the moment. Ah, you see, the blessed event, the blessed — well, he is taking the nourishment that is natural to him and Charlotte — er Mrs Collins, er, that is, she asks for you, cousin.'

Lizzy looked confused but obediently she followed Mr Collins upstairs. They all sat again. No one knew what to say. Georgiana swung her foot, looked around, and bit her lip. Mary found herself thinking only of the dirty tea things. She could not imagine Charlotte leaving the house so untidy. She must be very busy, she thought, trying to remember everything she had ever heard about lying-in and childbirth. The mamas spoke about such things in hushed tones and didn't let the young girls hear anything. But it seemed as if babies left one with very little time to take care of one's house.

Mary began to gather the tea things, half-expecting Mr Collins to pop out and cry, 'Don't touch them!' She carried on, cleaning up the crumbs and using a small napkin to dust. The table gleamed under her ministrations. She left the tea things on the tray and began to tidy the small parlour. Georgiana and Darcy looked at her.

'Mary, what — ' Georgiana began.

'Charlotte would never leave her house untidy,' Mary said, gaining more confidence as she neatened things. 'So she must be very busy with the baby and has no time for visitors. The least I can do is help to make things nice. Though I thought they had at least one maid.'

Georgiana looked at her brother and then stood up. She gathered up the tea tray. 'We should at least bring this to the kitchen,' she declared.

'Georgiana,' Darcy began. He said no more, but his tone of voice indicated that he expected that was all he needed to say, and that she would obey. Georgiana wavered, but held firm.

'Mary will help,' she said. 'I can't just sit by, Darcy.'

'You don't have to help,' Mary hurried to say. 'I can, only because old intimacy forgives impertinence. Not that it would be impertinent of you, Georgiana, but for poor Charlotte.'

'Mary is wise, my dear,' Darcy said. 'She knows what is due an old friend, but you are a guest.'

Mary took the tray from Georgiana's unwilling hands and went to the kitchen. Poor Georgiana, she thought. She had a generous nature but was forced by her station to remain aloof. Perhaps she should learn how to keep a house anyway. A girl had no control over her fortune or her fate. If Lizzy Bennet could marry a rich man there was very little to bar grand Georgiana Darcy from marrying a poor one, or one who became poor.

It was not a mean thought but it was a curious one. Mary was reminded of the old song that she had sometimes heard the housekeeper at her parent's house, Mrs Hill, sing.

I know where I'm going & I know who's
    going with me,
I know who I love, but the dear knows
    who I'll marry.

None of us knows, she thought. Well, she supposed that she would remain an old maid her whole life. She could count on one hand the young men that she knew — Charlotte's brothers, some of the young men in Meryton who gave her not a glance. The curious Mr Aikens. Mary felt an unaccustomed flush, remembering the way he had whispered in her ear, and their friendly intimacy on the grass at Pemberley. The curious Mr Aikens had not thought much of her at all, though. He had danced with Georgiana and all the other girls, his good humour and high spirits equal to them all. So why did her nerves turn cartwheels whenever she thought of him?

It turned out that Charlotte did have a cook. The woman was tending to the kitchen range and when she saw Mary she gave a relieved sigh and took the tray.

'The house has been at sixes and sevens these past few months, and poor Mrs Collins still not fully recovered from the birth of her great big boy. The girl who comes from the village to help has been ill and I've just had my hands full. Mrs Collins has been looking forward to your visit, I must say, for all that her own mother has just been here, but you know how young mothers and their mothers are, for they cannot agree on anything, and Lady Lucas was fair determined that Charlotte tend her baby her way. Mrs Collins couldn't be more relieved when Lady Lucas went. But you mustn't put yourself out any more, my dear. I will just take those things and be out in a moment with your tea. Then I'll help Mrs Collins down with her baby boy. He sleeps better in the parlour, poor thing.'

Charlotte did come down eventually, followed by Lizzy and the cook with the baby. Charlotte's cap was askew and her shawl had a stain. But her eyes were lively and she looked upon her visitors with a pleased smile.

Mr Collins fussed at her and admonished her with every other breath, and settled her into a chair by the fire. The cook placed the baby in her arms.

'So you've heard my fine Robert's cry,' Charlotte said, looking fondly at her baby boy. Charlotte had never been a pretty girl, but she had a pleasing plumpness now and the bloom of love lit her face that lent beauty to her countenance.

The parlour was a cheerful place now, a warm fire on the hearth, a simple tea on the table for them to enjoy, and the baby to admire. They spoke of all manner of things, but mostly oohed and ahhed over the little baby boy, who slept through it all. Mr Collins spoke in his most solemn tones and platitudes but even he would lose his train of thought as he gazed at his son.

Charlotte looked around at her clean parlour and smiled at Mary.

'Well, Mary,' she said. 'Cook said I have you to thank. A poor hostess I am, putting my guests to work.'

'Not at all,' Mary said. 'Idle hands are a devil's playground, as they say.' There was an awkward pause, as she reflected that she had just called Mr Darcy and his sister idle. 'I meant, only, that it was a pleasure to be able to help,' she added awkwardly. Her cheeks heated with embarrassment, and she could scarcely look up.

'Your impulse, dear cousin, was an admirable one,' Mr Collins said. 'A thrifty, industrious woman is a jewel, but perhaps one that shines all the more brightly for not calling attention to itself.'

Mary froze. She was hard put to keep from showing her disgust. Georgiana looked shocked, and Lizzy was angered. Mr Darcy had no qualms — he rolled his eyes. Charlotte looked ashamed. She hastened to fill the awkward pause. She held out the baby.

'Would you like to hold him?' she said. Mary opened her mouth but had no words, as startled as when Mr Aikens had asked her to dance. 'Oh,' she said. 'Yes. I-I think so. Would it be all right?'

Mr Collins almost yelped. 'Mrs Collins, do you think that is wise? For Miss Mary Bennet is hardly, that is, would it be wise to set a small infant, perhaps it would not be decent . . . ' He trailed off.

'Mr Collins,' Charlotte said, 'I have known Mary Bennet since we were small, and she is perfectly capable of holding an infant without corrupting herself or it.'

Lizzy coughed behind her hand. Following Charlotte's urging Mary sat next to her and Charlotte passed her the small bundle. The infant in his blankets felt warm and slightly damp. His few curls were plastered on his head and his little rosebud mouth quivered in his sleep. He nestled in her arms and she could feel the rise and fall of his chest.

She looked down at little Robert Collins's sleeping face. She felt nothing, other than a sense of disquiet. Her lack of maternal emotion was disturbing and suddenly frightening. Mary wondered when they would take the baby back. Not soon enough, she thought, panic suddenly rising.

'There! That is quite enough,' Mr Collins said, after the baby had been in Mary's arms for a few brief moments. 'Surely that's enough. Mrs Collins? Enough?'

'I wouldn't want to upset my cousin,' Mary said, trying to hide her eagerness to be rid of the infant. She lifted him to Charlotte. 'Perhaps Lizzy? Or Georgiana?'

'Oh! Not I!' Georgiana said impulsively. 'I am so frightened of babies. They seem so easy to break.'

Lizzy, laughing, reached out her arms. 'I would love to hold him again, now that he sleeps,' she said. 'I fear I gave some cause for his outburst upstairs.'

Grateful but trying not to be hasty, Mary transferred the baby to her sister. Little Robert whimpered and wiggled but lapsed into sleep in Lizzy's arms. Instinctively she rocked and crooned to the infant as Darcy looked stoically fond of his wife. Charlotte watched her friend with a smile that held a hint of sadness.

'You next, Lizzy,' she said softly. Lizzy looked up at her with a bright smile.

'I hope so,' she said. 'Mr Collins is right — it *is* a blessing.'

Mr Collins, hearing himself praised, gaped faintly at his cousin, to whom he had once declared a wholehearted avowal of love.

Unaware that he was the centre of all manner of feeling and admiration, not to mention the cause of a great undercurrent of sensibility of all kinds of meaning and portent, the baby boy slept on. Everyone kept their voices low out of respect for the infant and he would have slept for many an hour, giving Charlotte some blessed peace, had not a loud bang on the door caused him to awaken with a start and then cry.

Lady Catherine, her discontent with her visitors notwithstanding, had discovered that she could not be without them after all.

10

The baby, once woken, could not be consoled.

'Well,' the grand lady said as she settled herself in the parlour with the others, looking around with a suspicious eye, 'I see the boy has already set the household on its ear. I wonder at you, Mrs Collins, in not providing a more ordered household for your issue.'

Perhaps in sympathy for his poor discomfited mother, the infant bawled on. Lizzy hastily passed him to Charlotte, and Charlotte rocked him and cajoled but to no avail. The peace of a few moments ago was dispelled as everyone tried to think of ways to settle the infant down. Lady Catherine banged her stick on the floor and demanded that the infant should cease. Mr Collins raised his voice but could be heard mouthing only incomplete sentences as his wife tried in vain to calm both him and their son. At last Charlotte snapped,

'Mr Collins, call Cook!'

For a moment everything fell silent, even the baby, at her sharp tones. Then the baby broke into an even louder wail. Mary sat with her hands folded in front of her, the baby's crying setting every nerve on edge. Georgiana looked as if she wanted to run away. Mr Darcy held his wife's hand, his mouth tight. Lizzy looked discomfited but also on the verge of laughter. Mary was careful not to look at her more than once — she knew that if she did she would start to laugh herself.

Cook, whether she had been summoned or not, popped her head around the door. 'Mrs Collins, let me help you upstairs with the baby. Poor thing, he needs a change, doesn't he?' She caught sight of Lady Catherine and bobbed a curtsy. 'Your pardon, your ladyship, if I had known you were visiting I would have brought that cordial you like.' Her voice dropped to a whisper as though Charlotte could not hear her. 'Let me just bring poor Mrs Collins and her baby boy upstairs and then I will have time to treat your ladyship as you deserve.' She raised her voice again. 'Come Mrs Collins, let me help you up. There you go . . . ' She escorted her charges back up the stairs, the baby crying, Charlotte calling out her goodbyes and hopes that they would return when things were in less of an upheaval. Lizzy added to the chorus, assuring her that she would be back. Mary, Georgiana, and Darcy, prudently saying nothing, only waved and nodded. Through it all the baby cried unceasingly.

As the door closed behind them, Mr

Collins stood as a man torn between his duty to his wife and family and to his patronness. Mary could not think which was worse — if he stayed to serve Lady Catherine, or if he followed his wife. For she did not think that Charlotte cared for him much. But how much worse is it, she thought, that the man she married is more devoted to a sour old lady who treats him with such contempt and disdain? To be sure, Charlotte married for all the wrong reasons — it was not hard to see it. But so had Mr Collins. They had both done such a terrible, terrible thing, she thought. She thought of the little baby oblivious to it all and Charlotte's wistful smile as she looked at Lizzy with her husband.

We are all supposed to find someone to love, Mary thought, but it does not seem as if there's quite enough to go around. And so we make our bed and must lie on it. Even the marriage bed. And there she left off her shocking thought, for the idea of Charlotte and Mr Collins in their marriage bed was the most alarming thing.

Mr Collins walked them all to the door, stuttering over his obsequious apologies to Lady Catherine and Mr Darcy, and Georgiana. Lizzy and Mary walked behind as Lady Catherine heaped abuse upon her admirer.

'Poor Charlotte,' Mary muttered as they

waited for Lady Catherine to be helped into her carriage and give curt orders to the driver to drive on, leaving all of them to walk back to Rosings.

Lizzy gave her a look. 'How so? The baby? I saw you look at it as if you had a live snake in your hands.'

Mary was startled into a laugh. 'No, not the baby.' Her mirth turned into solemnity. 'Mr Collins is a very foolish man. It's not that he treats her ill, but . . . '

Lizzy sighed. 'I know. But I think she's made her peace with it. And children will give her further reason to . . . stand it better.'

Darcy turned to look back at his wife, who smiled gaily and waved at him, so far separated they were on the walk home. Mary suddenly gave a most unladylike snort. Lizzy looked at her with exaggerated alarm. 'Good God, Mary, what is it?'

At that point Mary was crying with laughter. 'Lady Catherine . . . ' she said between gasps. 'Banging her stick on the floor to make the baby stop.'

The Bennet sisters walked the rest of the way up the grand drive, laughing until the tears came.

★　★　★

The rest of the visit went as could be expected. Miss de Bourgh came down to dinner along with her companion, Mrs Jenkinson. Mary found Anne de Bourgh a wan, silent thing. Her complexion was pale and her eyes narrow, and her hair was dry and flat for all that it was curled to the highest fashion. Lady Catherine spent most of conversation either praising Anne or scolding her, so that her daughter could scarcely say a word. Mrs Jenkinson spent all of her conversation making sure her charge was comfortable. Miss de Bourgh never once looked at any of the party, and Mary could not fathom such gaucheness. To Mary, her lack of attention did not seem to spring from a sense of superiority but rather a lack of wit.

Nor did Lady Catherine pay much attention to Mary. She lavished her demands and conversation on Darcy and his wife and sister. Georgiana held up as best she could, though she was herself not in the habit of talking much in company she did not know. Mary watched and listened and ate little.

Mr Collins came but Charlotte did not, sending her regrets that she was still indisposed. Lady Catherine was most dis-pleased and she took it out on Mr Collins, rendering the hapless man into a quivering lump of apology.

'I can not abide a spoiled child,' Lady Catherine said. 'Mr Collins, you must take care that your child does not become a greedy petulant thing with airs of superiority, for you will find that such a manner in the lower orders is a sign of depravity.'

Mary wondered how an infant could show signs of depravity and tried to compose her expression so that Lady Catherine would not set upon her. As if by her design, Lady Catherine's eye swept over the table and settled upon shy Georgiana. Mary felt both relief and guilt.

'Georgiana!' snapped Lady Catherine. 'Do you still play the pianoforte?'

For a moment Georgiana froze. Then she recovered herself. She gave the smallest glance at her brother and he reassured her with a slight nod.

'Yes, Aunt.'

'After dinner you shall play for me. I hope that Mrs Darcy has not encouraged you to stop your practice.'

'No, Aunt, of course not.'

Lady Catherine harrumphed. 'When surrounded by those who will not improve their study, the weak-minded will often give up.'

'I continue to play, ma'am, for I do enjoy it.'

'I suppose, Miss Bennet, that you follow

the example of your sister and play ill?'

Mary felt the eyes of her sister, of her brother-in-law, and Mr Collins all upon her. She put her fork down and dabbed at her lips with her napkin, trying to hide her swelling anger and remain calm. How dare she. How *dare* she.

'I follow my own example, ma'am. But no, I do not play the pianoforte.'

'Your own example!' Lady Catherine's eyes bulged. Mr Collins made small ineffectual motions with his hands. Mary folded her hands on her lap to hide the trembling. 'Pray tell me, Miss Bennet, what is your own example?'

'I read sermons to improve my understanding, ma'am. I go to church to improve my soul. I attend upon my parents and my sisters and my friends. I do not play the pianoforte.'

Lady Catherine could not have been more surprised had Mary said she stood on her head and recited drinking songs. All she could say for several minutes was, 'Well! Well!'

Mary pretended to eat, cutting her meat in the tiniest bites. After a moment everyone returned to their meal. With all her courage Mary looked around. Lizzy glanced at her and the sisters shared a solemn nod. Only Lizzy's bright eyes indicated that she was hiding her laughter. Mary looked away before she betrayed herself with a laugh. In so doing, she caught Anne's eye. Despite her righteous anger Mary flushed. Anne regarded her with the same blank expression and looked away as if Miss Bennet ceased to exist.

Understanding pierced her and she felt a great and sudden sorrow. She had been right. Anne de Bourgh was simple, and all of Lady Catherine's bluster, all of her posturing and praise on behalf of her daughter, was to deny herself the knowledge. How the great lady's pride must sting her when she was alone at night, alone with herself and her terrible knowledge. There was no sermon that could comfort her, no words that Mr Collins could say that could make this all right.

The old Mary might have intoned to herself self-righteously, *pride goeth before a fall*. The new Mary simply thought, 'Who can have compassion on the ignorant, and on them that are out of the way; for that he himself also is compassed with infirmity.'

* * *

Young people, we know, are often corrupted by bad books; and have we not likewise known them improved by good ones?
Fordyce's Sermons for Young Women

The small party of the Darcys and Mary spent the rest of the fortnight with Mr and Mrs Collins and Lady Catherine. The days were filled with simple diversions and those small happinesses that comfort old friends as they visited Charlotte and Mr Collins or ventured into the small village. At night, Mary was thankful that she was staying at the parsonage, for dinners at Rosings were excruciating. They ate at Rosings almost every evening, but on those occasions when they dined at the parsonage, Lady Catherine and Anne never joined them. Even Mr Collins was a breath of fresh air compared to the household at Rosings.

It was not so bad staying with the Collinses. Mary, Lizzy, and Georgiana spent time alone with Charlotte and her baby while Mr Darcy and Mr Collins were thrown together by virtue of being men. Mary felt that the women had the better part of the deal. The ladies cooed over small Robert, dandled him, made much of his simple smiles. Mary even got used to carrying him, and his sleepy weight felt right in her arms.

One long afternoon the ladies were all gathered in Charlotte's parlour, the baby rocking in his cradle and the ladies with their books and embroidery. Mary sat with a book borrowed from Mr Collins's small library, his old copy of Fordyce's *Sermons*, for he had little else to choose from, but this time she had not done more than read the lengthy introduction. She looked up at the tableau before her. Lizzy and Charlotte sat in comfortable companionship on the sofa, their heads together in the way Mary remembered them when they both were still in Hertfordshire and were intimate friends. Georgiana plied her needle briskly, perhaps a little too briskly for she sucked a pricked finger now and again. Mr Collins had agreeably asked Mr Darcy to fish with him, though the quiet of the sport would no doubt be broken by Mr Collins's constant and incessant speech. If he had ever fished with the great fisherman Isaak Walton, Mary thought, that esteemed gentleman would very probably have drowned him in the first fifteen minutes of the exercise. She trusted that Mr Darcy would have more self-restraint.

There came a knock at the door and they all looked up.

Charlotte's cook bustled to the door and they heard the low tones of their visitor. Still, they could not make out the voice, and the expressions on all the ladies' faces were a combination of surprise and alarm. Cook filled the doorway and bobbed an awkward curtsy.

'Miss de Bourgh,' she said, her voice wobbling a bit, and then she stepped aside so that Miss de Bourgh could enter the room. She had come alone, without Mrs Jenkinson.

All the ladies rose at once and curtsied. Anne bowed her head.

'Miss de Bourgh,' Charlotte said with a gasp. 'What an honour! Indeed, I did not expect — that is, please do sit down. Cook, bring tea please.'

Without a word Anne sat down. There came an unhappy silence, the kind, Mary knew, that her mother was wont to fill up with silly chatter. For a powerful moment she wished her mother were there. At least her rattling could not have been anything nearly as embarrassing as sitting in silence with Anne de Bourgh. Charlotte gave Lizzy a desperate look. Lizzy gave the slightest shrug. There was little she could do — she was not the hostess. Charlotte plunged ahead.

'How is Lady Catherine, Miss de Bourgh?'

Miss de Bourgh ignored her. Instead she fixed her eyes on Mary. Mary felt herself redden. Anne nodded at the volume of sermons in Mary's hand.

'It's Fordyce's,' Mary said. 'Have you read them, Miss de Bourgh?' Even as she asked the question, she cringed with embarrassment. Surely Anne de Bourgh did not need lessons in how to be a virtuous woman.

'I have not,' Anne said, her voice quiet and thin. It was the first time that Mary had heard her say anything. From the looks of Charlotte and Lizzy, it might have been the first time they had heard her speak as well. Mary handed her the book but as Anne did not reach out to take it, she drew back her arm.

'Do you like to read, Miss Bennet?' Miss de Bourgh asked. She eyed Mary with an imperious look, quite like her mother's.

For the second time Mary had been asked that question. She wondered whether Miss de Bourgh thought reading to be as odd a pastime as Mr Aikens had. It was becoming tiresome. When Mary replied, she was short.

'Yes, I do.'

'I get such a headache when I read, that Mrs Jenkinson has told me I must avoid it at all costs,' Anne said. She spoke with pride, as if such an ailment was a rare distinction.

The other ladies hastened to agree with her, that reading could bring on a headache if one read for too long or in poor light, and Anne's expression grew more dubious.

'But I cannot read anything,' she said, and her words trumped their sympathy. *They* could read a little until they got a headache. *She* could not read for her headache would come on at once. Chastened, they all fell silent, until Georgiana said rather impertinently,

'Mary can read to you! Mary, have you read Mrs Radcliffe?'

A laugh went around the room. Even Charlotte laughed, though it was quite clear that she was scandalized. She said, 'Miss Georgiana, you cannot propose that Mary should read from the *Mysteries of Udolpho*!'

'Why not? It's nothing bad, you know. Just a silly little book.'

'I do not think Mr Collins would approve,' Charlotte continued doubtfully. Mary glanced obliquely at Lizzy. She merely gazed upon her friend with equanimity. But whatever gaiety Georgiana was feeling was not dampened. She slipped a hand into her reticule and drew out the novel. She lifted it triumphantly.

'Just the first chapter,' she said. 'Please, Mrs Collins. Mr Collins cannot consider it bad if Miss de Bourgh thinks it proper.'

Miss de Bourgh looked flustered but delighted to be asked to take part in the conspiracy. It was probably the first time that she had sat with women of her own age. She was usually surrounded by old women, Mary thought. She had never really been in company with other females. She knew that Lizzy and Charlotte, as married women, lent respectability to their plan. But what could it hurt, really? Fordyce would not approve, she thought, but Fordyce — goodness, what *did* he approve of? She thrust away her small sensation of guilt.

'I suppose it would be a diversion,' Charlotte said. 'If there is anything scandalous, of course we would stop.'

'It's a silly little novel, as Georgiana said,' Lizzy said, with a hint of impatience. 'There is nothing scandalous about it, except for the extreme absurdity of the story.'

Georgiana handed the book to Mary with a little happy cry, and for the second time, Mary began at the beginning of Udolpho. *I am beginning to know it by heart*, she thought.

She settled in, leaning back to catch the best light from the window. In truth, she enjoyed reading aloud, and the romantic sensibilities of the novel lent itself to great emotion. She often felt she could have been a curate had she been a boy, and when she was younger she would go out into the fields outside Longbourn and orate to the beasts and the birds. Only, one of the Lucas boys had caught her and teased her and she still burned with embarrassment to think of it. Now she read precisely and with clear enunciation, losing herself in the grand words.

She looked around now and again at her audience. Charlotte and Lizzy listened gravely, as befitted their matronly status and their personal natures. Georgiana attended with bright-eyed delight. Anne sat very still, her hands folded neatly in her lap, her back slumped as usual as if the weight was too much to bear. Her gaze was very distant, and Mary wondered whether she even listened. She read fluently, clearing her throat now and again, lost in the long story with its tale of a virtuous, accomplished heroine, everything a young woman should be in form, manner, and mind. It is easier for the beautiful to be good, she thought, because everyone expects it of them and forgives them for their lapses.

At last her voice gave up the ghost, just as young Master Robert woke up with a lusty cry. Everyone was startled and everyone laughed, including Miss de Bourgh. Mary was surprised to see how dark the room was — the sun had left the window and the shadows lengthened. The little room was almost dark without any candlelight.

'That was fine, Miss Bennet! That was very fine! Oh, what do you think will happen next?'

That was Anne. It was the most animated response that any of them had ever seen from Miss de Bourgh. But what happened next had nothing to do with young Emily of the novel. Instead, they heard the front door open, and the men came home, the deep voice of Mr Darcy and the more excited one of Mr Collins coming down the corridor to Charlotte's parlour. Mary closed the book with a snap.

'My dear Charlotte,' Mr Collins said as he pushed open the door. 'We have had a day of fishing, I tell you. Mr Darcy is a great fisherman, my dear. Mrs Darcy, your husband knows how to fish. Why, he had us separated and fish opposite ends of the pond, just so we could divide the catch between us. I caught quite a few, though I did need help in untangling my line from the willows once or twice. But Mr Darcy assured me, it happens to us all.'

He fell silent at last, as he looked at all the women, counting them all in the dimness. When his eye lit upon Miss de Bourgh, he gasped almost with fright.

'Why, Miss de Bourgh! I did not see you in the shadows at the end of the sofa. Charlotte, why does Miss de Bourgh not have the armchair by the fire? Miss de Bourgh, where is Mrs Jenkinson?'

Miss de Bourgh rose to her feet. She opened her mouth to speak, took a deep breath, gave an awkward curtsy, and fled, brushing past Mr Collins and Mr Darcy, neither of whom had the chance to bow. Mr Darcy looked gravely astonished. Mr Collins was near to tears.

'What were you doing?' he cried out. 'Oh, if Lady Catherine is to find out. Mrs Collins, what did you say to Miss Anne to put her to flight?'

'I? I did nothing,' Charlotte countered, dandling the baby, his long gown wet and limp down her front. 'It was Mary! She was just reading from a novel. Miss de Bourgh enjoyed it and she was startled when you came in.'

Mr Collins stared at her. Mary knew Charlotte hadn't meant to cast blame. Still, Mr Collins stared at her. She had to force herself to steel her nerves and show neither resentment nor contempt. Under her calm and steady gaze, Mr Collins's bumbling nature reasserted itself. He tittered and coughed.

'My dear cousin, I think you might be unaware of the fragile and delicate nature of the sensitive Miss de Bourgh. I cannot think that a novel, the reading of which is a pastime I do not favour for young ladies, would do her good. I know you mean well, but I fear that you may have frightened her unduly with your forward ways. And you my dear,' he turned with grave disappointment to his wife. 'I am sure you did not approve of this diversion, for you know that we do not keep novels in this house.'

Charlotte's eyes flashed with anger as she dandled the baby. She did not look chastened at all. Lizzy stood up.

'Mr Collins, really! It was a quite respectable novel by a respectable authoress. Charlotte said you would not approve, but Anne herself asked Mary to read.'

That was not quite true, but it was true enough. Mary glanced once at Georgiana, who looked as if she wished to run away from her part in the misdeed. The girl kept her head down and her hands folded as if she had taken some of Miss de Bourgh's nature. Mary saw Mr Darcy look at his sister with a considering eye, as if he didn't believe her sudden meekness.

Mr Collins looked most astonished.

'Miss de Bourgh asked Mary to read a novel? Why should she do that?'

'Perhaps it is my voice she wanted to hear,' Mary said.

With visible effort, Mr Collins gathered himself. 'My dear cousin. You have no idea of the damage — the turmoil you could have caused.' He attempted a smile. 'It might be best — you see, Lady Catherine is quite protective — perhaps, Miss Mary, you will not join us at Rosings, lest you upset Miss Anne again. You will be quite happy here on those evenings in which we are out, and perhaps, perhaps you can stay with young Robert, as he has grown to like you, I daresay.'

Mary was torn between her very natural inclination to feel slighted and her more honest response of relief. To be freed of visits to Rosings was almost worth the insult. But it was not to be.

Even as Georgiana gasped, Charlotte stood up angrily. 'Mr Collins! What do you mean, to say that Mary cannot go with us to Rosings?'

At the same time, Lizzy took a step towards him, bright red on her cheeks. She looked wild and angry. 'Mary did nothing untoward. Miss Anne asked her to read. How dare you imply that Mary injured her in any way!'

Confronted by two angry women, Mr Collins turned between his wife and his cousin and sought to placate them both. 'My dear wife,' Mr Collins said, flapping his hands. 'My dear cousin. I meant no insult or accusation. I merely thought that Mary was not aware of how delicate Miss Anne is. After all,' he gave a small titter again, 'she does not flee at my sermons.'

No one said a word; no one had to.

Mary stood up and handed him the book while Georgiana made a faint noise of protest. 'I am sorry, sir. Perhaps you should put this in a safe place so that I cannot use it again. If my crime is to be punished with exile from Rosings, be assured I will not dispute your decision.'

Mr Darcy coughed and they all turned to look at him, but he waved them off.

At Mary's apology, Mr Collins softened. 'You see, Mary, I feel that we all must play our roles to the best of our ability, and not endeavour to reach above them. Your passion for the written word is unseemly, if I may say so. Your father and mother have failed you as much as they failed your — well, we will not speak of *her*. They indulged your precocious reading when they should have turned you toward greater rewards. A woman should go to church, do good works, and not clutter her head with novels and poetry, but only concern herself with virtue and that modesty that is the best adornment of her mind and her form. Scholarship is for men, novels their province for amusement and education.'

'To improve themselves you mean,' Mary said, and he beamed.

'Yes, exactly, cousin! Exactly.'

'A pity it does not always work,' she said.

11

The Collinses and Mary were not invited to Rosings to dinner that night or the next, an omission for which Mary, according to Mr Collins, was to blame. Mr Collins could be counted on to allude to Mary's indiscretion at every meal, until one day, as he broached the subject, Charlotte stopped him with a sharp look. He looked abashed, muttered some thought or other about giving to his wife that honour that was due to her, and didn't bring it up again. He didn't speak much to Mary though. She felt his silence keenly, although with relief.

It had become abundantly clear that Mr Collins could not have been the husband for her, even if he had succumbed to her simple charms upon his first visit to Longbourn a year ago. She could not bear to be in the same room with him. His obsequiousness masked an inferior mind, made all the more proud because he had so little understanding. She flinched at the thought. How many times had she expounded in exactly the same way on a subject of which she knew little, but of which she had read something or other?

Oh to be a man, she thought with some hollow humour. No doubt Mr Collins had never been taken to task by his family but had been allowed to dwell in his misperceptions of his own superiority. *He should have had sisters. They would have taken care of him.*

Even if the Collinses were left wondering at their being cast out from the inner circle at Rosings, they were not left to wonder for long. Lizzy, Georgiana, and Mr Darcy visited every day. Mary knew from Lizzy and Georgiana that Anne could not have told her mother anything and that their exile had little to do with the escapade of Udolpho.

'She is her same imperious self and speaks not at all of Mr Collins or Charlotte or you in any particular way,' Lizzy said, when they walked arm in arm in the park at Rosings. There was a little wilderness there that she had become acquainted with on her last visit to Rosings and she introduced Mary to it. Mary enjoyed the peacefulness.

'And Miss de Bourgh?' Mary asked with some trepidation.

Lizzy smiled. 'Anne says nothing. Anne is the same as she ever was. She sits with her head bowed, and Mrs Jenkinson dotes upon her. So unanimated! I pity her, Mary.'

'And Lady Catherine,' Mary agreed. At her sister's wondering glance, she said, 'She must see how wanting Anne is. Anne must feel it, the difference between who she is and that which her mother is so desperate that she should be. Every compliment would be a cut, every praise an insult. Anne is the one thing Lady Catherine cannot change to suit herself.'

Lizzy smiled at her. 'Mary! Now you make me sad and I wish to be merry! At least, as much as I can be until I get home.'

Mary wanted her home as well, but she knew Lizzy meant Pemberley, not Longbourn. 'Do you know when Lady Catherine will release us?'

'Ah, no one knows. Darcy waits upon her, and therefore so must Georgiana. I am merely the wife, so I must wait upon the others.'

'I fear I am imposing too much on Charlotte and Mr Collins,' Mary admitted. Lizzy's face darkened.

'I know, and if Lady Catherine were not Darcy's aunt, I would call her a wretched, spiteful woman. Is it so bad, Mary?'

'Charlotte is kind, but Mr Collins cannot stand the very sight of me. And I think it has begun to tell on Charlotte.'

'Cannot stand the sight of you! Mary! He was going to fall in love with you next, you know, if Charlotte hadn't stepped in to save you.'

'Charlotte saved herself,' Mary said. She *had* half-expected that Mr Collins would pay his respects to her next, and she *had* wanted a beau for herself, even if he had professed his love for her sisters first. To hear that Charlotte had swooped in ahead of her was both a shock and relief. 'But it was at the expense of her own happiness.'

'Perhaps,' Lizzy said. 'I was dreadfully shocked and angry with her at first. How she could marry a man of such poor understanding, one whom she could hardly esteem, was not the Charlotte I knew. But she is happy in her way, she has a great deal of independence for a married woman, for he follows her lead in most things, and she has a child. I begin to think that Charlotte had the right of it after all.'

'Lizzy!' Mary said. Lizzy laughed, but she turned grave and held Mary's hand tight under her arm.

'Mary, that is not to say that I think you or Kitty should make such a choice. I would not wish it of you. *You* can be easy now. You can make a choice of a husband based on love and esteem, and a compatible nature.'

Mary sighed. 'I have not studied men much, you know, but sometimes I think they have more of Mr Collins in them than of your Darcy.'

'Women live quietly, it is true, and often are not able to compare all the samples of the species that they should. But I think you should not judge all men by Mr Collins or by Mr Darcy, just as, it must be hoped, *we* are not all judged by the worst or the fairest of our sex.'

'Are we not?' Mary said. 'A woman's virtue is so easily lost. One false step, one stumble, and she is judged, and judged harshly.'

Lizzy was silent for a long time. They were both thinking of Lydia. 'You are right,' she admitted at last. 'I cannot deny it. Yet we have a choice, and we are not completely fettered. A well-regulated mind, practised in reading and understanding, will always find a way to thrive, even under the meanest conditions.'

'Lizzy,' Mary said patiently, 'one cannot eat or put a roof over one's head, with only a well-regulated mind.'

Lizzy laughed. 'You are determined to be low, Mary, and I am equally determined to raise your spirits. But I can't. You win. Please, may we talk of something less dreary? Look — here's Darcy. He's come looking for us.'

He had come with good news. Lady Catherine had decided that they should go at the end of the week, for that would have made their visit exactly one month. That left them with three more days to enjoy the charms of the local hospitality, but they had one more hurdle to overcome. They must dine once more at Rosings.

12

Mr Collins was ecstatic at the lifting of the exile from his beloved Rosings. He hurried home with the news, gasping with eagerness, his expression fawning.

'Be easy, Cousin,' he said to Mary. 'You have done no permanent ill, or at least, the consequence of your whims have not been damaging. We have been invited to the farewell dinner at Rosings, before your removal to Darcy's ancestral home. Charlotte, we will not have to cook the joint after all.'

'I will tell Cook,' Charlotte said, her lips twitching. Mr Collins, unaware that he had insulted his cousin with the suggestion that she was eating him out of house and home, turned to Mary. His face had grown solemn.

'Cousin,' he said. 'We must have a serious talk.' He took a breath and turned to his wife. 'My dear Charlotte. If you could leave us for a moment for a conversation that I think Miss Bennet would like to hold in private. We are family after all, and thus it cannot be improper.'

'Whatever you wish to say can be said in

front of Charlotte, Mr Collins,' said Mary. 'We are family, but she has been a friend since we were children.'

'That's all right, Mary,' Charlotte said. She rose. 'I hear Robert stirring anyway.'

Mr Collins waited for her to leave, and even after the door closed behind her he paced in front of the fireplace, as if unable to find the words. Mary waited. She was actually curious. What was he going to try to tell her?

'My dear cousin,' he began, and then stopped as if choked with emotion. He was not a man who had much skill as an actor, though, and she was hard put to keep from laughing. 'My dear cousin. I will not ask you to lie. If you feel you must tell Lady Catherine that you read a novel out loud to her daughter, then unburden yourself of the truth and ask forgiveness for the sin. I understand the need to clear one's heart and soul of such a misdemeanour. Oh, I see by your expression that you don't understand the grave impropriety of what you did. Miss Mary, you read a novel to Miss Anne de Bourgh under my roof. Lady Catherine cannot do other than blame me, as head of this household.'

'Mr Collins, it was a novel written by a respectable lady for respectable ladies. It wasn't Swift, after all.' He gasped at the thought. 'But if you think it best, I will confess to Lady Catherine that it was all my doing.' Mary knew better than to bring Georgiana into it.

He looked as if he was finding it difficult to order his thoughts.

'It is up to you, of course. I could not, in my capacity as a cleric, tell you to withhold a truth. On the other hand, it would not be *such* a lie, unless Lady Catherine asked you directly about the matter. I am only saying that if you wish to tell Lady Catherine what happened, if you felt the heavy weight of your transgression, your unthinking action, then by all means you should tell her ladyship and hope for her forgiveness. But if you feel that it would be better left unsaid, that we should talk no more about it, then perhaps that could be forgiven as well. For it was not so very bad, except that Lady Catherine might think I had something to do with it.'

Mary's mouth dropped. Mr Collins didn't want her to tell Lady Catherine anything! He was afraid that Lady Catherine would blame him! For a moment a mischievous impulse rose up in her. After all, she would be leaving in a day or two and Lady Catherine's wrath would be nothing to her.

'Oh,' she said, as if considering the matter. 'I had better tell, don't you think? Because as you say, withholding the truth is as bad as lying.'

'*Not* as bad,' he corrected, holding up a hand. 'Not as bad, in many instances. You misunderstood me, Mary. Unburden yourself, if you must, for it was a transgression, I cannot advise you otherwise, but be aware that the censure of Lady Catherine will fall on me.'

The poor man was tied up in knots. Mary decided to have pity on him.

'If you are sure, Mr Collins, that it is not a sin to not tell — '

'Not at all a sin.'

'And you think it won't be so very bad — '

'No, no, not at all.'

'Then I won't tell.'

'An excellent conclusion, my dear cousin. So long as you can rest easy in your decision and not think that I swayed you in any way.'

'I may not rest completely easy,' Mary added thoughtfully, only to see him blanch. 'But if I feel I must clear my conscience, I will write a letter.' She smiled at him. His returning smile was sickly. 'If you will excuse me, Mr Collins. I must finish my packing.'

The Collinses and Mary walked over to Rosings at the appointed hour. Dinner was always early at Rosings, for Lady Catherine always dined at an unfashionable hour, and retired at the chiming of nine of the clock exactly. At least, thought Mary, the ordeal will be short. She was most eager to be leaving. She shivered in her spencer, for a wicked little wind had come up and ruffled her gown and petticoats. Night had fallen, for it neared summer's end, and the path, though well trod, was in darkness. She stumbled in her dainty slippers and hoped that she had not stained them too badly.

The grand front entrance of Rosings was lit by two small lanterns at the door, where a footman stood waiting for them to lead them in. Mr Collins beamed and remarked upon Lady Catherine's thoughtfulness. Mary thought it disdain instead, but she kept her counsel. It no longer mattered.

Within, the lights were ablaze, and the glory that was Rosings opened before them. They were led into Lady Catherine's presence immediately, and Mary hoped they didn't look too wild after their walk in the windy darkness. She glanced at Charlotte as they curtsied to Lady Catherine. Charlotte's hair had escaped her neat bun and hung limply around her face, and Mary knew she looked much the same.

They were seated almost immediately at Lady Catherine's impatient summons. Mary was seated across from Anne. Miss de Bourgh surprised her with her direct look. Mary smiled nervously.

'How do you do, Miss de Bourgh?' she said. Anne merely bowed and looked away, and Mary thought, ah, back to life as usual. Lady Catherine wasted no time in interrogating her captives.

'Miss Bennet, your sister told me at her visit last year that you had no governess nor were you taken to town to expand your education there. Yet you enjoy reading? How did you manage that?' She sounded more accusing than curious, as if Mary had performed a trick.

What on earth? Mary glanced at Lizzy. What had she told Lady Catherine? Lizzy looked at her with exaggerated alarm.

'We had no governess, it is true, but we were allowed to study whatever we wished, so long as we did not neglect our other duties and chores,' Mary said.

'I see.' Lady Catherine sounded dubious. Mr Collins seized an opening.

'I think I can say that my cousins have had the benefit of a sizable library at Longbourn, Lady Catherine. Quite provident of my kinsman, Mr Bennet, to install such a large endowment of books.'

Mary and Lizzy exchanged small glances. Mr Collins had no doubt added the

Longbourn library to his accounting of his inheritance.

'*I* saw no sign of such a library,' Lady Catherine said. 'It is a smallish house, Mr Collins. Yet you say it has an admirable collection. Astonishing, that so much care should be put into books, but for many country gentlemen, books are more for show than for reading.'

'That may be true of many other country gentlemen, but it is not true of my father,' Mary said. 'He has read all of the books in our library, and has read many more besides.'

'I meant only to say,' Mr Collins said, reversing himself in the face of Lady Catherine's argument, 'that it is *large* for so small a country house.'

'I'm sure the Rosings library is magnificent,' Lizzy put in. Mary almost applauded. It was not possible to spend a month in Lady Catherine's presence to know that if she had a choice between insulting someone else's station and praising her own, she would choose the latter.

'It is the best library in the country and serves as a model for the kingdom,' Lady Catherine said. 'The de Bourghs have been adding to it for generations. I send my steward to London once a year to purchase the most important works in French, Italian,

151

and German. Anne will add to it in her turn.'

The Mysteries of Udolpho will be the first volume, Mary thought. She dared not glance at Georgiana, as the girl appeared to be having difficulty in maintaining her composure. Troublesome, to be thinking the same thing. It made solemnity most tiresome.

After dinner the entire party retired to the ladies' drawing room as neither gentleman expressed a desire to smoke or drink. Mr Collins made his protests with many flourishes and bows whilst trying to convey simultaneously that as a clergyman he did not drink or smoke but that he would be flattered to do both in Darcy's company. Darcy merely said that he would rather join the ladies that evening. They sat in an uncomfortable silence, making small talk, while most of the party wished they could depart at that instant. Mary found herself beside Anne. She wished she had something to do with her hands, but she had forgotten the small bit of embroidery that she often carried when she couldn't have a book. For the first time, Mary saw that someone was missing. Mrs Jenkinson was such a silent presence after dinner, for she never dined with the family, that it wasn't until Mary realized she was in the woman's usual place that she knew she was missing.

'I hope Mrs Jenkinson isn't ill,' she remarked to Anne. With the attention of an eagle, Lady Catherine heard and responded.

'What, Miss Bennet? Why do you care for Mrs Jenkinson? She is not ill. She has gone away.'

'Gone away? Has she taken another position?'

'I did not send her off without a reference, and with my recommendation she will find a new place quickly.'

She could hardly ask if the loyal servant had committed such a dreadful crime that she must be turned out. She also couldn't commiserate with Anne about losing her faithful retainer, if it turned out that Lady Catherine was the one who wanted her to go.

'Oh,' she said. 'She was such a devoted companion.'

'*I* did not wish her to go,' Lady Catherine said, and she rested her baleful eye upon her daughter. Anne shrank under the haughty gaze.

So it was Anne who had expressed her dissatisfaction with Mrs Jenkinson. Mary wondered whether she had had to stand up to her mother to win that small bit of independence? Mary gave an encouraging smile to Anne, who almost smiled in response.

'Yes, but now Anne requires a companion. I am most particular about my requirements, and I can see it will be difficult to find another creature such as Mrs Jenkinson. We had to turn away twenty to find her.'

'Yes indeed,' Mr Collins said. 'Anne is such a flower, Lady Catherine, that in the wrong hands she would wilt and wither, rather than bloom.' He beamed beatifically. Lady Catherine waved an impatient, beringed hand.

'Perhaps a younger woman,' Charlotte ventured and she too gave Anne a kind smile. Anne did not respond, having retreated into her own thoughts, as she almost always did.

'Young women are flighty and inconstant, and would trouble Anne no end,' Lady Catherine said. 'Anne would not like a young woman, would you, my dear?' Anne said nothing. Lady Catherine warmed to her theme. 'The proper young woman would have to be well bred, yet not too highly bred, impecunious no doubt, so that she may be properly grateful for her position, soberly dressed with a well-regulated mind, a lover of books and music but not so fine a dancer that she is in demand as a partner. Service, not marriage, must be foremost in her mind, and yet she cannot be one of those independent-minded women who believes she must earn a living. Finally, she must be quiet and biddable. But where in England can such a paragon of service and humility be found?'

The drawing room fell silent. Not a single person looked at Mary. Mary felt the colour drain from her cheeks, and knew how the mouse felt when the shadow of the owl fell over it. Mr Collins appeared to be thinking hard over Lady Catherine's imploring question, his lips moving as if he were adding up a difficult sum. Suddenly his head lifted in triumph. Lizzy jumped in just as he spoke and their words tangled with one another.

'You are absolutely right, Lady Catherine, such a person would be impossible to find.'

'I have it!' Mr Collins cried. 'Miss Bennet would be just the thing!'

13

The post brought two letters to the Bennet household, a small one from Mary to her mother and a more lengthy one explaining matters to their father from Lizzy. Those simple missives had to wait, for the news came to Longbourn in a more accustomed matter.

'Mr Bennet!' his wife cried when she came home from visiting Lady Lucas. 'Have you heard the news? Why, Mary is to be the companion of Miss Anne de Bourgh, and it may be because she read her a sermon! Our Mary!'

Mr Bennet put down the letter he had just received from Lizzy apprising him of the same situation, although with rather less emphasis on the sermon.

'Ah, I see you have received the word via Lucas post, my dear. She is efficient, to be sure.'

'But Mr Bennet, don't you know what this means?' Without waiting for him to guess, Mrs Bennet plunged on. 'We have no need to worry about Mary finding a husband!'

'As I hadn't been, I can't be as delighted as

you, Mrs Bennet. But I congratulate you on your triumph.'

'Oh Mr Bennet, of course you must know that I have been very worried about what will happen to Mary after you die and all we own passes to Mr Collins. For she is not likely to have found a husband and now she will remain with Lady Catherine and Jane will not have to take her in.'

Mr Bennet considered that. 'You have been planning, my love. But what if Mary should not like it?'

'Well, she must like it! She has no other choice. My nerves would not stand it, if she first takes the position as the companion to Miss de Bourgh and then decides against it.'

Mr Bennet knew better than to argue, but he frowned as he folded the letter and set it down on his desk.

He hadn't thought much about all of his daughters. He had heard them described as beauties, but to a man of his years, such distinctions no longer interested him. To him, all girls were alike in silliness, including his own, except for Lizzy. But what it all meant was that by the standards of society; that is, the ladies who determined who was a beauty and who was not, and often by the most arbitrary of details, he supposed that Mary wasn't as pretty as Lizzy or Jane. On the other hand, neither was she as simple as Lydia or Kitty, which attribute could recommend itself to more discerning husbands. Those, however, were as much at a premium in the current day as in Mr Bennet's youth, and so he expected that his wife was right. Mary would have difficulty in finding one such, she was so little in company beyond that of Meryton.

And yet he was neither pleased nor satisfied. For a daughter of his to retire as virtually a servant in the household of Lady Catherine de Bourgh ruffled his self-esteem in a most unaccustomed manner. Certainly Mary would not make a spectacle of herself as Lydia had, but somehow, this was worse. Well, it could not be helped, he thought. Foolish girl. Just when she was becoming interesting. For he had noticed that she was also no longer as silly, no longer as eager for attention as she had been nor as intent on exposing her awkward talents as she had been used to do. Though it seemed more martyrish than usual for Mary to consider becoming a companion to Miss Anne de Bourgh, a companion it would have to be.

It did not occur to Mr Bennet that he could put a stop to Mary's decision. Shortly after the unpleasantness concerning Lydia's impetuous marriage that had bid fair to ruin them all, he had returned to his customary indolence once the hubbub was over. Mr Bennet easily adjusted to his new circumstances, of having put himself in serious debt to his son-in-law, then cast off the uncomfortableness of his situation with the air of one who allowed himself not to think of uncomfortable things. With little effort on his part he could remove Mary from the danger of fading into obscurity. He chose not to make that effort.

Unaware of his musings, Mrs Bennet chatttered on.

'So we must send her things. She doesn't have much — she took most of what she had with her to Lizzy's. With all the girls gone, I am not sure we even have a trunk to pack for her.' Mrs Bennet bustled off, calling for the servants to help her pack Mary's meagre belongings, leaving Mr Bennet to contemplate a much quieter house. It had contained just himself and his wife these past few weeks, but he had tempered that with the knowledge that his daughters would soon be home. Now, he had to revise his expectations. Soon, there would only be Kitty at home, a thought which did not please him much.

Ah, Kitty. She was off to London with Jane and Bingley for a taste of the Season. Although all his daughters were out, Kitty had never been to town, and once more Mr Bennet thanked God that Bingley would be the one to introduce Kitty to London, or rather London to Kitty. The thought of himself bringing his daughters to town, there to find husbands, had been a distasteful idea to him, so naturally, he had made no effort to do it.

He did not expect Kitty to take London by storm and be married before the end of the summer, for all that Mrs Bennet hoped she would. He knew there was not much wrong with Kitty that a few years and separation from Lydia would not cure. She was very young, after all, and that was a fault that time fixed all on its own. But her youth was not likely to attract a London beau. Mr Bennet hoped only that Jane kept a tight leash on her young sister and made sure she didn't expose herself to any more ridicule than could be expected for a younger Bennet, and finish the work of destroying the Bennet name that Lydia had begun so thoroughly.

So Mr Bennet had few hopes for Kitty and equally few expectations for Mary. But he thought, 'We ought to have sent Mary to London with Jane and Kitty to stay with Lizzy. In that way, Mary would eventually have acquired a certain amount of polish, and Kitty would have been so cowed in the presence of Lady Catherine that she could not possibly have got into any trouble.'

He knew better than to give voice to such thoughts to Mrs Bennet, for she would have been by turns astonished and disdainful that he thought Mary would benefit more from London than Kitty would. It was just as well that she supervised the packing of Mary's few things.

Mr Bennet turned back to his book on his desk. With the door closed the room was blessedly quiet, even as the excited voice of Mrs Bennet wafted down the stairs. It turned out that there was a trunk, in the attic. The last one, it seemed. The thought was disquieting. For an instant his wife's voice fell silent, and all that was to be heard was the ticking of the clock on the shelf by the window, and the song of a few birds outside his window.

Mr Bennet was not used to melancholy. His was a silent nature, though he was quick to voice his opinion of others, especially his family. But he felt lonely at the thought of his quiet house, a quiet that he often had longed for when his five daughters had all been at home. He could almost hear the ghosts of their presence from when they were little children, now long gone. No more girls. No more chatter, no more laughter, no more bursts of energy and exasperation over typical girlish things. No more surprising conversations with Lizzy or tender ones with Jane, not unless he travelled to meet them. He missed Lizzy, he decided. Yes, he missed Lizzy. All of these strange sad thoughts of his daughters he'd experienced lately had everything to do with Lizzy, and nothing to do with the passing of time and children growing up.

Mr Bennet closed the book and set out in search of his wife.

'Mrs Bennet,' he said. 'How would you like to go on a trip? We shall visit my heir Mr Collins as well as Lady Catherine, and deliver Mary's trunk ourselves.'

14

'I have it!' Mr Collins cried. 'Miss Bennet would be just the thing!'

Upon Mr Collins's exclamation, Mary's protest died on her lips. She looked at once at Miss de Bourgh. The young woman's expression was one of surprise and, to Mary's astonishment, growing delight.

'Miss Bennet?' said Lady Catherine.

'Oh, I think not,' Lizzy said quickly, but she was at a loss for words with which to turn down Mr Collins's suggestion without offending everyone in the room. As the hubbub rose Mary and Anne looked at one another. Anne's delight turned to apprehension and she ducked her head, fading back into the withered little thing she had always been, except for the day of the dreadful reading.

Don't, Mary told herself. *Don't agree.* But she could not forget Anne's look of delight. She bit her lip, knowing she would say yes, and knowing she would be made miserable by an impulse of charity that could not end other than badly.

'I — I would like that,' she said quietly. The animated conversation died away. 'If Miss de

Bourgh would enjoy my company,' she added. She looked at Anne. 'I would not wish to impose. Perhaps I could stay until you found a companion more suited to your liking?'

Anne de Bourgh sat up a little straighter. She looked over at her mother, who was struck dumb.

'I would like that, Miss Bennet. I would like that very much.' Anne de Bourgh spoke quietly and with halting words, but she spoke firmly.

Still, how quickly it had all happened. Charlotte announced in her placid way that she had written to her mother with the news, and then Lady Catherine had said that Mary would have to move into the house as quickly as may be, now that Mrs Jenkinson was gone. Lady Catherine supposed that Mrs Jenkinson's small apartment near Anne's chambers would suit Mary quite well.

'It has a piano,' Lady Catherine said, 'but you will not mind that, of course. You will scarcely need the space yourself. And the view is quite spectacular — it looks over the wilderness at the back of the house, and you have a view into the valley and the fields and the farms. I think it quite the best view from the house, Miss Bennet. I wonder that I don't take it myself. You will be at home there.'

Darcy and Lizzy and Georgiana delayed their departure long enough to help Mary settle into her new apartment. As Lady Catherine had said, the small rooms were airy and open and looked down into the valley so that she could see the villages and farms all around. The rooms were along the side of the house and down the hall from Anne's apartments, which overlooked the well-kept park to the front of the house. As promised there was a small piano in the sitting room.

The room had a melancholy air of having been recently abandoned. As Mary put away her few things, she was reminded of Mrs Jenkinson's former presence by a slight aroma of pomander in the cupboard and a hairpin left in a crack on the dressing-table. Lizzy and Charlotte helped her and exclaimed over the windows and the large bed; all to herself, they kept saying, Charlotte with more wistfulness than Lizzy. Mary found herself wishing for privacy. She realized that she might never have another moment to herself again. It's not for ever, she thought. I may leave and go home at any time I wish. Well, perhaps her mother would not wish it, but she could always go to Lizzy's if she needed to. Or Jane's.

How very odd, to go from houseguest to something between servant and companion. For how long will Anne de Bourgh want me? Mary thought. She hoped she and the other young lady could be friends. She did not much have the habit of friendship, and perhaps that was why something was wanting in her own life. Mary Bennet and Anne de Bourgh — it would be an unlikely alliance, but there was something about the other girl that, when she became animated, was pleasing. Certainly she, Mary, was here not so much for herself, but for Anne, to help draw out that best part of her that appeared cowed by her mother and her own frailty, Mary thought. She thought of her own life and how she had just recently moved beyond her own small society into the larger world. She even enjoyed dancing. Maybe much the same could happen for Miss de Bourgh.

Well, Mary thought, straightening her dress and smoothing back her hair. She smiled at Lizzy and Charlotte and they went back down the grand staircase. Bennets had a way of surprising one. She herself was surprised at the turn her life had taken.

At the top of the stairs Mary halted a step behind the other two. She was not given to flights of fancy, but for a moment her thoughts flew to the heights of the decorative ceiling, painted in gilt, red, and blue. How would it feel to be mistress of Rosings, and not just a poor companion under its roof? Then she giggled.

She would, at least, read all the volumes that her servants brought back from Europe.

'Mary?' Lizzy said, looking back at her with a quizzical eye.

Mary started, and hurried down the stairs.

'Lizzy, you must not let me languish here,' she whispered so that Charlotte couldn't hear.

'I will not,' Lizzy said. 'But it would not be right to leave just yet.'

'I know. I will tolerate it for a few weeks. If Anne is as unbearable as her mother, perhaps just one week.'

Lizzy tucked her hand under her elbow. 'Mary, why are you doing this, really?'

Mary bit her lip. Charlotte, hearing them speak in confidence, quickened her pace down the stairs, letting them talk in private. They stood on the landing, sister to sister.

'It's an adventure, in its way. I've never been on my own, among people outside my own family.' She added with daring, 'It is my pilgrim's progress.'

Lizzy arched a brow. 'And Rosings is your Slough of Despond?'

Mary blushed. Was Lizzy making fun?

'Don't tease, Lizzy. I haven't been anywhere or done anything, as you have. This is the most of the country I've ever seen. You all may think that I care for nothing other than my books, but I too would like to see fine things. Even London, though I am not so enamoured of balls and teas, but to see the Court of St. James and Parliament and all the grand buildings. London is more than just the Season, Lizzy.'

She stopped herself from telling Lizzy exactly how London was, acutely aware that she had never been there, and that Lizzy, as the wife of Darcy, was more acquainted with London than she would ever be. She must think I am a little fool, as always, Mary thought. Thinking this is a stepping stone to London when I am nothing more than a lady's maid. She will tell Darcy and I will be exposed once more to his astonishment. She sighed. She should be used to it by now, but she had only become more aware of it.

Lizzy said nothing, just looked at Mary.

'Well,' her older sister said at last, and she gave Mary's hand a little squeeze. They began to descend the stairs. 'Even the pilgrim had to start somewhere.'

★ ★ ★

When at last they reached the entrance hall, they found that all was in uproar. Darcy and Georgiana were waiting for Lizzy so that they could all leave for Pemberley. Mr Collins paced anxiously with his wife, looking up at the staircase and wondering what could have kept Lizzy and Mary. And Lady Catherine was in a deep displeasure. She held an opened letter in her hand and when eventually she saw them, she shook it at Lizzy.

'I cannot understand what it means,' Lady Catherine said, and it was clear that she had been saying it for some time. Both Lizzy and Mary looked at her with astonishment and confusion. Lady Catherine thrust the letter at them as if they would learn its contents just by gazing upon it. She looked reproachfully at Lizzy as if it were her fault. 'What can your parents mean by coming here with your sister's things? For she will want for nothing while she is here, and I do not propose to support a houseful of her possessions. She will have to be satisfied with what she brings. And now, Mrs Darcy, your mother is bringing a trunkful of belongings? I cannot understand such a thing. And what do your parents mean by coming? It puts me out, Mrs Darcy. It puts me out indeed.'

Mother and Father coming here? Mary

looked at Lizzy, astonished.

'I think, ma'am, that my parents mean to bring Mary her books and other things because they are hers and she should have them,' Lizzy said. 'I cannot think that there is any other intention.'

'But it does not suit me, Mrs Darcy. It does not suit me. And they are already on their way, so I cannot tell them not to come.'

Mary gave a small smile that she hid by bowing her head. That was her father, she thought. He must have known that he would be unwelcome to Lady Catherine and rather than wait for permission had decided instead to seek forgiveness.

But she herself was pleased by their decision. To come themselves, rather than sending her trunk, made her realize that she missed them and they her.

★ ★ ★

That first night at Rosings, the house spread out in darkness all around her, Mary slept ill. The bed, though grand, was uncomfortable, and the window let daylight in early, as it faced east and the curtains were not thick enough. As a result, she woke at dawn and sat up in her dressing-gown at the little table, her dark hair coming out of her braids because she had tossed and turned so on her pillow. She decided to write of her experiences and, accordingly, she pulled out some letter paper she had brought with her, wet her pen, then paused. What could she say? Was it really her own pilgrim's progress that had led her here? What could Anne expect of her, or Lady Catherine for that matter? Not quite guest, yet more than servant, she thought.

What do I expect for myself? The thought arrested her pen still further. This first step, a journey away from her home, could, if she were not careful, imprison her even more securely than if she remained an old maid at home. The first necessity, then, was a strict timetable for her sojourn.

She dipped the pen again and set it to paper.

I do resolve that I will spend no more than three months at Rosings as Anne de Bourgh's companion and friend. It not yet being Michaelmas, I will therefore leave the week before Christmas.

And what will she have learned by then? She considered once more, and then wrote,

I do resolve that I will have learned in that time the customs of different families, great

and small, and write down my observations.

And what would she try to accomplish?

I do resolve to be a good companion to Miss Anne de Bourgh and help her achieve some measure of independence from her mother while still giving her the respect and affection which is due to her.

And what would she do well to remember? Lady Catherine would say, her place. Mary smiled, and wrote instead,

I do resolve to remember that I am a Bennet, and whether I am placed high or low, a Bennet is good, and useful, and true.

Such sentiments may not please Lady Catherine, Mary reflected, but Lady Catherine was not her only judge.

15

The decision of Mr and Mrs Bennet to pay a visit to Rosings caused the party's leaving to be delayed further. It was decided that the Darcys would stay a few more days, until the Bennets came. It could have been no surprise that Darcy expressed his displeasure to Lizzy that they could not depart for Pemberley any sooner. Lady Catherine too was quite ungracious about having her guests linger far beyond the time she thought it necessary for them to stay, not quite unreasonably, Mary thought. It was now two months since the visit had begun, and Michaelmas was drawing near. The travellers were all anxious to leave. At least, no one had to stay with Charlotte and Mr Collins, except for Mr and Mrs Bennet when they arrived. And they would stay no more than one night, for neither of them enjoyed being away from Longbourn for very long. For Mrs Bennet, it was her nerves. For Mr Bennet, it was Mrs Bennet's nerves.

Still, they managed to cause great hubbub when they alighted from the carriage at Mr Collins's house. Charlotte came out to greet them with great feeling but equally great uncertainty. Mrs Bennet kept her feelings in check, but it could be seen that she looked over the small house with narrowed eyes and a pursed mouth. The only balm to her soul was that Lizzy and Jane lived in far greater houses, but there was still the matter of the entail. Young Robert Collins was another cause of smarting pain, but Mrs Bennet took a deep breath, announced him a dear little boy, and made much of him.

Mr Bennet shook Mr Collins's hand, ignored his blandishments, gave Charlotte a heartfelt greeting as befitted his daughter's best friend of so many years, and then gave each of his two daughters a hearty kiss.

'And so, Mary,' he said, eyeing his daughter from beneath his thick eyebrows. 'You have decided that it's best to live in the grandest house in the country even as a servant than to come home to comfortable old Longbourn?'

'Do you not wish me to stay at Rosings, Papa?' Would her father put his foot down and tell Lady Catherine she could not have Mary? She half-hoped he would, half-feared it, but his next words relieved her own indecision by their professed indifference.

'You, my dear, can live wherever you like. If Longbourn is not to your liking, then Rosings may keep you.'

He gave her another brisk kiss and Mary bit her lip as he went off to greet his son-in-law as best he could with Mr Collins bobbing around them as if eager to insert himself between Mr Bennet and Mr Darcy.

At length the family moved inside the house, filling Charlotte's front parlour with laughter and conversation. Mary's plain trunk was pulled down from the top of the carriage and left waiting by the door, to be carried up to Rosings. She looked through it while the others talked, curious to see all of her belongings in this new setting.

There were her few books, her winter clothes that she had not expected to use since she was to have returned to Longbourn before the summer ended, and a few pretty things that she possessed. Gloves, with small pearl buttons. A garland of dried flowers. She remembered that. She had been no more than ten years old when all her sisters made garlands for some pretty play or other. She lifted it to her nose; perhaps it was her imagination but she thought she could smell the faintest remnant of sun-warmed straw and sweet roses. There was an old fan, its colour faded like the garland's. It was stiff and she tugged it open gently. She had meant to carry it to her first ball, but there had never been a ball grand enough, and then, when there was — Bingley's ball at Netherfield — she had found out that she was not meant for sentimentality. She smarted at her remembrance of the embarrassment of that event, when she had hoped and practised so hard at the piano so that she would, at last, be noticed for her own accomplishments, meagre though they were. Instead, she had reaped only laughter. It would be a long time before the sting would fade. She set the fan aside. It would not have done, in any event — the fan was so cracked and faded that carrying it would have only garnered its own ridicule. I am not meant for balls and such entertainment, she thought. Though dancing with Mr Aikens had been pleasurable enough, it had been more an exercise in stamina than a graceful dance.

At the bottom were her books, old friends that had kept her company many a long night when the candle had burned so low that she had had practically to hold it over the book in order to read the words, but she had been determined to read just one more page . . .

There was a new book, too. Curious, Mary picked it up. She recognized it — it was from her father's library, one of his books on the natural history of beasts and birds in their part of England.

'Papa?' she said, holding up the book.

Everyone turned to look at her. 'Did you mean to pack this?'

'Goodness, how did that get in there?' her mother cried. 'For I did not pack it, Mary. Perhaps Cook did. I could tell she was grabbing things quite at random. I can tell you, it was no easy thing to fit everything in.'

'I packed it, my dear.' Mr Bennet smiled. 'I thought you would like it, Mary. I have done with it. I thought it might be a relief from sermons and being agreeable.'

'Thank you,' Mary said, still a little confused. It was not like her father to think of her as wanting to read something, and the fact that he had given up one of his books for her was most unusual. He was very protective of his library. She wasn't sure that she wanted a book on beasts and trees, but all knowledge could be enlightening. She resolved to read it and write to him, giving her opinion. She set it back carefully in the trunk.

While she did this, Mr Collins coughed into his hand. When no one looked at him, he coughed harder until Mrs Collins said, 'Yes, Mr Collins? Have you something to say?'

'Thank you my dear. Mr Bennet. Mrs Bennet. Please allow me to address your daughter on the eve of this momentous change in her life. Miss Bennet. Cousin. You have put yourself in a position that will provide you with excellent opportunities to improve yourself far beyond the accomplishments that most young women achieve. To be the companion of Anne de Bourgh! To live next to her, and be a part of her most intimate moments — it is with great regret that I, as a man, am barred from the orbit of such a star.'

Everyone looked down and away from him, but heedless of what effect he was having on his audience, Mr Collins continued his praise, enumerating the great benefits that Mary would enjoy in living under the same roof as Anne de Bourgh. To think she would be allowed to live in the small room next to Anne! To think of what she must no doubt imbibe from the very air of nobility that graced the de Bourgh family. She would become kind, modest, good, and humble, just by being in their proximity. And it had all been his idea.

'But you should be very careful, Mary,' he concluded earnestly, 'not to lose Lady Catherine's regard and take for granted any thing that she should give you. For you see, what Lady Catherine elevates, she can cast down. She would not wish you to become proud. Be humble, Mary. Stay humble, as befits your position. You cannot then go wrong.'

Mary really had no idea what to say. She looked around her at the rest of her family. Mr Darcy's face was filled with disgust. Mr Bennet likewise had a look of tired contempt. Her mother did not seem to have been listening very much, and Lizzy had cast her eyes at the ceiling but made no other sign. Since she did not feel that she was expected to say anything to Mr Collins's extraordinary speech, Mary kept her silence. Mr Collins didn't seem to mind. Cheerful that he was able to discharge his thoughts in this manner, he turned to his wife.

'Well, Mrs Collins? Shall we all march up to Rosings?'

* * *

Mary's trunk was so small that they made a parade of it, the men holding the handles between them, and the rest of the party straggling behind. The twilight was only just settling over the country. A few stars poked out, and the sunset glimmered on the horizon. Insects buzzed, and the cool air washed over Mary's flushed cheeks. Up ahead, the torches of Rosings already lit their way. The beaten path was a pale road that led them on to the house. The path was dry and the way was clear. Most of the company was in a good mood. Her mother was in the throes of heightened anticipation at finally seeing Rosings, of which she had heard so much. She seemed to have forgotten Lady Catherine's impetuous visit to Longbourn last year, that had left Lizzy in such a temper.

Mr Darcy's visage had lightened, no doubt because he would be departing on the morrow. Mr Collins was lecturing Mr Bennet and any and all who listened, and Lizzy and Georgiana exclaimed over young Robert, who was well wrapped against the chill and safe in his mother's arms, looking at the strange world with wide eyes and peaceful babbling.

Mary dawdled a little behind. Mr Collins's voice rose over the others as he declaimed to his captive audience.

Once I could have been married to that man, she thought. *I, of all the Bennet sisters, would have made the best match for Mr Collins*. Their interests and their temperaments matched exactly. She had entertained dreams of playing a simple pianoforte to him, whilst he wrote his sermons. She had thought — before first he fell in love with Jane, and then with little effort, adjusted his heart to accept Lizzy and presumably with very little uneasiness after that, Charlotte — that surely he would see she was the Bennet for him.

It was laughable now, in the face of the

reality before her. She despised him for his pedantry and his slavish attachment to Rosings. Poor Charlotte! She pitied her old friend once again. She would always be tied to a man who would for ever place her and her son beneath his patroness in esteem. Yet, Charlotte had *known*. She had known before she decided to make Mr Collins fall in love with her what kind of man he was.

And what of me? Mary thought suddenly. For if she were truthful with herself, she had just allowed herself to be put on the same plane as he, a useful servant for Lady Catherine de Bourgh, submissive to her wants and needs, and never once to be considered as having any other use or future or want or need herself. She hadn't *married* Mr Collins: she was about to become him.

16

Their arrival at Rosings went as well as Mary expected. Lady Catherine greeted her parents with condescension and bullied Mr Collins unmercifully. Then she called on the footmen to carry up Mary's trunk, and though she had first feared that Mary would bring too much now seemed to think she had brought too little.

'Miss Bennet!' she said to Mary. 'I cannot imagine what you are thinking, for your dress reflects my household now. Pray assure me you have not stinted on your clothes, for I will not buy you new ones. A companion should have a simple dress, always clean with modest lines and very little ornament, for her position is to remain in the background waiting to be called upon. You should have taken your tone from that of Mrs Jenkinson. She was always proper in her dress and comportment.'

As Mrs Jenkinson was at least four decades older than Mary, even her unvain heart sank. But in keeping with her new determination not to let Lady Catherine cow her, for Anne's sake of course, she spoke up before her mother, father, or sister could defend her

— or before Mr Collins could leap in with his anxious exclamations in support of Lady Catherine.

'I have never been one to seek ornamentation, Lady Catherine,' she said, and her ladyship widened her eyes at Mary's temerity. 'But I do know how to dress as befits a young lady of my breeding and background.'

There was a silence. Lizzy and Mr Darcy exchanged glances, which Mary saw from the corner of her eye. Her mother sat as if turned into stone. Mr Bennet looked pleased. Mr Collins gazed wide-eyed at his cousin for a few moments and made a few sputtering sounds, but could produce no other vocalization.

Lady Catherine recovered first. 'My word, the Bennets do seem to have a very high opinion of themselves.'

'We have indeed, ma'am,' Mr Bennet said heartily, as if she had made a compliment rather than a complaint. 'The girls learned that themselves, you know — if one did not speak up, one was not heard.'

Mrs Bennet put in, 'But they are good girls, Lady Catherine, and most gently brought up. Mary is a reader, and plays the piano, and she will be a good, quiet sort of girl for your Anne.'

Lady Catherine leaped on the mention of

the piano with the air of a small terrier. It was an alarming expression of animation for one so overwhelming.

'Mrs Bennet! What do you mean, the piano! Your daughter most assuredly does not play, for she told me so herself.'

Where her daughters were concerned, Mrs Bennet felt herself to be on solid ground. 'Does not play! Goodness, Lady Catherine, we almost couldn't stop Mary from playing! She could be quite insistent upon it.'

Lady Catherine stumped her cane on the floor and turned to Mary. 'Miss Bennet! Answer me this instant! Do you play the piano, or do you not?'

There was a ringing silence. Mrs Bennet looked at her daughter as if she just then realized that the young girl was a cuckoo and not really a Bennet after all, but a strange bird of plain plumage.

'I have given it up, ma'am,' Mary said with calmness. 'My mother did not know, for it was after I left home to visit my sister.'

'Given it up?' cried Mrs Bennet. 'Well, Mary, I think that you might have told me. Very well, but I can't imagine why, except, my dear, that you were never quite that proficient. So I suppose it is for the best.'

Lady Catherine had a look on her face that could best be expressed as second doubts.

She had offered the position of companion to Mary, knowing it would humiliate the Bennets whilst she got her revenge for Mrs Darcy marrying Mr Darcy. Now she wasn't sure that the revenge was worth it. The Bennets were as changeable as the wind, it seemed, and seemed to weather all manner of disgrace and good fortune with equal parts of luck, humour, and decidedly odd behaviour. They did not stay put in one's estimation, but went about doing things, or not doing them, or deciding differently what they should do. It was hard to keep up.

And now this strangely self-possessed girl, who was more plain than Anne, had a past life that included playing the piano, but she had not even told her mother that she had stopped! She was on the verge of calling the footman for Miss Bennet's things and dismissing them all from her house, when she noticed Anne sitting quietly next to Miss Bennet.

Anne was smiling.

* * *

Mary went up to her little suite next to Anne's. The maid had already put away her things and so the room, in which she had already spent her first nights, was now more familiar and more comfortable. There were her books and her few belongings, the fan, a little statue of an elegant lady, and small round hatbox with her sewing things, all set out on the dressing-table by the window that overlooked the garden. The cupboard held her clothes, serviceable and plain, as befitted Mary herself. There were a few pearls and a round brooch with a faded picture of flowers, but, as she had promised Lady Catherine, very little ornamentation.

She had said goodbye to her parents and the Collinses and the Darcys and was now blessedly alone.

A knock came on the door and a head poked in. It was Lizzy.

'Goodness,' Mary said mildly. 'Darcy must be hard-pressed to not leave without you.'

Lizzy laughed. 'I only came to see how fares the pilgrim.'

Mary swept her hand around, indicating the room. Lizzy cocked her head. 'It is dreadful,' she said. 'You must come away at once.' She tugged her sister's hand. Mary smiled but released her.

'I know you have not the temperament for it, but I do,' Mary said. She looked at Lizzy, wondering whether she could tell her sister what she meant. But Lizzy was too set on her objections.

'She's not worth it, Mary. Not even for a pilgrim. Anne de Bourgh is too much like her mother to be worth this.'

'Everyone has worth, Lizzy. *She* is not bad. She has never been allowed to be anything but a poor shadow of what her mother wishes. I have seen in her some spirit and independence and I am convinced I am not just seeing what I wish to see. There is a woman inside the shell, and I think she wants only a sympathetic friend to allow her to bring it out.'

'Perhaps she is not completely hopeless, but don't try to tell me that you think her mother can be mended.'

Mary laughed. 'No, Lady Catherine is most decidedly fixed.'

Lizzy sighed. 'You should have stayed with us. I feel myself at fault, Mary. I feel as if I've let you down, as if I have abandoned you here.'

'Don't,' Mary said. 'This is — and don't tease, Lizzy — this is my own establishment. As I've said, there's work to do here. I am needed here, where I am not so at home or at Pemberley. No, Lizzy. You know it's true. Papa doesn't really see anyone and Mama can only look at me and think, '*she* won't get married'. At Rosings, no one expects me to be married — I can just imagine Lady

Catherine if she heard that news.'

Lizzy laughed. 'You shouldn't give up all hope of marriage,' she scolded. 'I think Mr Aikens could be tempted by a bookish girl — his horse, after all, vouched for your character.'

Mary pushed away the last bit of longing at hearing Mr Aikens's name. Let me just forget him, she thought. And then I can be calm as before. 'Give him my greetings and to his horse too. I believe the creature had an unimpeachable character.'

The sisters hugged, and then Lizzy left her, promising to write and to visit often.

Mary sat at the window and looked out into the darkness. The cool air wafted in through the curtains. She could smell the farmlands, rich and fecund, and was comforted. It smelled like Longbourn. In the daytime she would see the farmlands, and beyond them the hills in the hazy distance.

Mary sighed. It wasn't that she had given up on marriage; marriage had given up on her. Her view from Rosings would be equally fine whether she were a companion or a chatelaine.

17

The journey home to Pemberley was welcome. Everyone breathed a sigh of relief once the horses were finally under way. The Bennets followed in their carriage until it was time to turn off to Longbourn. Then the horses could be encouraged to move faster, almost as eager as their master to be going home. It was a day and a half of travelling before they drove along the drive at Pemberley and pulled up at the steps of the house. Lizzy and the rest alighted with thankfulness. Still, Lizzy was not quite easy. Happy as she was to be home, she could not help but worry about Mary. She had told Darcy of Mary's decision, of her 'pilgrim's progress', and Darcy had listened gravely. Then he said,

'I cannot understand it. It is a fanciful conceit, and I have no head for such a thing. But you should rest easy for your sister. My aunt has her faults, but she will provide Mary with the care and chaperonage that is her due, if only to preserve herself from the censure of society.'

By which Lizzy, ever sensitive, thought he

might be comparing Lady Catherine to Colonel Forster. She gave him the benefit of the doubt though, and owned that he was right. He knew his aunt. Ill-tempered she was, but as she was so protective of her own daughter she could hardly put Mary in any danger. The only concern was that Mary would be so unhappy or so stubborn, as she could be, that she would infuriate Lady Catherine or Lady Catherine her.

In such a case either Mary will leave in the middle of the night, or Lady Catherine will send her away, Lizzy thought. Or perhaps Mary will become an indispensable part of Rosings. She might just be what Anne needs. And either way, there was Charlotte close by. She would see to it that Mary knew she had a friend, even if Mr Collins could be infuriating.

Georgiana ran ahead of them into the house, exclaiming her pleasure at being home, calling out to the servants and housekeeper, all of whom welcomed her with fondness. Lizzy and Darcy followed more slowly, but smiling upon the young woman's impetuosity.

'She has changed,' Lizzy commented to Darcy. His expression lightened.

'She has. She has become happier, less nervous. Her trials have left her and she enjoys herself again. I think your presence has much to do with it.'

'I have done nothing at all!'

'I have not said you had *done* anything. Now you think I insult you — I merely speak the truth. You, by your presence and fresh way of thinking, have provided her with female companionship that wants nothing from her except to be cheerful. And so she is.'

'Yes, you insult me. When I demurred, you were supposed to tell me that I had through cleverness and diligence wrought such a change in your sister for the better. Instead you agreed with me.'

'Forgive me. I am a simple man and I never know what to expect from a woman when she speaks at cross purposes. You will have to instruct me in what you mean.'

He lifted her hand to his lips and she knew what he meant, and the instruction he expected. For a moment the world dropped away, and then with a start they became aware of the servants unloading the coach and standing at the head of the horses, waiting to lead them away. Darcy gave the order and they went into the house, where the servants greeted them. Georgiana came skipping back into the grand hall.

'Home!' she cried. 'It is so good to be home. I was so afraid of putting a foot wrong at aunt's! And Mr Collins looks so disapprovingly on me! Except when he praises so effusively. I couldn't make him out at all.'

'Did you know that he once proposed to Lizzy?' Darcy said, still in a playful mood, in expectation of delights later that night. 'Can you imagine that she turned him down?'

Georgiana was startled into a laugh.

'Oh, Lizzy! How could you have broken his heart so!'

Then she darted off, and soon they heard the piano from the drawing room, sounding out a gay march. Lizzy was reminded suddenly of Mary, and the way she would turn to the piano as soon as they returned home from some small outing, to Meryton perhaps, as if to quiet herself after the excitement. Since Mary didn't play the piano any more, what would she do to calm herself? she wondered.

Oh, Mary. I hope you have done the right thing for yourself.

★ ★ ★

The very next day Mr Aikens and Hyperion called at Pemberley. The young man swept in after the butler's quiet announcement, his greatcoat sweeping along the parqueted floor. Its hem was crusted with mud, as were his boots.

'Capital! You've returned! It has been deadly dull without you, Darcy! You have an excellent chase across your estates. Did you know that Hyperion took the stiles at the cattle crossing with at least two feet to spare? Landed in the mud but kept his feet and almost threw me off, he was so proud of himself. Ladies! Pleasure.'

He bowed.

'Mr Aikens, so good to see you,' Lizzy said, now that he had stopped and she could catch up. Mr Aikens looked around with some puzzlement and a growing alarm.

'Where's Miss Bennet? Did you know that Hyperion had grown deuced fond of her? He moped awfully when I told him she was gone. Couldn't wait a moment when I told him the carriage had returned and you were back.'

'Mary stayed at Rosings Park, Mr Aikens. She has become a particular friend of Anne de Bourgh.'

Mr Aikens was for once wholly at a loss for words. That is, his lips moved but he was silent, as if he could not fathom Lizzy's meaning. And then she felt another pang. Had they crushed Mary's one chance at joy with this strange man who loved horses and dancing and never opened a book?

It was Mr Darcy who spoke first in his dry way. 'Yes, we left her behind in the dragon's den. She said she wishes to remain there — and I think she will do well, to draw my cousin out of her solitude and loneliness.'

'A companion,' Mr Aikens repeated, and his eyes darkened. He spoke with great distinctness. 'So she will fetch shawls and fans and read out loud and sit quietly by. Mrs Darcy, had she given up?'

Georgiana was looking rather frightened by Mr Aikens's turn from amiable to angered. Lizzy shook her head.

'Mr Aikens, you — and Hyperion — seem to have taken with great fondness to Mary and I know she is grateful for your friendship. She has not given up. She took it as a challenge. I think she liked the idea of winning over Lady Catherine and she has grown fond of Miss de Bourgh.'

Mr Aikens snorted. Lizzy grew angry herself. 'Excuse me sir, but I believe I know my sister better than you do.'

'No you don't,' he said flatly, and Lizzy's eyes widened. 'You don't because you think of her only in one way, as the quiet bookish one. I see now what it is. She hadn't given up. You had. Good day, Mrs Darcy. Miss Darcy. Sir.'

He turned on his heel, leaving a clod of dried mud on the floor, and left, his capes swinging.

In the echoing silence that remained, they all looked down at the mud.

'Shall I call Mrs Reynolds?' Georgianne ventured. Rather than ringing, she fled at once to find her directly.

Lizzy and Darcy looked at one another.

'Oh my goodness,' she said. 'What have we done?'

He pulled her close and kissed her. 'The only thing we could have done — support Mary in her decision,' he said firmly. 'Tom will get over his anger as quickly as he got into it. A new fancy has probably already come into his head in the time it took him to mount his horse. If I truly felt he had fallen in love with Mary, I would drive to Rosings to bring her back at once.'

Lizzy gave him a look to remind him of the last time he had misjudged a friend's heart, and Darcy acknowledged that with an inclination of his head even as he defended himself.

'If you want me to go, I will,' he said. 'But I think Tom Aikens will only raise her hopes and break her heart. He doesn't even *read*, Lizzy. I am not even sure he knows how.'

She had to laugh at that.

'I will defer to your judgement this time, sir. But you have not yet redeemed yourself. I will keep an eye on Mr Aikens and if I see any signs of steadfastness, any at all, you will drive to Rosings at once to bring back Mary.'

★ ★ ★

Once Mr Aikens had taken his leave, and Pemberley had returned to its usual quietude, Lizzy sat down to read several letters. She hadn't had a chance to skim a welcome letter from Aunt Gardiner when the footman brought her another one, from Jane. Lizzy set aside her aunt's letter and opened Jane's with eagerness.

Both the eldest Bennet daughters had been keenly aware of Lydia's fall and took pains that Kitty should not, through the neglect of one parent and the encouragement of the other, find herself in the same predicament. Accordingly, when Jane invited Kitty to stay with her and Mr Bingley at their establishment, it was to impart to Kitty some acquaintance with society and conduct. Only Caroline Bingley was not pleased with the arrangement, but she had never been able to forgive Lizzy and thus her whole family from ruining what she had thought were her chances with Darcy. And Kitty, admittedly, could wear on anyone's nerves. However, Kitty had already improved immeasurably, now that she had been away from Lydia's influence, and Lizzy opened up Jane's letter, expecting nothing more exciting than that she had taken Kitty shopping for a bonnet and that the girl had attended one quiet ball.

Dear Lizzy,
Oh dear, after writing you so recently, now I find I must write you again, and I don't know whether to laugh or cry.

I am afraid that Kitty got into the most awful scrape and it was while she was under our care. I feel so ashamed of myself and, at every turn, Caroline is making it worse, as she is wont to do. But you see, a London gentleman — I can hardly call him such — gave Kitty too much to drink at a ball, and then took her off to see the tigers in Mr Kent's menagerie. Oh Lizzy! It was dreadful. If Bingley had not come in time, the tigers would have eaten Kitty! At least there was an Indian servant who held her back, but you can imagine my fright.

I know I am hardly making any sense, but I can hardly believe it myself. And poor Caroline — I know, Lizzy, but she is poor Caroline — she is beside herself. Mr Kent is a special friend from when she and Bingley were young, and he returned to London from India with an astonishing fortune. That I believe is the reason for the menagerie. And then when Kitty made a spectacle of herself, I think Caroline felt that she had lost her only chance of re-establishing her friendship with Mr Kent. Her hopes have been dashed, and we have been quite feeling it as well, as she makes her discontent known. I own, I was quite upset when she said that Kitty would go the way of Lydia, but dear Lizzy, I can understand her concern.

For, much as we were injured by Lydia's fall, so too was Caroline and I think she feels it keenly. She had requested that we keep Kitty in hand and we tried, Lizzy, but we thought, what harm is in just one ball?

I must close, but first I beg you, not to tell Mama and Papa about Kitty. I will, in my own way. And secondly, have you any advice for us on the matter of Wickham?

How is our plan for Mary? And do give my love to Darcy and Georgiana.

All my love,
Jane

Lizzy's eyes widened. The matter of Wickham? She searched through the other letters and found an earlier one from Jane.

Dear Lizzy,
Oh dear, I don't know what to do.

Wickham is in London! Without Lydia apparently. And he has been seeing Kitty, or at least, she has been seeing him, and only just now has she told us. He met her along the promenade when she was out with some young friends — good people, the Cranes, they have a daughter and son, Kitty's age — and then he left his card at the house! We were not at home to him, of course, but then Kitty met him again, and she said he was with a strange woman.

Oh Lizzy, Kitty has also been writing to Lydia, and Lydia said that she was to be in London and gave her an address, and Bingley said it was a very bad address. He has gone to investigate, but do you think, perhaps, that you could speak to Darcy and see what he could make of things? If you think he won't be too angry. I don't know. Please do what you think is best.

Lizzy folded the letter carefully and set it down on her little table next to her little figurines from Longbourn.

'Wickham,' she said out loud. The man could not leave them alone. He had not just ruined Lydia, but bid fair to ruin two families. She had not thought much of Caroline's predicament, but she could see it now. Caroline was a grand lady who was now tied to the Bennets and could do nothing about it. She would think every move the Bennets made reflected poorly on her. She makes it worse for herself, Lizzy thought. I will not be held to blame for every fault and failing of Caroline Bingley's life. But she could not but admit that Caroline had a point.

And something must be done about Wickham. If he had taken up with another woman and abandoned poor Lydia, it was but a predictable result of his actions. He had never loved her — indeed, their elopement had been less about love than about embarrassment of Darcy. She was an expedient, and a willing target, though she loved Wickham, in her careless saucy way. She loved him, and would be devastated at his betrayal. Lizzy had a wistful moment, indulging a dream that Lydia could be returned to Longbourn, to live out in quiet company with her mother, who had always loved her youngest best, and her father, never to stray in company again. But Mr Bennet would not allow it, and so Lydia was banished from her childhood home.

Nor would she be welcome at Pemberley or with Bingley and Jane. Lizzy felt a pang of sadness for her exasperating little sister.

'Lydia, what is to be done with you?' she said out loud again. She did not want to talk to Darcy. She understood Jane's reticence.

Darcy could call out Wickham, less to avenge Lydia than to have reason at last to avenge Georgiana's near disgrace. Wickham should have realized that, Lizzy thought. So what is his game, to be openly seen in London with another woman and knowing the word would get back to his arch enemy?

He wishes to wring money from the family again, she thought. After all, it worked so well the last time. Her anger rising, Lizzy got up. If I were a man, I would call him out myself, she thought. She went off in search of Darcy. He might want to call out Wickham, but she had faith that he would not let his passions overrule him in this matter.

She found him with Georgiana. She was playing for him in a desultory fashion, more extemporizing than playing one of her pieces. Darcy was reading. They both looked up at Lizzy in relief.

'My dear,' he said. He held out his hand. 'Come.' She sat down with him.

'I'm glad you're here,' Georgiana said mournfully. 'I miss Mary. I can't believe we abandoned her to Aunt de Bourgh. I think Mr Aikens was right.'

'We didn't abandon her,' Lizzy said with exasperation. 'Goodness, Georgiana, please don't take it so.'

'But what if Mr Aikens wanted to marry

her? Now he'll forget all about her.'

'Mr Aikens does not want to marry Mary!' Lizzy said, feeling quite like her mother and guiltily so. For Mrs Bennet had often discounted Mary in this very same way. Oh bother, she thought. If we don't restore some sense to Kitty and deal with Wickham, never again will a Bennet get married.

'Mary felt that Anne de Bourgh wanted a friend, and I own that I agree with her, though the sacrifice may be too great,' Darcy said.

'And there is the matter of Hyperion,' Georgiana went on disconsolately, or so it would have seemed if Lizzy had not caught a gleam of mischief in her expression.

'Hyperion will recover, Georgiana. And Mary was quite determined. She is very independent in the matter. In fact, I wouldn't be surprised if Lady Catherine decides that she is too independent for her Anne and sends her home to us. I also wouldn't be surprised if she wins over Lady Catherine and Anne with her sermons and speeches. Either way, we did not abandon Mary, she may come home any time she likes, and Hyperion and Mr Aikens may fall in love with her as soon as she returns. But Georgiana, may I borrow Darcy for a time? I must talk with him.'

Georgiana pouted and went back to her piano. 'I have the fidgets,' she said. 'All this talk of Mr Aikens, I expect. I want to go riding — may I?'

'Make sure Jameson goes with you,' Darcy said, and she slid from the piano stool and went off to change into her habit. He pulled Lizzy towards him, and she sat on his knee. 'As for you. Why must you interrupt all the terribly important things I am doing?'

Lizzy made an unladylike expression. 'Be forewarned. I give you one chance to escape, Darcy. You should go riding with Georgiana and leave the groom to his work.'

'I will take my chances.'

She took a breath. 'It's Wickham. He's returned, and if possible it's worse than before.'

She told him all, not omitting Kitty's escapade among the tigers, though she was not entirely sure what that was about. When she finished, Darcy sat for a moment, staring off into space. At last he helped Lizzy to her feet.

'My dear,' he said. 'I can see nothing else to do but go to London and meet Bingley.'

'I'm so sorry,' she said, and her voice broke. But Darcy kissed her.

'It is not you who needs to be sorry. Wickham came into your life because of me.

He would never have run off with Lydia, never would even have looked at her, if I had just told you the truth, all of you, sooner. This would not have happened.'

She didn't quite agree but she didn't disabuse him. The Bennets were at fault too, and she knew, if it had not been Wickham, it would have been someone else. It had only been a matter of time before Lydia followed her untamed nature.

Georgiana came rustling back in, dressed in a smart dark-green riding-habit with epaulettes and braid. Her hat had a sweeping green feather and her riding crop had a silver handle.

'I'm ready! And Lizzy, you should learn to ride. I am tired of going out with the grooms. They are always telling me not to jump this or not to gallop there.'

'And do you listen to them?' Darcy said sternly.

'Of course, because I know they will carry tales. But my sister wouldn't tell on me.'

'Indeed I would, if you were unsafe,' Lizzy said. 'And if I learned to ride you would be bored to distraction. I would have to sit on the smallest pony and be led around.'

Georgiana giggled.

Darcy said, 'Come give me a kiss before you go. I have had some news and must go to

London immediately. But do not use this as a time to disobey the grooms, because I will hear about it when I come back.'

Georgiana looked as if she wanted to take her chances, but at last she said, 'All right. Lizzy, are you making him go?'

'Indeed I am not. It's his decision.'

'But this is what you wanted to talk to him about?'

Lizzy nodded.

Georgiana tilted her head, then said, 'And you have no plans to tell me, do you.'

'I promise you won't remain in the dark if it turns out there's any news I can tell you,' Darcy said. Georgiana was almost a grown woman and they could not keep news from her for ever, but Wickham had been such a bad man, better to allow her some peace.

Knowing that Georgiana would continue to tease, Darcy kissed Lizzy and said, 'I must be off. Georgiana, be good. My dear.'

He left them. Georgiana watched her brother go, a considering look on her face. 'You won't tell me, either?'

Lizzy didn't reply. Instead, she took the young girl's arm. 'Come. I will walk to the stables with you and then we can watch Darcy out of sight.'

Georgiana let herself be persuaded, and they went off to the stables, there to watch

Darcy depart for London.

When Georgiana had set off in another direction, riding her sprightly bay mare, followed by stolid Jameson on a grey gelding, Lizzy had the house to herself. Now she really felt lonely. She returned to her parlour, missing everyone. She sat and reread Jane's letter, still puzzling over the tigers. What on earth could Jane mean? She sat down to write a reply to her sister, wishing the house were not so very quiet.

18

Mary's new life was hard, much harder than she had ever suspected it would be. It should be hard. Lady Catherine ruled her daughter's every waking moment with a fist of iron and if she could have ruled Anne's sleep she would have done so. As it was, if Lady Catherine could have ordered it so, Anne would have received all manner of unsuitable physic. Instead, she was attended almost daily by the doctor, a learned man who quickly understood that his real patient was Lady Catherine herself. So his nostrums were mostly wholesome and anodyne, for he knew that Anne suffered from nothing but too much maternal attention. His remedies provided a sop now and again to Lady Catherine's desire for dosing.

Each morning, before Anne dressed, this gentleman came up, and in the presence of Lady Catherine and Anne's maid, he checked her pulse with utmost attention, looked at her tongue, and prescribed something or other. Anne dutifully swallowed all that he gave her, while he checked her pulse again, his eyes closed, as if communing with her humours, and then pronounced her well.

Mary, upon first witnessing this scene, tried to discern what the doctor was doing, but could come to no conclusion other than that he meant only to allay Lady Catherine's fears whilst doing as little harm as possible, to his patient or his purse. Lady Catherine spoke throughout the examination, telling him his business, and he remained calm and collected throughout.

So that is how her ladyship must be handled, Mary thought. She resolved to follow his guidance. The doctor, on being introduced to the new companion, gave her a smile and a grave adjuration not to tire Miss de Bourgh unduly and to ensure that her charge was always well protected from draughts and ate no food that was too hot-natured. Meat must be well boiled, and cold drinks should be avoided. Yet as he gathered up his supplies and packed them away into his valise, he said something remarkable for her ears alone, as the others bustled around to help Anne into her morning dress.

'I would like it very much, Miss Bennet, if you can induce Miss Anne to join you for a gentle walk in the gardens around Rosings as often as the weather permits. The exercise will do her good and put roses in her cheeks, I am sure.'

'I will do my best, sir,' Mary promised.

Unfortunately, Lady Catherine managed to hear her words over the general hustle and bustle.

'What is that Miss Bennet? What do you say?'

Mary had never told such an untruth so quickly in all her life.

'The doctor bade me again not to tire Anne, ma'am,' she said.

Lady Catherine eyed them suspiciously, but just then Anne said querulously, 'Mother, attend me. Why do you not listen to me?' She turned her attention at once to her daughter.

'Yes, my pet. What is it?'

Anne gave some complaint and Mary schooled her expression into one of complete innocence. Had Anne also taken part in the little deception? The doctor finished packing and gave her a wink. Mary blushed.

The advice from the doctor gave Mary her course of action. If she acted the part of a companion and guardian, for she understood that her position was to be something of both, then she would have to bring about the separation of Anne from Lady Catherine, and thus make her own life bearable. She thought she could do something about that, and resolved to put it to the test as soon as she could. Accordingly, one morning during her first week at Rosings, after she learned the routine that Lady Catherine and her daughter kept, she made her first proposal.

'Lady Catherine,' she said at breakfast. 'I thought that perhaps Anne and I could drive out in the carriage today, since the weather is so fine.'

'Anne does not drive without me or Mrs Jenkinson, Miss Bennet. I do not think that you should be thinking up amusements but should leave that to me.'

'Of course, ma'am.' Mary nodded but she caught Anne's expression out of the corner of her eye. The young woman looked distressed, as if there was something she wished to say. Small steps, Mary thought. Small steps. They finished their breakfast mostly in silence and then retired to the sitting room, where Mary picked up the book she had been reading out loud to Anne, a small book of learned essays, written by men who evidently thought literary merit lay in soothing thought rather than exciting it. Lady Catherine attended to her own business, and the two girls sat together, separated from each other by a small table. Mary read with as animated an air as possible, but the book was boring, and even she had trouble stifling her yawns. Longbourn was never this still, she thought, hard put to keep her mind on the solid book of sermons that neither challenged nor pleased. While the grandness of Rosings never failed to overwhelm Mary from the moment she woke up to the moment she laid down her head on her pillow in her small room, the house oppressed her in a way that Pemberley never had and Longbourn never could. Comfortable old Longbourn! So crowded with five sisters! She had wished for solitude all her years before Lydia, Jane, and Lizzy left. Now she had all the solitude her heart required, and she found, as so many do, that one could have too much of a desired thing.

No wonder Anne was so ill — it was the only thing of interest to anyone here.

'You read that sentence twice, Miss Bennet,' Anne said, breaking into her reverie. Mary blushed at having been caught. She closed the book.

'Perhaps we could do something else,' she proposed hopefully. 'A walk in the gardens?' The doctor would be pleased.

'Walking gives me a headache,' was the querulous response. 'I think I will retire to my room for the morning.' Anne rang for her maid. Mary's heart sank. She had been one week at Rosings and had never sat so still in her life. Dutifully she gathered up Anne's shawl and followed behind as the maid helped her to her feet and led her up to her bedroom.

★ ★ ★

As it turned out, Mary did not have to persuade Anne to take exercise or air. Anne persuaded herself. Mary was surprised to see the spark that she had known was within Anne made manifest so soon, and it was lit by none other than Lady Catherine herself.

Mary had long suspected, and her suspicions were borne out, that Lady Catherine would be more demanding of her time and attention than would Anne. Most of what Lady Catherine required was simply admiration.

'Miss Bennet, have you seen the fresco over the great hall? It was commissioned especially by my father after his visits to Italy. Miss Bennet, you must tell me what you think of our gallery of portraits. They show a true nobility in the de Bourgh line. Miss Bennet, I pray you will not write letters boasting of your new position at Rosings — the charms and delights of Rosings are not for gossip. Miss Bennet, tell me — have you ever seen a park as beautifully ordered and well-maintained as the grounds here?'

At first Mary had tried to make an intelligent comment, but it was soon evident that no actual opinion was required other

212

than Lady Catherine's own. Then she tried to respond politely, but there was never any time, as Lady Catherine furnished both her observation and Mary's response. In the end she stopped looking up, and continued with her embroidery.

On one occasion she was reading out loud to Anne while Lady Catherine started up her conversation with no regard for Mary or her daughter. Rather than stopping, Mary raised her voice.

'Miss Bennet! Are you even listening to me?' Lady Catherine snapped. Mary stopped her reading and closed the book, marking the place with a ribbon. Anne waited, apprehensively.

'I was not, ma'am,' Mary said.

'You were not?'

'No. I was reading to Miss de Bourgh.'

This had an unexpected but wholly desirable effect, for it stopped Lady Catherine cold. She had engaged Mary to be a companion to Anne. Mary could hardly perform her duties if Lady Catherine continually sought her attention. Lady Catherine's two guiding motivations, her demand for attention and her love for her daughter, warred with each other, and love won.

'Well? What are you waiting for? Anne is waiting, Miss Bennet.'

She sat down and made a great show of arranging her shawls and skirts and settling herself in, fussing over her spoiled lapdog, and Mary found her place again. No sooner had she opened her mouth to read when,

'Miss Bennet!'

Obediently Mary stopped.

'Are you sure this is the book Anne would like to hear?'

Mary turned to Anne. Anne sat straight up. She started to say something, stopped, and then burst out, 'Miss Bennet, let's go for a walk.'

Had the tiny dog nestled in Lady Catherine's skirt spoken up the effect could not have been more startling. Lady Catherine's eyes popped in a most unladylike fashion.

'Anne!' said her mother, gasping quite like a fish.

Anne stood up and Mary followed suit.

'I think that's a splendid idea,' Mary said.

★ ★ ★

It was a lovely day to take some air. Rosings was such a grand estate. Mary had taken for granted the rambles in Longbourn that were enjoyed by the Bennet family. She also found much to admire at Pemberley, with its long avenues lined with stately trees, and its gardens and fields. Rosings was even more extravagant so it was a shame that so little use was made of its grounds. The house was sited on the top of a rise, so that all might look upon it, and it might survey all of its holdings and be satisfied each day that everything was in its place, at its feet.

Not far below Rosings was the village of Hunsford and Mr Collins and Charlotte's little house and the well-trod path that wound from Rosings to the parsonage, well worn by Mr Collins's feet. Anne and Mary did not walk that way. By mostly silent agreement they wound along the gardens that spread out behind the house. As Mary noted from her window each day, it was untamed here, less groomed, more tangled and wild. There were the fields and the farm buildings and cattle and sheep. Deer stepped gently through the untidy pastures at twilight. This path was rough and rocky, and both women were breathing hard when they stopped to sit on a natural stone bench halfway down the hill. Mary looked back up at the house once.

'It will be a very hard climb to go home,' she said dubiously. Mary had only lately started to enjoy walking, when she had begun to sort through the loneliness and uneasiness that had plagued her when her sisters married. She did not necessarily enjoy the heat the exercise brought.

'Indeed,' Anne said. 'We shouldn't have come this way.' But her eyes were bright and there was red in her cheeks, so unusual for the pale, still, quiet girl. She smiled now, shading her eyes. 'I never come this way. We should walk here every day.'

Well, she was the companion. Mary smiled gamely. 'It has a certain grandeur, a wildness as if it were an older England.'

'One day it will be mine,' Anne said. 'Or my husband's, though I don't know if I will ever marry.'

Mary supposed that she should make consoling noises and assure Anne that of course she would marry. Instead she let the wind rush over her and lifted her face to the sun, playing with the clouds. A shadow swept over the two women and raced over the fields, the wind bending the grasses before it. From far away came the baahing of the sheep and the lowing of the cattle, a man's rough voice and a dog's bark.

'Must you? Marry, I mean?' Mary said instead. Wasn't one perquisite of the wealth and status of a de Bourgh that she did not have to marry?

Anne gathered her shawl around her and shrugged. She looked away from Mary. 'What else is a de Bourgh to do? We marry and we

216

lord over Rosings and take our place among the highest in England. My mother was most displeased with your sister when she became engaged to Mr Darcy. He was supposed to marry me.'

Mary remembered Lady Catherine's startling visit and Lizzy's anger afterwards. She hadn't found out until months later what Lady Catherine's purpose had been, for Lizzy had kept her counsel out of anger and embarrassment. 'I think we were all surprised, since they did not seem to like each other one bit at first,' she said instead. When she had heard the news, she thought that she had been once again left out of being told anything important. Then she quickly learned that in fact, they had all been deceived.

Anne gave a thin little sort of laugh. 'You were surprised at their attachment? I was not. The first time I saw them together, in this house last year, I knew they had very high regard for one another. I sit quietly, you see, but I pay attention.'

'They must have been more forward with each other then,' Mary said, still puzzled.

'Hardly. They barely exchanged two words, but Mr Darcy took pains to stand next to your sister at every opportunity, and she could scarcely look up at him. I don't need to read a novel to know what that means.'

So the attachment that the two actors hid from all their nearest relations had revealed itself to one silent girl. Then Mary thought of the implications of Anne's observations. She, sitting silently, watching Mr Darcy . . .

'Had you — been in love with him?'

It was an impertinent question, but she felt she had to know.

'Love does not enter into it.' Now Anne sounded like her mother. 'I hardly knew my cousin. We were pledged from infancy, and I grew up thinking our match was inevitable. I still wonder at your sister for going against my mother's wishes.'

Mary was startled into a laugh. 'I wonder at your mother thinking she had the right to stop Lizzy and Darcy from marrying.'

'She had an obligation, Miss Bennet. If Darcy were not to marry *me*, he should not throw himself away on someone so very unsuitable.'

Mary felt herself grow dangerously angry. Her voice was quiet with her attempt to control her emotions. 'Miss de Bourgh, I would rather you not insult my family. My sister is not unsuitable. The Bennets are good people, better perhaps than some that interfere with the lives of others. Your mother showed her breeding when she intruded into our lives so rudely and told Lizzy not to marry Darcy.'

Anne stood, and her small eyes glittered. Her face was pale again, except for two spots of colour high upon her cheeks. The two ladies faced each other on the side of the rocky slope.

'How dare you speak of my mother in that way. You are low and plain, and I only took you as my companion out of pity.'

'Amusing. Pity for you is the only reason I took the position.' Mary's own response took her by surprise and she stopped abruptly. Anne seemed equally startled. For a moment they both looked at each other, then looked away in embarrassment. They had declared in anger what they had conceived privately and had never meant to reveal.

'I can dismiss you any time I wish,' Anne said. 'I will tell my mother you are no longer suitable.'

'Good,' Mary said. 'I will write to my parents and start packing at once.' She picked her way back up the hill, stumbling a little over the rocks in her angered haste, her thin slippers inadequate for the going underfoot. It was not long before she took a careless step and slid, rolling on her ankle, and she fell into the dust. Mary gave an involuntary cry and stopped herself from sliding back down to Anne.

'Miss Bennet! What have you done?'

Frightened, Anne made her way back up to her. Mary sat up, rubbing her ankle, her stockings and slippers covered with dirt and mud.

'Nothing permanent,' she said, her voice quivering. Her ankle hurt dreadfully. 'I will be able to walk in a minute.'

Anne looked as if she were going to cry or rage. She chose the latter. 'Miss Bennet. How could you! You are supposed to help me!'

Mary laughed out loud though she herself felt like crying. 'I am sorry, Miss de Bourgh. I don't know what I was thinking.'

'Now what am I supposed to do? If my mother finds out we walked this way — Miss Bennet! I demand you stand up at once.'

'I don't think I can,' Mary said. What were they to do? This was the furthest Anne had walked by herself for months. How could she climb up the hill for help?

'If I help you up, could you walk home? Oh please say yes, Miss Bennet. For I don't know what else to do.'

Mary agreed to try, and she let Anne help her to her feet. But Miss de Bourgh had very little strength, and the hill was so steep that they both fell back. The pain increased.

'You will have to go back to the house and fetch someone,' Mary said at last. It was mortifying. Anne would not have to dismiss her after all. After this, Lady Catherine would set her in a milk cart and send her home that way.

'I suppose I will have to,' Anne said resentfully. 'Wait here.' She gathered her skirts and marched back up the hill, looking rather like her mother.

Mary sighed and put her forehead in her hand. How could she have done such a thing? In all the stories, it was the rich heiress who hurt her ankle, to be rescued by the gallant hero. She was the companion, for goodness' sake. What was she thinking? Her lips quivered again, but instead of crying she found herself laughing. Mary Bennet, can't you do anything right? She couldn't be pretty, she couldn't play the piano, and she couldn't even be a companion to a rich selfish girl who would grow up exactly like her mother.

A noise caught her attention and she looked down the trail. Two farmers came huffing and puffing up the hill.

'We saw you was in trouble, miss,' the old man said. The younger one was a sturdy fellow who looked to be his son. 'Came as soon as we could.'

'Thank you sir,' Mary said, heat rising into her cheeks. 'I turned my ankle.'

'Saw that. The shoes you ladies wear are nothing for this ground. I wonder that you came this way. You should stick to the footpaths. Robert, help me here.'

Roughly but not unkindly they soon had Mary to her feet. They escorted her up the hill, speaking kindly and encouragingly. Mary was relieved that she was not to be carried. That would be much too — too overwhelming, as if she were heroine and the young farmer her handsome hero.

Mary Bennet, you should stick to your sermons, she told herself. Novels are no good for you.

19

Lady Catherine's eyes fairly popped out of her head when her daughter recounted Mary's mishap and told how she had gone for help. She sent for Mary, but her housekeeper told her that Miss Bennet was hard put to manage the stairs, and could they send for the doctor to have a look at her ankle? With due resentment Lady Catherine allowed the doctor to be sent for. The good man came at once, for he thought it was Miss Anne who had been hurt. When he found it was the new companion he breathed a sigh of relief. He bound Mary's ankle, scolded her loudly for her clumsiness, and told her to stay off her feet for the next few days.

'If you can, that is,' he said *sotto voce*, as he packed his satchel. 'If I know Lady Catherine she will send you packing. I'll see what I can do to prevent that. But there's nothing wrong with you that a bit of rest won't put right. I must say, Miss Bennet, this wasn't what I meant when I said you should try to get Miss de Bourgh out and about. What led you to try that path?'

Mary could hardly tell him that it had been

Anne's choice. After all, she should have been wise enough to counsel a different walk. She apologized and he patted her hand kindly.

As promised, his manner was more stern when he spoke to Lady Catherine in the hall outside Mary's room, telling her that if she did not want to be responsible for an amputation Miss Bennet should be allowed to rest as long as she needed. Lady Catherine's response was most gratifying, for she told the doctor that she would ensure that Mary rested and had the best care, along with advice for healing a hurt ankle and a discourse on proper shoes and any number of suggestions on how best to wrap her ankle so as to heal it best. The doctor listened gravely, and Mary closed her eyes. She was quite tired from her adventure.

Lady Catherine's voice signalled its mistress's progress down the hallway and Mary was left in silence. Her ankle throbbed and the emotion that had been kept under a tight rein now exposed itself, leaving her weak and tired. She had almost fallen into sleep, when a knock came at the door.

It was Anne.

Mary struggled to sit straight. Anne had a most peculiar expression on her face, one that Mary had never before seen her wear. She twisted her hands in her little lacy shawl, and she looked everywhere but at Mary. Eventually she burst out, 'I should not have said those things. I insulted you and your family and you should not have borne it.'

'I didn't bear it,' Mary pointed out. ' 'Twas why I fell.'

Anne gave a choking little laugh. 'Miss Bennet, you are strangely forthright with me. I wish — I wish more people would be. Please don't go.'

Mary frowned. 'I don't know but that your mother will make that decision for me,' she said. 'She's very angry.'

'If you wish to stay I will talk to my mother.'

Mary was at a loss for words. Did she want to stay? Miss Anne was a strange girl indeed. She was prickly, like Mary, and she was awkward, and she didn't seem to have any friends, not that she had the opportunity to make any. Despite their recent falling out, though, Mary thought that she and Anne could come to understand one another. Other people know how to live in society, but we two do not, she thought. Dances, flirting, all the parts we are supposed to play — it's as if we were thrust on stage with no time to learn our lines, and our whole lives depend on how we play our parts.

'Do you want me to stay?' she said.

Anne nodded. 'I understand if you wish to go home. But I would like to start again. On another foot, perhaps.'

It was a very small joke, but it might have been Anne's first one and it so surprised Mary that she laughed. Anne laughed too. It was a very good thing that Lady Catherine had not yet come back from advising the doctor on his profession, for if she had heard the two of them laughing she would have dismissed Mary outright. Grand ladies do not like laughter, especially in their offspring. It betokened a dangerous ease and carelessness. Anne laughing was Anne unaware of her high position. But Lady Catherine was safely out of earshot and so not able to save her daughter from her downfall, and when Anne spoke to her mother later at dinner, and told her that Mary had apologized thoroughly for her clumsiness and would not be so careless again, and had begged to stay on, Lady Catherine unbent enough to allow it.

'But you must take care, Anne,' she told her daughter. 'She is a Bennet, after all, and they are dangerous. They don't know their place, and they have been given unwarranted freedom to make their own decisions and think for themselves. I allow it only with the greatest of caution, and with the belief that you can teach her much. She must be made humble, you know.'

Anne agreed with her mother and they supped in silence.

★   ★   ★

Mary's injury kept her in her room for two days, but she was not left alone. In fact, when Mr Collins came to visit, she rued that she could not flee but had to sit and receive him. He paced in her small room, ducking when he came to the eave at the far end, nervously holding his hat while he berated her.

First it was her clumsiness, then her temerity, then her carelessness — what if it had been Anne who had fallen? Had she not been aware of the risk? And Anne had to go to fetch help. Was cousin Mary not aware of how beneath her status that was? Was this how she repaid the great attention that was bestowed upon her by Lady Catherine? Did she not see how this reflected upon Mr Collins himself, and his wife and child, by virtue of her relationship to them? And what of her sisters? Mr Darcy was a relative of the de Bourghs — could she not see that her mishap also dishonoured him and, by extension, his wife and so her other sisters?

As he went on, Mary listened, fascinated. Would Mr Collins even relate her slip to

Lydia's downfall? Indeed he would, with many flowery allusions to a woman's carelessness and a single slip that could bring her low if she did not place her feet carefully on the path of virtue. Just when she expected that he would warn her that her twisted ankle could bring about the downfall of the kingdom, rather like the want of a nail, he changed tack.

'I told Lady Catherine that it would bring me honour if I could assist her in this terrible task and relieve her of your presence, which must be so odious to her. But she told me in no uncertain terms that you are staying. I do hope, cousin Mary, that you did not beg, but that you are aware of the great honour — nay, the great mercy — that has been shown you.'

'Miss de Bourgh asked me to stay,' Mary said. He stared at her, thunderstruck.

'Miss de Bourgh!' he said, his tones excited and reverent. 'Miss de Bourgh! So she shows as great a forgiveness as her mother. She is a Christian indeed.' He took on an expression of deep thought. 'Yes, *there* is a sermon — I can turn that into a sermon that will be one to reckon with on Sunday!' He turned to her. 'You see, from even the most dire calamity can be brought forth the great blessing of a lesson for us all. A sermon indeed!'

Mary could hardly wait for him to go; she

was not disappointed. He swept out with scarcely a farewell, and she was left alone at last.

* * *

Her ankle healed quickly. She soon was able to put on her little shoes and go out on gentle walks with Anne, and their lives took a regular turn. They never went down the steep hill again but rather walked to the village, or to visit Charlotte, or took the carriage for rides further afield. In the evening, Mary read, while Anne embroidered, for as Anne had avowed, she hated reading. It made her head hurt. And Mary had never had the skill to set stitches or net purses. Lady Catherine sat with them often, and when they took the carriage she came as well, facing the two of them with her hands in a muff and well wrapped against the chill. Her conversation was chiefly to the point of making sure that Anne was kept warm and to admonish both girls on many subjects. Mary suspected that Lady Catherine was not so sure about leaving her only daugher in the careless hands of a Bennet. It was only when Lady Catherine managed her accounts, as she called her afternoon naps, that they were left alone.

During those moments alone, Mary and

Anne had a more amiable friendship. It was hard to speak freely with Lady Catherine interrupting every minute, so they saved their conversation for the afternoons when they had time to themselves. On fine days they walked in the garden, achieving that kind of intimacy that like-minded friends fall into. Anne wanted to hear all about Longbourn and Meryton, for she had had even less exposure to varied society than Mary. She became deeply involved in all of the doings in Mary's little village, and she often ventured an opinion of her own. It was deeply gratifying to have an audience and not have to vie with four other voices for someone's ear. Anne at least listened when Mary told her things. Everyone else just said, 'Oh Mary.'

As the days passed, Anne became less grave, more lighter of spirit. Although she was apt to shrink into herself when her mother was about, she became open and lively with Mary. Little did Mary see it in herself, but she too became more open and lively. It took Mr Collins, of all people, to bring it to everyone's attention.

★ ★ ★

True to his threat, Mr Collins wrote a sermon extolling Anne for her mercy and pity and nobility in forgiving Mary for her fall. He did Mary the courtesy of not mentioning her by name, but the effect was coy rather than mannered, as he kept winking in her direction in church and nodding until everyone turned to look at her. Mary felt the blush rise from her throat to her forehead, and she took a deep breath, wanting the pew to fold into the floor with her and never let her loose. Little did she know, however, that the looks of the parishioners were sympathetic rather than judging, and a few of the young men in the church even thought that Miss Bennet was being treated rather badly by her cousin and that it would have gone better had one of them come to her rescue when she had fallen. When the end of the sermon came and they all filed out of church, Mary thought at first that the young men bowing to her were like the Lucas boys, all teasing and horrid rather than nice.

As they stood about talking with Mr Collins and Charlotte and doting on Robert, now grown into a lusty little infant, a few of the young men paid her their particular addresses. Now she could see that they were not like the Lucas boys at all, but were vying for her attention. One or two laughed at everything she said until Mary began to blush again.

But Lady Catherine was longing to go, so Mary made her bow, said goodbye and was helped into the carriage after Anne and Lady Catherine. Mary held her head high, never once guessing that her profile was proud and her figure remarked upon. A village is nothing without gossip; everyone already knew that the young companion was Mr Collins's cousin, and that her two older sisters had married two fine young men, that she was the daughter of a gentleman and that she was the particular friend of the daughter of the grandest family in the county.

Even a plain Bennet is a Bennet, and though Mary was used to being overshadowed by her pretty sisters, she was not so plain on her own account.

Charlotte remarked on the transformation after church as she sat down to dinner with her husband.

'Have you noticed Mary Bennet, Mr Collins?' she said. 'She has become rather pretty, I think. I can't see why I hadn't noticed it before. Her complexion has become quite rosy and her hair shines so in the sun. It is unfortunate that she has bad sight, but she doesn't squint so much any more.'

Mr Collins was astonished that his wife asked his opinion on such a thing as the prettiness of the cousin he spent most of his time overlooking, except when he could expose her to the censure of her society.

'My dear! I cannot imagine what you mean. Mary Bennet is not pretty! She cannot be pretty. She is Anne de Bourgh's companion. She should not become pretty, and indeed I will warn her against any such notion.'

Charlotte thought about remonstrating with him, but she knew that it would do no good. Mr Collins had taken into his head one idea, and that idea was that Mary Bennet was plain. It would not do to confuse him with an alternative view.

The secret of Mary's transformation was simple. Her life at Rosings, despite Lady Catherine and despite Mr Collins, had become happy and so her outer person reflected her feelings of contentment.

20

To her credit Lady Catherine also marked Miss Bennet's new demeanour and gave it her approval, for as Miss Bennet changed for the better, so did Anne. She was no longer so silent and backward or so querulous as she once had been. Manner and constitution being intertwined, as Anne grew happier, she became healthier and as her health improved, so did her happiness. Proud and condescending as Lady Catherine was, she loved her daughter, and she could see the effect Miss Bennet had on her. She congratulated herself on her foresight in engaging Miss Bennet as Anne's companion, conveniently forgetting that Miss Bennet had agreed only until another such treasure as Mrs Jenkinson could be found. As far as Lady Catherine was concerned, Miss Bennet could stay, and there was little need to look for another treasure.

With Anne's health improving so clearly, Lady Catherine also could entertain thoughts of Anne's future, plans the considerations of which the great lady had found so unbearable not so long ago. Anne was meant to marry Darcy, but when that scheme was foiled,

Lady Catherine had to admit to herself that, despite what she and her sister had planned for their children, it could never be. Happiness in marriage was never to be considered, as happiness would come with duty well done, but Anne's health and temperament were to be thought of, and she could not have been a good wife, to Darcy or to any gentleman.

Watching the two young women come inside the house from a walk in the park, talking animatedly, with colour in their cheeks, brought up emotions in Lady Catherine that she thought she had long forgotten. Love, tinted by ambition, fuelled her new plans for Anne.

It was time that Miss de Bourgh was introduced to a larger society than Mr Collins and his wife, or even Miss Bennet. She was not yet ready for London — Lady Catherine would not risk Anne's new-found health and happiness on a London season — but the society of Hunsford and ————shire were not so small that Lady Catherine could not bring suitable company to Rosings.

* * *

All in Hunsford were agog to hear that Lady Catherine planned a small assembly, with just five tables, for an evening of dinner, cards, and dancing. Mr Collins was aquiver with trepidation until his household received an invitation, and then flushed with triumph to discover that very few from the village had been so blessed. News came from Rosings of meat being ordered for the table and musicians hired for the dancing. The servants dropped bits of gossip and hints about the rare occasion, and some of the more excitable villagers were beside themselves upon hearing that the Prince himself would be dining that night at Rosings.

'Dancing!' Mr Collins said. 'Dancing at Rosings! What do you think of that? I do believe that we should dance, my dear. It will not be amiss, I think, for us to join in this entertainment, for it is at Lady Catherine's invitation, and she would not steer us into anything lacking in propriety.'

'I would love to dance,' Charlotte said, a little wistfully. Her family had held many assemblies such as the one that had Hunsford so set on its ear. She missed the dancing and the fun for which Lucas Lodge was so well known. Her parents had loved to see young people at their liveliest, and the lodge had been the gathering place of much happiness. She knew better than to expect the party at Rosings to be in any way similar, but it would be nice to dance, even for a matron as settled as herself.

Then again, Mr Collins was not quite as good a dancer as his enthusiasm would make one expect. Still, Charlotte looked forward to the assembly, and set about thinking what she could wear. As the wife of a clergyman, she had been used to plain dress, and again she wished she had a bit more finery in which to appear.

Mr Collins then said something quite unexpected. He took his wife's hand, and said, 'I will dress in my sober clothes, my dear, but you must dress in your finest. It has been too long since I have seen you at your most adorned. Lady Catherine will not mind — indeed, I cannot think she will notice you among the illustrious company. But I know that females often miss the opportunity to peacock a little and I will not deny you this if you so wish.'

Oh Mr Collins, Charlotte thought with rueful amusement. Her heart softened towards her husband. His words were condescending and insulting, and yet she knew with the understanding of a wife that he meant well. When Charlotte had set out to secure Mr Collins and ensure a place for herself, she always knew that she would have to be a very good wife. Mr Collins could never know that she did not love him and could never love him. At that moment, however, she began, just a little, to like him.

* * *

As the day of the assembly approached, Mary felt a little wistfulness herself. How nice it would have been if Mr Aikens were invited. But she could allow herself no apprehension, for compared to Anne, Mary had been to so many parties as practically to be a lady of highest society. Anne was almost frightened back into ill health at the thought of meeting so many people, and it was up to Mary to calm her nerves and help her face the ordeal with poise and equanimity.

'I don't know, Miss Bennet,' Anne repeated as they walked in the gardens at Rosings. They were bundled now against the chill, in thick cloaks and sturdy shoes, their hands in muffs and their faces protected by warm bonnets, for autumn had come. The gardens were withered and the leaves turned brown and lay wet on the muddy ground. The gardeners had cut back all the plants in preparation for their winter sleep, and the garden was sad, as winter gardens always were. 'I don't know why my mother thought an assembly was the thing. I am not quite sure that I will like it.'

What could Mary say? Although she agreed with Anne, she felt sure that Lady Catherine would wish her to encourage her otherwise. 'I think that an assembly is quite a good thing,' she said. 'It can be a diversion from other duties. We find delight in reading and study, to be sure, but a rest from work can make work all the sweeter, I find. We two are in little danger of falling prey to frivolity and dissipation.'

Anne eyed her doubtfully. 'I do suppose that you are right,' she said. 'But must I dance, Miss Bennet?'

Mary had a most uncharitable thought — if Miss de Bourgh had danced with Mr Aikens poor Anne might have to take to her bed. She pretended to adjust her bonnet ribbon as another thought struck her.

'Can you not dance, Miss de Bourgh?'

Anne's expression was reply enough. Mary's heart sank. Had she more proficiency, she supposed she could teach Anne to dance, at least a simple country dance. But she was barely a dancer herself. And the assembly was less than a week away. They would need experienced help.

'Miss de Bourgh, I have an idea. Mrs Collins is quite a good dancer. Perhaps we can enlist her help.'

★ ★ ★

Charlotte was delighted at the idea and entered into the spirit immediately. They pushed back the furniture in the little parlour. The cook held on to Robert and watched the fun, as first Mr and Mrs Collins demonstrated the steps to a simple country dance. As the Collinses had no pianoforte, Mary clapped out the beat.

She was not so sure that Anne could see what the patterns were, as Mr Collins lost his place several times and Charlotte had to scold him, but they were all breathless and good-humoured.

'There, you see, Miss de Bourgh?' Charlotte said, stopping, breathless. 'Now you and Miss Bennet must try. Mary, take the gentleman's part.'

'Oh, of course,' Mary said with a droll face, and everyone laughed. She bowed to Miss de Bourgh, who, also entering into the fun, though she blushed, responded with a credible curtsy.

Charlotte began tapping her foot and Mr Collins to clap his hands, and Mary talked Anne through the dance.

They practised several times before pronouncing Miss de Bourgh a lovely dancer, quite graceful and light of foot. Mr Collins would have gone on about it overlong but for Charlotte's interrupting him and saying they should have tea so that the ladies could rest and refresh themselves before venturing out into the cold afternoon.

Over the next several days, Anne de Bourgh expressed concern more than once about the dancing. 'What if I forget the steps, Miss Bennet? I do have the most abominable time remembering the turns.'

Mary assured her that the rhythm of the music and the other dancers would remind her of all the steps, and that she would simply follow her partner through the patterns. Uncharitably she thought that the assembly could not come too soon for her own nerves. She was tired of leading Anne in practice and playing the gentleman.

★   ★   ★

The day arrived and Anne was as full of anticipation and apprehension as if she were being presented at court. Her querulousness had returned and Mary had to prevent herself from snapping at her waspishly. It was only when they retired to their rooms to dress that she had a moment to herself.

She dressed in the same gown that she had worn to the Greys so many months before. It was freshly pressed, and the blue over-dress and the lacy petticoat were as simple yet as pretty as she remembered. She had no maid to help her dress her hair this time, but Mary thought she could reproduce the braid that Lizzy's maid had done for her. With much use of hairpins and the looking-glass she was quite pleased with the results. She regarded herself in the mirror. Her face was no longer thin and pale. Her complexion was quite pink. The cluster of curls at her temple drew out her eyes and Mary smiled experimentally. Then she blushed. What had Fordyce said about the perils of the looking-glass? She would do well not to dwell on her appearance, for beauty faded soon enough. Better to cultivate that inner beauty of a soul well nourished and an intellect well nurtured. Mary turned the glass over and gathered her gloves. Anne might need her help.

Next door in Anne's room, the maids bustled in and out with petticoats, lace, and jewellery. Mary rapped gently at the open door and let herself in. Anne was being dressed by her maid and several undermaids. Her dress was much richer than Mary's but, to Mary's relief, Anne was not being done up like an artificial popinjay. Lady Catherine's good sense, for all it was self-congratulatory, at least led her well with regard to her daughter. Anne wore a pretty washed-grey-silk dress that revealed a plain white underdress. The ribbon under her bosom was a darker grey, and simple earrings, though sparkling with emeralds, were her only adornment, save for the hairpins that were set here and there in her dark hair. The colour was a good choice, for Anne's pale complexion was not yet sufficient to set off the yellows or pinks that became other women.

Anne looked up at Mary with relief.

'Oh, you are here! Thank you, Miss Bennet! I cannot go downstairs alone. I cannot!'

Mary came over to her and took her hand, pressing it comfortingly. 'Miss de Bourgh, you look lovely,' she said. 'If you would like, I will walk downstairs with you.'

Lady Catherine might not like it, for she would want all eyes on her daughter, to give her the attention due to her, but Mary felt that that might be too overwhelming for Anne. Poor Anne. She seemed to be on the verge of hysterics.

'Oh, Miss Bennet,' she whispered. 'The steps have flown completely out of my head. I cannot remember any of the turns. Oh please, you must help me.'

Mary pressed her hand once more. 'Once more, then. Shall we?'

Anne nodded, her eyes filled with abject terror, and Mary led her through the dance, humming the little air. And now, she thought, Anne needed a little confidence.

'When you hear the music, the steps will all come back to you,' she told her. 'Simply listen to the music and it will guide you, I promise, Miss de Bourgh.'

Anne nodded and took a deep breath to steel her nerves. 'Shall we go downstairs, Miss Bennet?'

Mary held out her arm and Anne took it. Together the two made their way downstairs.

21

The assembly was not the grand event Mary had half-hoped and half-feared it would be. There was none of the liveliness as there had been at Lucas Lodge or at the Greys, for many of the company were of Lady Catherine's generation rather than her daughter's. The Collinses were there, Charlotte looking handsome in one of her old ball gowns. Mr Collins was quite staid as befitted a clergyman, telling all who would listen that he was gratified to be part of such an illustrious company.

There was that awkwardness that falls over a gathering of people who have very little to do with one another generally. Anne had retreated into her usual silence, which Mary had taken for being simply hauteur upon their first meeting, but had come to learn was caused by a strickening shyness that rendered her incapable of speech. So it was up to her. Accordingly, she thrust aside her own tendency to talk too much and show off her own learning, and tried to make such conversation as would put Anne at her ease. She did not have Jane's sweetness nor Lizzy's wit; she could only be

Mary herself, and it would have to do. She almost wished for Lydia and Kitty, as their youth and vivacity, although forward and at times vulgar, at least would have enlivened the evening out of its dullness. That is beyond my power, Mary thought. Nor would Lady Catherine approve. *But how I wish this were more lively, for Anne's sake.*

Little did she know that to many guests she was the grave young girl who behaved quite nicely and made a dull evening more bearable with her quiet and sensible conversation.

The musicians whom Lady Catherine had engaged struck up the opening bars for the first dance, and all the company looked at each other uncomfortably. Mary saw Charlotte whispering to Mr Collins and nudging him forward. He coughed into his hand, then approached Anne and bowed.

'Miss de Bourgh,' he said clearly. 'Would you do me the honour of giving me this first dance?'

Anne started violently and began to shake her head in terror. Mary was struck with a sense of disaster. Not Mr Collins! He would lead Anne into such difficulties, for a bad partner was no good for an inexperienced dancer. But oh, how much worse it would be if Anne didn't dance. Mary nodded at her encouragingly.

'Do go, Miss de Bourgh. Listen — they are playing the same dance we practised.'

Anne stood at last and followed Mr Collins to the one set that was forming. Mary crossed her fingers in her gloves. Oh please, Mr Collins, she begged silently. Please dance better than you ever have before.

An older gentleman, in his mid-thirties, stout and whiskered, came up to Mary and bowed, as if he were reporting for duty. He mumbled something by which she was made to understand that he wished to dance with her. Hoping that that was what he meant, she curtsied her assent. It would do Anne good to have Mary in the set. She and the gentleman, who muttered that his name was Mr Stevens, or something like it, took their places. Anne gave her a look of such relief. Soon Charlotte found a partner, and the music came round again to the beginning and the dancing began.

The first dance passed this way: Mary kept up polite conversation with Mr Stevens, who was very difficult to draw out, whilst keeping one eye on Anne. Anne could be seen counting turns and steps, but she rarely put a foot wrong. Mr Collins was surreptitiously guided by Charlotte, who made sure she was near him for the whole dance. On the whole, with each looking out for the other, it was as much of a success as a dreadful experience could be.

When the music ended, Mary was sure the entire company breathed a sigh of relief, each for their own reasons, even the silent Mr Stevens, and applauded heartily, though it could not be sure whether that was because the dance had been pleasant or because it was over. Be thankful, Mary thought. It could have been much worse.

As no one else of the company wished to dance, when the music struck up for the next air, the dancers looked about one another but felt compelled to continue. Mary caught Charlotte's eye. Her old friend mouthed the word *help*! with such an expression of merriment mixed with droll terror that Mary almost laughed out loud. Here they were, unable to stop dancing, even if they wished.

After they had danced only a few more dances, with Anne gaining proficiency with every new air, Lady Catherine came to their rescue, and the company was called into supper. The dancing helped guests unbend, so now they at least had something to talk about in conversation that was both polite and desperately stilted. That topic exhausted, Mary was almost relieved that Lady Catherine held forth in her usual manner. She expounded on almost all topics, and all that remained was for her guests to agree with her. Anne sat at the place of honour by her mother's side, almost as silent as when they had first met, and Mary pitied her, for she could not possibly be enjoying it. Mary shared a table with Mr Stevens and others, and in between Lady Catherine's commentary they exchanged the dullest pleasantries imaginable. When Lady Catherine signalled supper was at an end, she almost despaired of how much longer the evening had still to go.

Here the evening took a turn for the worse. The ladies went to the drawing room, the men to play billiards and smoke. While waiting for the gentlemen, the ladies decided to play at cards. Cards held no interest for Mary, however, she was placed at a table in which several of the guests considered themselves very good card-players.

'Do you not play, Miss Bennet?' one lady said, a vision of glittering adornment in a too-youthful gown. 'My word, how do you keep from dying of boredom in Hertfordshire?'

Another lady at the table laughed behind her hand. 'I imagine Miss Bennet has simpler pleasures to keep her busy. Whenever I find myself in the country, I never can be persuaded to play cards or stay indoors, but must always be about walking, and imbibing the fresh air, and looking at the darling cows and pigs.'

Mary wondered what country she could possibly be referring to but only rearranged her hand.

'Now my dear,' said the third lady, and she laid her hand on Mary's arm. 'You can be quite at ease with us. We know you must be longing to spend some time away from your duties.'

Ah, Mary thought. That was what they were about. They wanted to quiz her about her relationship with Miss de Bourgh, without asking Mary directly to gossip about her.

'So ill and frail, poor Miss de Bourgh. She should have taken the waters at Bath or Harrogate. Yes, Bath would have cured her. But she danced so well tonight, so perhaps she was improving? Would she go to London soon? Surely Lady Catherine would take her to London, the town would be much improved by her presence.'

'Don't you think, Miss Bennet, that Miss de Bourgh would make a vast improvement on London?'

'My opinion is of no matter,' Mary said, disgusted by their gossip-mongering. They were grander than her Aunt Phillips and would no doubt have condescended to the vulgar old lady, but they were behaving in the same way themselves. Fordyce had warned against such examples of her sex, those matrons who sought only to draw a young lady into their own circle instead of guiding her appearances in society. Besides, she really didn't like them at all. She continued, 'But as you believe it to be so, I own it must be true.'

The ladies laughed again. 'It must be difficult, to be the companion of Miss de Bourgh,' one said, her eyes bright and eager. 'Lady Catherine is so demanding.'

Mary folded her cards and simply looked upon her companions. They watched her avidly. 'Lady Catherine,' she began, warming to her task, 'is, I believe, a most singular female. She is proud and condescending, to be sure, yet she is honourable and most respectable. She has decided opinions but her counsel is, in my experience, always good. I can give you many examples. First.' She paused to see how her pronouncements were being taken. The ladies looked at her with expressions of alarm. Mary tried to keep from smiling. She could keep this up for ever. After all, she had practice at it. She took a breath, when one of the ladies interrupted, asking one of the others about an acquaintance. They continued that conversation and Mary fanned open her cards again with quiet satisfaction.

★ ★ ★

The evening broke up at an early hour, in keeping with Lady Catherine's schedule. Mary rose from the card table with relief. Anne was exhausted. The evening's exercise has not been very taxing, but the accompanying terrors and apprehension had been more than her nervous disposition was equal to. She had very little to say to Mary or even her mother, and once she was safely ensconced in her bed Mary sought hers. As she took down her hair and stepped into her dressing-gown she thought with satisfaction on the evening. She had acquitted herself well against her interlocutors, who must have hoped she was a silly girl eager to talk about her benefactors. Instead, Fordyce had armed her and armed her well.

As for Anne, the evening could be considered a success. Mary resolved to ask her on the morrow, when she was refreshed, what her opinion of the evening was. It had not been a very diverting night, and the second half of the evening was more of what Anne was used to, for she and her mother often played cards, but the dancing! Anne had done very well with the dancing. She should be well pleased, Mary thought. She yawned, braided her hair loosely, and blew out the candle. As she slipped into her bed, she thought that Lady Catherine should be pleased as well. Perhaps one Bennet she could approve of, Mary thought, and drifted off to sleep.

22

Mary thought later that it was the assembly that was her downfall. From the hours spent in friendship at the Collinses, teaching Anne de Bourgh to dance, to her charge's successful, quiet debut into the small society of the country, all had gone towards putting Mary at her ease, the better to lure her to her doom. No evil snare was better set to entrap her — she walked into it with her eyes open and confident.

Anne was not the only one who came out that evening. Mary had impressed many of the gentlemen at the party, especially one of her partners, Mr Stevens. The portly gentleman came calling two days later and left his card. Lady Catherine grew thunderous, thinking the poor man meant to call on her daughter, when he was in no wise grand enough for a de Bourgh. She was only somewhat mollified when she discovered that he expected to pay his addresses to Mary. She called Mary into the drawing room.

'Miss Bennet, I cannot be expected to chaperone your courtship. If you encourage Mr Stevens, it will be under your parents' roof, not mine.'

Mary endeavoured to assure Lady Catherine that she had no interest in encouraging Mr Stevens and that she was sure the gentleman was just being polite.

'And yet you danced several dances with him, Miss Bennet. If that's not encouragement, I don't know what is. I will not harbour a flirt or a coquette. It is a bad example for Anne, though her reputation cannot suffer for it, except by connection.'

'It was the nature of the assembly, Lady Catherine,' Mary tried to explain. 'We all danced with the same partners, for there was only one set.' And none of us could sit down, she added silently.

'You should have sat down, Miss Bennet. A young lady can always choose to sit down.' Lady Catherine sounded appeased though, and her voice became more gentle. 'My Anne danced, did she not?'

'She danced very well, Lady Catherine. She was quite pleased with herself, as she should be.'

When Lady Catherine spoke next, she took Mary by surprise. 'Miss Bennet, your presence here has done Anne good.'

Mary managed to stammer out her thanks and Lady Catherine waved a beringed hand at her.

'No more suitors, Miss Bennet. You are warned.'

Lady Catherine should have warned the suitors. For it was not just Mr Stevens, but two or three young men from the village who were eager to talk to Miss Bennet after church and when they intercepted the two young ladies on their walks to the village. Mr Stevens was nothing — unsuitable for Anne. But the young men, closer in age and in lineage, and being that sort of person with whom young ladies prefer to fall in love, were to be prized. Yet none of them had much interest in Anne, who reverted to her bashful countenance, barely able to bow, when they drew near. They vied instead over Mary.

Mary took no pleasure from the attention. She used to wonder how Jane, who attracted suitors the way flowers attracted bees, could not be proud of the distinction. Now, she felt how it must have embarrassed her sister, not to say annoyed her. Mary and Anne could go nowhere without it being assumed by these young men that they would stop and talk. And the men would speak nothing of interest and they would ignore poor Anne. They showed off their horsemanship but they could not be compared to Mr Aikens. He would not have spurred or whipped his horse so — she could not imagine him treating Hyperion that way.

Unwelcome male attention was of the

utmost lack of interest to Mary. She knew that it hurt Anne terribly, though. Anne never spoke of it, and as far as Mary could tell, she did not complain to her mother, but she lost interest in going out. Though they tried other walks it seemed that they must be confined to the garden to avoid the assiduous attentions of the young gentlemen.

It is very annoying, Mary thought. If Lady Catherine finds out, she will think I encouraged them, just as she thought I encouraged Mr Stevens.

She discovered exactly what Lady Catherine would think very shortly afterwards. It was a rainy autumn day, when there was no walking that day at all. Lady Catherine was managing her accounts, and Anne herself dozed away the afternoon. Reading had palled and there was nothing else with which to amuse herself. Restless and bored, Mary sat down at the pianoforte in her little suite, left from Mrs Jenkinson's day, and began to play.

The instrument sounded much better than the tinkly little spinet at Longbourn, though it was not as grand an instrument as Georgiana's pianoforte at Pemberley. It was so long since she had played that her hands were rusty and she made many mistakes, but she was well on her way to regaining her skill. Rather than rush through the simple exercises as she was used to do, she took her time, and was rewarded with suppleness and a better sound than she had ever produced before.

Mary knew she would never be accomplished, and in the knowing gave up the ambition. Instead, she took joy and comfort in the simple tunes. Some she managed from memory, others from the yellowed sheet music left on the piano. She continued playing softly, now and again darting a glance at the door with a little bit of alarm, afraid of being discovered. If Lady Catherine heard her play, she would not know what to think. Mary could almost hear her complaints. 'Miss Bennet! What is the meaning of this! You expressly told me that you do not play!'

Soon she forgot her apprehension and was lost in the music, and even tried a more difficult composition than she had ever played before, puzzling out each measure as carefully as she could. She almost forgot where she was. It was one of the maids who interrupted her.

'Miss,' the woman said from the doorway. Mary jumped, taken by surprise. She had a dim awareness that the maid had been standing there for some time and had even knocked, but she hadn't noticed.

'You have a visitor, miss,' the woman said,

and the disapproval in her voice said all that her actual words could not: that she wondered what Lady Catherine would think.

'A visitor?' Mary said blankly. Could it be Mr Stevens again? Her heart sank. Had she not made it as clear as possible that his attentions were unwelcome? Or was it one of the young men from the village? Not on such a day as this — it had not stopped raining all day, for it was well on its way towards winter and the first frosts.

'Yes, miss. A young gentleman. Mr Aikens.'

Mary stared at her, her mouth opened in a most unbecoming way.

'Forgive me,' she said. 'Did you say Mr Aikens?'

'Yes, miss. He waits in the hall.'

Mary felt as if she were walking in a dream as she followed the maid to the hall. A figure stood there, his greatcoats dripping on the parqueted floor in gleaming puddles, the butler and the footmen waiting by to wipe the water as soon as he handed them his coats. He turned from contemplating a bust of some great man that guarded the front door when she approached.

'Miss Mary!' He stepped forward, holding out his hand. She took it, hardly knowing what to do. 'I knew I would find you here! What a ride! What stables! I took Hyperion round first thing, just to make sure, you know, that he would be well cared for. You don't mind, do you? Since you didn't know I was coming, that is. I hoped it would be a surprise.'

'It is,' Mary said faintly. She curtsied awkwardly, well aware of the servants watching without appearing to. *Lady Catherine will be livid.* But she couldn't turn Mr Aikens away. 'Mr Aikens, how wonderful to see you. Why?'

'Came to see you, of course. Your sister said they left you here.' He leaned forward with an exaggerated whisper. 'I've come to rescue you. It was Hyperion's idea.'

Rescued? Whatever could he mean?

'I am not a prisoner, Mr Aikens.'

He looked crestfallen. 'I didn't think you were really a prisoner. It's not like that book, you know. I know that. But you don't want to stay, do you?'

Mary hardly knew what to say. Luckily, the butler did. No doubt hoping to hurry the dripping young man out of his hall, he said, 'Would the young gentleman like to sit by the fire in the small parlour? I can have tea sent in, miss.'

'Oh! Yes, oh of course. Please forgive me! Mr Aikens, please do come in.'

'Fine by me,' Mr Aikens said cheerfully. 'I

260

suppose a rescue can wait for tea.'

Mary wasn't sure if she had the right to ask him in for tea, but the butler took care of things. He had Mr Aikens's coat and soon they were settled in the small parlour with a cheerful fire and tea things. Mary poured, praying she wouldn't spill a drop. Mr Aikens sat back with a sigh, a small teacup in his large hands.

'Now that's the thing,' he said with satisfaction. 'Tea on a day like this. I daresay I could eat all of those sandwiches.'

'Please do help yourself,' Mary said. She had a sense of great contentment as she watched him eating with gusto.

'You should jump in, you know,' he said, chewing and swallowing.

Mary selected a sandwich. The small parlour with the crackling fire and the rain sliding down the windows was pleasantly comfortable. For a moment she had a wonderful thought. If she were mistress of her own establishment: nothing grand, not at all, nothing like Rosings or Pemberley but more like comfortable Longbourn, but if she were her own mistress — how agreeable that would be.

'Now,' he said, washing down the last sandwich with tea. 'Do you wish to be rescued? Is all this a gilded cage?'

'Mr Aikens, I don't know what my sister told you, but I am here as a friend of Anne de Bourgh. It's really quite pleasant. We're friends.'

'Nonsense,' he said. 'What about me — and Hyperion? We're your friends too. Have you ever thought of that?'

She coloured at his forthrightness. 'I do apologize, Mr Aikens.' She wondered what she was apologizing for. 'I did not know — that is, I did not think — '

'You didn't think we are friends. Why? Because I don't dance with as fine manners as a gentleman should, or sit indoors but must always be outside in the weather? I daresay you think me too wild and wind-blown with my hair in knots and up to my topboots in mud to be a friend. I'm not a fellow who sits in a salon and reads fine books, so we can't be friends?'

He was quite beside himself. Mary stared at him.

'No,' she said, and she could barely force the words past her unwilling lips. 'No, it's because — I am none of those things. I never thought we could be friends because I scarcely do go out of doors and I don't ride and I thought you were just being a gentleman and kind.'

He snorted a laugh. 'That's amusing. Even

my mother says I am no gentleman.'

And my mother thinks I am no lady, or at least, not a marriageable one, Mary thought.

'I meant no disrespect or injury,' she said. 'I think — if you wish it, I would like to be friends.'

'Good! Then you'll come back. You have to finish the book, you know.'

Mary looked at him suspiciously. He looked quite pleased with himself. Had he set a trap for her?

'Mr Aikens, I am Anne de Bourgh's guest. I promised I would stay with her, and it has hardly been more than a month and a half, and they believe in long visits here. I can scarcely run off . . . '

Run off. Good God. He wasn't asking her to elope, was he? She set down her teacup with a shaking hand so that it rattled in its saucer.

'What is going on here?'

Lady Catherine stood in the doorway to the parlour, the housekeeper hovering behind her, as were the butler and the two footmen. Mr Aikens stood hastily and for *not a gentleman* made a quite credible bow.

'Ma'am, your servant,' he said. 'Thomas Aikens, ma'am. You must be Lady Catherine.'

She glared at him sourly. Now the housekeeper and the footmen stood aside and Anne came to stand next to her mother, looking from one to the other in fright. Lady Catherine spoke up icily.

'What do you mean by bursting into my house and speaking with Miss Bennet?'

Mary stood. 'We're friends, Lady Catherine. I met Mr Aikens when I stayed with my sister at Pemberley this spring. He came to resc — visit me.'

'Impertinent girl! Have I not expressly told you that I will not permit you to entertain your suitors in this house?'

Mary reddened. What would Mr Aikens think of Lady Catherine's accusation? She would not cry. She would not cry. But I will not apologize either, she thought firmly, and clamped her lips shut. She was not a servant girl. She might not be one of the *ton*, but she was a respectable young lady and she could have visitors if she wished. Mr Aikens made as if to speak, but she interrupted before he could come to her defence.

'I can see that I have angered you, Lady Catherine,' she began. Indeed she could. Lady Catherine was not as pettish as she was usually when Mary put her out of sorts. She was angry. This must be how she had been when she came to see Lizzy, Mary thought. 'But I was not aware that as Anne's guest I was to have no other company while I lived here at Rosings. As for Mr Aikens, he is a friend. He is not a suitor.'

Again Mr Aikens opened his mouth to say something, but was again interrupted. Lady Catherine swelled in her anger.

'You make yourself at home here, Miss Bennet, far too easily. This is not your home. You were given a place at Rosings to be my daughter's companion, not her equal. You are a Bennet; no Bennet is the equal of a de Bourgh. Your youngest sister is proof of that.'

That was enough. Mary was acutely aware of Mr Aikens standing by mutely, his every suspicion of her position confirmed by Lady Catherine's hateful speech. She burned with shame but also with anger.

'Then, Lady Catherine, I will trouble you no more. I will pack my things at once and remove to the parsonage where I will stay until my parents can send for me.' Oh dear, she thought. What will Charlotte think?

'No!' That was Anne. 'No! Mother, you must not send her away.'

'That is enough, Anne. My mind is made up. This girl — this abominable girl — is an ungrateful spoiled fool. She thought nothing of you, Anne, or your position, only of herself. No doubt she thought of this as a comfortable sinecure and that she would live on my hospitality till the day she died. No! I will not have it.'

'Oh, that is quite enough,' said Mr Aikens. 'Ma'am, how dare you! How dare you insult Miss Bennet, who is nothing but good and kind and even can bear one such as me? You are very wrong, Lady Catherine. You are very wrong about Miss Bennet. I thought that someone who had such stables could be a kindred spirit, but it's clear to me that you care nothing for your fellow creatures, only for yourself. To treat Miss Bennet thus — if you were a man I would call you out.'

Everyone in the room gasped, possibly even the two footmen. In the stark silence that followed, Mary turned to Anne and curtsied.

'I am sorry. I wish you to know that on my part, I thought we had become friends. I will miss you, Miss de Bourgh.'

'I know,' Anne said, and her weak eyes brightened with tears.

'Enough!' thundered Lady Catherine. 'You will pack immediately Miss Bennet, and leave this house at once. You will never set foot inside Rosings again. And you sir, will remove your horse from my stables immediately, and depart, never to return.'

23

How Mary was to carry her trunk by herself down the stairs, let alone to the rectory in the pouring rain she had no idea, but she must consider one thing at a time. She set to work packing her belongings neatly and carefully, placing the book and her small things on top of her few clothes. Then she closed the trunk and looked around her in the empty room. It had become comfortable, even welcoming but now that she was forced ignobly from it, she could see that the striped wallpaper was dingy and grey, and that there was an air of must that no pomander ball could disguise.

She pressed a key on the piano so quietly that it made scarcely a sound. She could hardly believe she had just begun to play again, after so many months.

There was such a feeling of unsettlement in the pit of her stomach that it took her a moment to identify it as fear. She was frightened. Where would it end? Where could she live? Her parents were growing old. Longbourn would soon pass to Mr Collins and Charlotte. If she did not marry, would she wander from small room to small room like this one until she died?

How could I have thought that this was my life? she asked herself. She had been frightened, that was all. She was frightened by Pemberley and the life Lizzy led there. It was a life of great consequence, but it was not for Mary. And so when the chance came to live in a small room she chose that instead. But a small room, even in a great house, was much too confining. I do not want much, she thought, but even a cloistered nun would find Rosings confining. It was not just the room, it was the box that Lady Catherine was determined to put her in, sitting on the lid until Mary inconvenienced her no more. Mary had not liked the fact that Mr Aikens had thought he should come to rescue her, and little did she like his seeing her humiliation at the hands of Lady Catherine, but he had at least known what she had wilfully closed her eyes to: just because she was not meant for a great life it did not mean she was meant for a small life.

She was meant to live one life only — her own. Mary looked around the barren little room and shook her head. When she spoke it was out loud, and the room gave back a dusty little echo.

'I have been a fool, as great a fool as any when I was determined to be known for my singing and playing and my sermons. At least this time I have inconvenienced no one but myself.'

That was not quite true. She was now about to inconvenience Charlotte and Mr Collins, once she could work out how to get her trunk downstairs. Mary looked at the little bell pull next to the door. She had never used it; she had known even then that although she was one step above servant she could not summon one of the housemaids as if she were a member of the household. This was her last hour at Rosings, however, and she could not carry her trunk by herself. Surely she could call upon one footman. Lady Catherine would begrudge it, but Lady Catherine begrudged the air she breathed, and there was little Mary could do about that.

She pulled the tasselled rope. It promptly broke off in her hand. Mary stared at it, and laughed out loud. She gathered up her gloves and shawl and small reticule and went off to find a servant.

★　★　★

Neither Lady Catherine nor Anne was there to see her go. Mary was let out by the side door near the stables, where a cart waited for her, drawn by a fat and patient farmhorse that shook the rain from its blinkers. One of the men carried her trunk, threw it in to the back of the cart and helped Mary on to the seat next to the driver. He grinned kindly at her.

'Like the good Lord decided on another flood, eh Miss?' he said. He clucked to the horse and slapped the wet reins against the animal's hindquarters. The cart rumbled forward. Mary held on with one hand and pulled her bonnet over her eyes. Her head was soon soaked. The rain was unrelenting.

'The Lord gave us a rainbow,' she said but she didn't think he heard. She heard wet hoofbeats and looked back. There was Hyperion, tossing his head against the rain. Mr Aikens's coat was draped over the horse's flank. He pushed the horse up next to the cart. His expression was serious, and Mary felt dreadful once more that he had to see her in exile. What was more, her nose was probably bright red and her hair hanging in lank strands under her wilting bonnet.

'Miss Bennet, where will you go?' he called out.

'To my cousin, Mr Collins,' she replied. It would be the stuff of embarrassment, but it was her only option. 'And thence to Longbourn.'

'I will escort you there,' he said, and fell in

beside them, the spirited Hyperion jogging light-footed even in the muck of the road next to the plodding farmhorse.

Mr Aikens was one of that sort who can talk to anyone. He was soon in deep conversation with the driver over the carthorse and its breeding, Hyperion's own bloodlines, and the general merits of the English horse compared to horses of other countries. The two discussed matters of founder in the hoofs, and horse draughts and colic while the rain hammered down and Mary despaired of her bonnet, her gown, her slippers, and her trunk, for no doubt it was drenched in the back of the cart. There was no help for the situation, however, and despite her despair over her things, her heart was becoming light. It was as if Rosings had oppressed her spirit without her even being aware of it, so that leaving Rosings, even though it meant she must bear Mr Collins next, was the best thing she had ever done. She would miss Anne, though. They had become friends. Well, perhaps I have given her the strength to be herself and she can stand up to her mother's wishes, Mary thought. She knew better, however, than to place any dependence upon Anne's strength. The poor girl had had too many years in her mother's house to suddenly straighten up under her thumb. She will always have my best wishes, Mary thought. And I think I will have hers. Perhaps we will meet later and can be friends again.

It might be pleasant to meet Anne de Bourgh again on an equal footing. She called herself Anne's friend, but she knew — and Anne knew — that Mary had occupied that uncomfortable place between friend and servant. No good could come of that, not in the long run.

★　★　★

The distance between the great house of Rosings and the Collinses' humble abode was not far. They soon arrived, and Mr Aikens helped the driver with the trunk. Charlotte was most astonished as she stood in the doorway and watched Mary step down from the cart, splashing into the muddy lane. Mary told her what had happened in as few words as possible. Mr Collins appeared behind his wife, for once rendered silent by surprise. The men set the trunk inside the little hall, Mr Aikens paid the driver, and sent him off with a promise to try some horse draught or another, and then Mary was able to introduce Mr Aikens. She was keenly aware of all their eyes upon her.

'Charlotte, you may know Mr Aikens. I met him first at Lucas Lodge in the spring,' she said. *Had* Charlotte known him? Mrs Collins eyed the young man doubtfully and so it appeared that she did not.

Mr Aikens cleared up the mystery. 'Will Lucas is a friend of mine,' he said. 'Or at least he would be, if he didn't ride so badly. No idea you were his sister.'

'Oh, of course,' Charlotte said. 'I think my brother has spoken of you. How do you do?'

Behind his wife Mr Collins burst out, 'But how did you come to Hunsford, sir? Have you come to visit my wife?'

'Never met her before,' Mr Aikens said. 'No, I came to visit Miss Bennet at Rosings.'

'Visit Miss Bennet?' Mr Collins could scarcely credit it.

'Mr Aikens is a friend of Mr Darcy as well, and we met a second time at Pemberley,' Mary said, her irritation rising at his disbelief. Why did Mr Collins always manage to bring out her anger? He could never stop insulting her, it seemed. And now the Collinses made no move to invite them into the parlour; in all fairness, this was the second house Mr Aikens had dripped all over, and Mary was well aware that her dress clung to her most unbecomingly.

'I'm afraid it's my fault that she was driven

273

from Rosings,' Mr Aikens said. 'I came to visit and that old harridan threw her out. Had no idea that would happen or I never would have come, but I still think Miss Bennet made a terrible mistake. Lady, indeed! Who can stand her?'

Mr Collins' mouth worked. To hear his patroness be so maligned required him to make some address to the young man dripping in his greatcoat on his floor, but he could not summon a sound. If the truth were to be told, the young gentleman *was* a gentleman, after all, and Mr Collins was in the habit of approaching such a gentleman with flattery and obsequiousness. How to manage such flattery and self-abasement and at the same time correct his judgement of Lady Catherine was beyond his powers. Mary took matters into her own hands.

'Charlotte, I apologize, but may I presume upon your hospitality? It will just be until I can take the mail to Longbourn.'

'Of course, Mary! Please, you are both drenched. Come and warm yourselves in the parlour.'

'The idea of a fire and chance to dry off is too good to be true,' said Mr Aikens. 'But I wouldn't want to sit down on your furniture, Mrs Collins, and you have no stable for Hyperion. I will just go on down to the inn in the village and put up there.'

Mary was almost relieved at his decision. She wanted him to stay, but she could not bear it if Mr Collins was rude to him. She turned to him. Conscious of her audience, she held out her hand. He took it, and despite the cold and wet his hand was warm. He held her hand tight and did not appear to want to let her have it back.

'Mr Aikens, thank you. You are a good friend to help me. Please do not blame yourself. It was only a matter of time before something of this sort happened.'

Behind her she heard Mr Collins gasp.

'So you did need to be rescued,' Mr Aikens said with a cheerful grin. 'I made a mess of it, as usual, but that's me. I mean well, but I've been told I'm like a bull in a china shop, and though I've never been in a china shop, I can see how that could be. Mrs Collins. Mr Collins. Miss Bennet.'

Mr Aikens let her hand go, though the sensation of his rough palm remained with her for a few moments longer. He made another rather wet bow and took his leave, Hyperion splashing off to the village inn. Charlotte took Mary's other hand and drew her into the house. The housekeeper took her up to her room to change. It was the same room that she had stayed in when Lady

Catherine had refused to offer her a room at Rosings. Mary undressed quickly, and Charlotte knocked on the door, pushing in a warm wrap to her.

'I will ask Mr Collins to bring up your trunk and leave it outside your door and you may change your clothes. Please come downstairs when you wish. Oh, dear, Robert's woken up.' The baby's cries filled the hall, and Charlotte hurried away. Mary wrapped herself in Charlotte's robe and then heard a laboured thumping and dragging and heavy breathing. Mr Collins was not a strapping young footman, and the trunk was too much for him. A louder thunk indicated that he had dropped it outside her door. Mary waited, nervously. Surely he could not think of coming in. He did not; he coughed once in his hand. She waited. He waited. Then at last he spoke through the door: 'Miss Bennet, er, Mary. When you have, er, decently covered yourself, you may come downstairs. I think we have much to discuss over your intemperate remove from Rosings. I cannot tell you how upset — nay, disappointed, I must say — yes, harsh as it is, disappointed, and yet not surprised, that your adventure ended in such a bad way. I fear, however, that it may have caused grave damage to your family — '

'Mr Collins, I am coming out to get dry clothes, if you please,' Mary called out.

There came an unhappy silence from the other side of the door. But she had no indication that he had moved away. She reached out for the doorknob and rattled it, without opening the door.

'Mr Collins, I am coming out now, sir,' she warned. At last she heard what sounded like a frightened gasp and the creak of floorboards as he moved away. Mary pushed open the door and peeked out. Her trunk stood there, damply, but the hall was empty. She knelt and with shaking hands opened the trunk and fished for dry clothes and a dry shawl. Her trunk had kept her things mostly dry, for which she was grateful. She grabbed her things, closed the door, and dressed gratefully.

★   ★   ★

The parlour was everything she could have wished: a cheerful fire, aromatic tea steeping in Charlotte's porcelain teapot, and biscuits. Charlotte sat with Robert in her lap and the little boy gave a great toothless grin when he saw Mary. She looked around warily, but Mr Collins was not present. Charlotte saw her look.

'I asked Mr Collins to let me talk to you

first to find out what happened. He's most disappointed.'

'Yes, he is.'

Charlotte nudged the teapot towards Mary. 'Please, Mary, will you pour? I have my hands full at the moment.' As Mary poured the tea and set a biscuit on a plate for Charlotte, her friend added, 'He is a very interesting young man, Mr Aikens. So he came to visit you at Rosings? You are particular friends, then?'

Mary blushed. 'He's a particular friend of Mr Darcy I should say. We became more acquainted during my stay at Pemberley, while he put up at the inn at Lambton.'

'And he came all this way to Rosings to visit you,' Charlotte said, smiling at her over the tea things. The Charlotte Mary knew, when she had been Lizzy's best friend, would have considered such things as matchmaking to be nonsense. Is this what happens when women marry? she thought. Even those who marry such a man as Mr Collins? Perhaps it is a way to ensure that all women enter their state so that none might judge them by their choice. The uncharitable thought was an indication of her tiredness and irritation.

'Yes,' Mary said. She didn't say anything about his plan to rescue her.

'What happened, Mary? What made Lady Catherine so angry?'

Mary told her the story in a few short words, including Lady Catherine's admonition against suitors. When she was finished, Charlotte fussed with her tea.

'Mr Aikens is not like any gentleman I've ever met,' she said at last. 'He is quite original. But he came unannounced to Rosings? Surely you should have realized that it was not your place to have visitors without Lady Catherine's knowledge or permission. You of all people, Mary. You see how it must have looked.'

The room was no longer so pleasant but had become uncomfortably warm. Had she fallen, much as Lydia had? There was such a narrow path alongside a chasm of disaster.

'I offered him tea,' Mary said, aware of how inadequate it sounded. Well-intentioned though her motives had been, no matter how she had meant not to flirt, Lady Catherine would think the worst of her, and so would anyone else who heard the tale. Those Bennets! the story would go. The companion to Anne de Bourgh, meeting men on the sly.

'It was just — terribly forward, Mary. I know you meant no harm, for we have been friends for our whole lives. But Mr Collins — Lady Catherine — they will judge you. They *have* judged you. I think it was an unfortunate *faux pas*. We shall have to consider how to remedy this.'

Judgement from Charlotte made Mary even hotter.

'Charlotte, you of all people should know that anyone can look at the actions of others and think the worst.'

Charlotte stopped stirring her tea and grew very still. 'I'm sure I don't know what you mean,' she said.

Mary had not meant to say it out loud and she regretted the words even as they burst from her.

'What actions of mine do you think the worst of?' Charlotte continued. When Mary said nothing, she pushed further. 'Do you mean my marriage to Mr Collins? Go ahead, Mary, tell me.'

'And what do you know of me?' Mary said. 'Tell me, Charlotte, what do you know of me? A friend came to visit me and I offered him tea in the house where I was something between a guest and a servant. My crime, if crime it can be considered, was to have a society beyond the one selected for me. Yet you have been judging me and judging me the moment I arrived on your doorstep with nowhere else to go. The old Charlotte would not have judged me. This new Charlotte — I no longer know this person. But I can tell you this. In order to live your life, you had to slough off the old Charlotte and become this new person, who looks upon old friends and judges them not with her eyes but with her husband's and that of his patroness.'

The words were quietly spoken, but they rang in the parlour. For a few moments the only sound were the mantel clock and the hissing of the fire in the grate.

A knock came at the door and Mr Collins came in. He looked grave indeed, and quite wet, and for a moment Mary feared that he had heard them quarrel. She felt quite ill at the thought. He was a foolish man, but no doubt he loved Charlotte as best he could, despite all his faults. If he had heard her accusation that Charlotte had merely made sure of him to secure herself an establishment, it could turn out very badly.

Mr Collins's next words laid her fears to rest. He only had Mary's transgressions on his mind, not his wife's esteem of him.

'Mary,' he said very soberly. 'It is as I have most desperately feared. Nay, it is worse. I have been to Rosings,' he said, rather as if he were telling her he had been to war, or to Hell. 'Lady Catherine is most upset. Mary, you have achieved what your unnamed sister could not. You have incurred Lady Catherine's full wrath and displeasure.'

Charlotte looked frightened. Mary was a little apprehensive too, until she remembered that she had always incurred Lady Catherine's displeasure and wasn't sure what more was expected.

'I do not know how to mend this thing. You will have to go home, of course,' Mr Collins continued, with the air of one thinking out loud. 'Though I am not sure that will be enough. Your parents would do well to seclude you. I think it best you never set foot in society again, where your paths and Lady Catherine's — or Miss de Bourgh's — might ever cross.' He lowered his voice. 'She did not want me to shelter you, cousin, but I prevailed upon her mercy and her just temperament.'

'Is it really necessary that I cloister myself as if I were a Spanish nun?' Mary asked, with some acidity. 'Surely England is big enough for both Lady Catherine and myself to move in the society to which we are accustomed.' Not, she thought, that she was accustomed to society, but Mr Collins didn't need to know about that.

'Oh Mary,' Mr Collins said mournfully. He paced in front of the fire. 'Oh Mary. You still do not understand the gravity of your situation. For you see, Lady Catherine will not cut herself off from her nephew, Mr Darcy, and so you must cut yourself off from Pemberley and your sister. I suggested it myself as a way to assuage Lady Catherine's understandable outrage, and she agreed that it was the only solution.'

Mary had not felt her temper boil so since Lydia had seen fit to tease her.

'Mr Collins,' she said, and her voice sounded unlike her own. 'If Lady Catherine deems it necessary that we never cross paths again, she may sit in Rosings for as long as she likes. I will not cut myself off from my family for all the de Bourghs in England.'

She rose to her feet, gathered her shawl and went off to bed.

The rain had stopped except for the uneven beat of the last raindrops falling on the eaves. Mary huddled in the cold, damp, spare room under her blankets, smelling the wildness of the wind and the cold summer rain, and the mustiness of the blankets and the room that was little used and little aired. She knew she would get no sleep that night. It had all been such a day. Mr Aikens coming to visit, her banishment from Rosings, and her fight with Charlotte. Shame, tiredness, and regret conspired to torment her, until at last hot tears rolled down her cheeks into her thin pillow. I don't know what everyone wants of me, she thought, wiping away her tears. I have been cast in a mould and have come out with an ugly crack. But this is me. How could I be other?

24

As Mary was driven from Rosings, Mr Darcy
returned to Pemberley with news of Mr
Wickham, Lydia, and Kitty. Mr Wickham had
approached Kitty and Jane in London with
the object of ingratiating himself with them,
especially Kitty, in the hope that they would
give him money, but then he had disappeared. Darcy drove to Bingley's town house
and from there the two men went all over
London together to find him, looking into all
the disreputable places in town where he
could be expected to be found. They
eventually came across him at a gaming hell
where he was adding to his debts. There they
put it to him forcefully that he was not to
approach Kitty or Jane ever again. Mr
Wickham was dutifully impressed with their
manner, but he also gave them the astonishing news that Lydia was expecting their first
child. He hoped that the families would see
fit to provide more money to help support
this heir. As he was in the process of gambling
away what little he had anyway, neither Darcy
nor Bingley was inclined to accede to his
request. However, both felt ill at ease with

their decision. Any child brought into this marriage was innocent. How could they not do all in their power to make sure the infant was supported?

They made Wickham take them to see Lydia, and so they journeyed north. There, they could see for themselves that she was expecting. She was as wild as ever, angry and flirtatious with them both by turns, abusing Wickham terribly for his abandoning her for London and leaving her out of the fun, and threatening to go out and enjoy herself without him. Bingley's compassion overcame him and he pressed some money into Lydia's hands, knowing that one or the other would gamble it away or waste it on fripperies.

Both Darcy and Bingley went away, satisfied that Wickham would no longer dare to ask them for money, but uneasy about the couple's burgeoning family. Darcy, when he returned to Pemberley, asked Lizzy what they should do about Wickham and Lydia now that they had this new intelligence.

'First,' Lizzy told him, 'a kiss for your good sense in asking for my advice.' She suited action to words. 'Second, I will have to tell my father. He may have prepared for this, he and Uncle Gardiner, and well he should have, but if it comes as a surprise he will like to know.'

'I did not think it out of the possible,' Darcy admitted. 'If anything, I hoped they would have tired of one another by the time they reached —— in the north, and so Wickham's profligate habits would no longer be of any concern to us.'

They both thought the same thing, that Lydia might have lost all consciousness of her reputation and carried another man's by-blow, but said nothing to one another because it was clear by their expressions that each knew what the other thought.

Lizzy resolved to go to Longbourn and tell her father in person. *He* could tell Mrs Bennet for Lizzy would rather not have that commission. She thought of her own situation. She and Darcy had still not been fortunate in that respect, though she hoped for it as much as she could. Especially since she had met little Robert Collins, her hopes for a happy event in her own house was foremost on her mind. So it was bad that Lydia would be the first one, even before Jane and Lizzy, to bring a small heir. Whether an infant would bring a reconciliation or lead only to greater distance, Lizzy could not foretell.

★　★　★

While Lizzy packed for her journey to Longbourn, news of Mary came in a letter from Mrs Bennet, filled with wild misspellings and much underlining. The gist was plain to see, that Mary had been driven from Rosings after she had entertained a young man in the parlour there. Lizzy covered her mouth with her hand, not sure whether she would laugh or cry. So Mr Aikens had done as he had threatened and had ridden off to Rosings to rescue Mary.

There was one good thing to come of all of this, she reflected. Her mother's nerves would be fully engaged upon Mary and she would not have the slightest interest in what her second eldest daughter had to say to her father. She could relate her news of Lydia and Wickham in relative peace and in turn learn something more of Mary. She sighed. *Oh Mary, whatever have you done?*

It was as Lizzy expected when she was handed down from the carriage at her family home. Mary was nowhere to be found. Mr Bennet was closeted in his study, and Mrs Bennet could not refrain from making meaningful remarks from the moment she kissed Lizzy in welcome.

'You talk to her, Lizzy,' Mrs Bennet said immediately. 'For my poor nerves cannot bear it. She is an impossible girl. How she could have thought of doing such a thing! Mr Collins said Lady Catherine was beside herself, and that Mary was impertinent! And the wild young man! How did Mary meet such a creature! Why ever would she invite him in to tea! He was a highwayman, I am sure of it, and no doubt he has gone back to Rosings to steal all the silver! And Lady Catherine will blame us! Oh and Lady Lucas has been in and out with all the news and I just cannot bear it any more.'

Lizzy kissed her mother. 'Where is my father?'

Mrs Bennet waved a hand. 'Your father! Your father has been no good at all! He stays in his study and hardly comes out! I am all alone, Lizzy! All alone, with my nerves!'

'I'm here now, Mama. You may be reassured I shall talk to Mary.'

'Oh, it's too late now. Little good will talking do. She never had any sense. What was she thinking!'

Lizzy knew that she would continue in that vein for some time, so she made her way up the familiar stairs to Mary's room. She knocked gently. There was no answer. Lizzy waited a moment, then opened the door. The room was empty save for Mary's trunk and her things. Lizzy waited a moment. She hadn't heard the piano — and then she remembered that Mary no longer played.

She looked for her sister in the parlour anyway, then in the kitchens and finally out in the gardens. But she did not find Mary until she started along the path to Meryton. There was a figure ahead of her, wrapped in a warm pelisse, walking briskly down the path.

'Mary?' she called out.

Mary turned and stopped and came towards her eagerly.

'Lizzy!' She came to give her sister a kiss. Lizzy hugged her and then held her by the shoulders so that she could see her. Whatever disgrace she had brought upon herself, it had done her good. Mary had roses in her cheeks and her eyes were bright. Her hair had loosened from her bun and caught the wintry light.

'Mary, why did you let a highwayman into Rosings?'

Mary gave a rueful laugh.

'So you spoke to Mama.'

'I could hardly avoid it. She wrote me such a letter that I was hard put to make it out. I had to come to Longbourn at once to make sense of it all. Was it so dreadful?'

'Not at first, but then it became so much worse. Oh Lizzy, I was such a fool. How could I have thought that that was the place for me?'

Lizzy listened as her sister spilled her tale. Something had changed about Mary. She still had her same thin, dark, intense frown, but her face was lighter none the less.

'When I drove away from that dreadful house and those dreadful people, I felt so ashamed, but the longer it is left behind the more I feel as if I could fly, and I have not come down since.'

So that was it. Mary was happy. Lizzy smiled back.

'Don't blame yourself entirely. We encouraged you into it.'

'I let myself be encouraged. I know you all wanted a place for me. 'Something must be done about Mary',' she said in a droll voice. 'What can it be?''

That stung, but Lizzy knew it was true. 'What did Mama and Papa say?'

'Oh I suppose Mama will resign herself. I expect to hear no end of it. It will be referred to at unexpected moments whenever I do something else that disappoints her. Papa said only that he hoped I brought his book back. But I think he approved.' Mary smiled at that, and Lizzy felt once again a mixture of sadness and exasperation that her father had brought upon her lately.

Lizzy had grown up the favoured daughter of their father and not for the first time she was aware that her sisters had not had that advantage. Mary's learning and earnestness had been a way to capture his attention, but even if he was aware of that he gave her neither encouragement nor guidance. And Lydia and Kitty felt his lack of interest the most keenly — perhaps Lydia would not have fallen had her father been more attentive. She felt a spark of anger. All Mary wanted was his approval and he barely deigned to notice her. And now he approved of her precipitous action, which could have been avoided altogether. I can't blame him for it entirely, Lizzy thought. But oh, for a good man he is most astonishingly an indifferent father.

'So tell me the rest. How did you manage your remove from Rosings?'

'Mr Aikens helped very much. I would have been entirely at a loss had he not seen to it that my trunk was carried down. I spent the night at the Collinses, which was awkward as you can imagine. And then he escorted me home the next day. My pride was hurt, and my vanity both — I could not tell them apart in the event, and all I kept thinking was, that my troubles would soon be over and I would be at Longbourn again. Dear Longbourn!'

Lizzy could imagine the embarrassment and the wounded pride.

'That was very kind of Mr Aikens,' Lizzy

said, resolving that she would write to him at once to thank him. He also deserved an apology. He was right. He knew Mary better than any of them. 'He was most displeased when he found out you were at Rosings and he was quite wild in his accusations.'

Mary blushed and looked away. 'He did say he had come to rescue me. He is quite an unusual gentleman.'

Lizzy saw fit to tease her a little. 'Just an unusual gentleman? Or something more?'

But Mary became uncertain almost at once. 'Oh Lizzy, please don't,' she said. 'I have never liked any young man before and I am so afraid that he cannot possibly like me in return.'

Lizzy was reminded that Mary had never had beaux and that she was so little in society, except among the Lucas boys and her sisters' husbands, that she had little experience with them. And she did not want to encourage an attachment if there was no hope that Mr Aikens really was in love with Mary. He was such a strange young man. He was loyal, but he treated everyone with the same brash heartiness. Perhaps he was just friends with Mary, and nothing more.

'I don't pretend to understand his heart or his affections,' Lizzy said. 'But I think you may allow yourself to like him a little bit, and know that you have a loyal friend in him. Not many men would go to rescue a friend from the dragon's den, after all.'

Mary sighed. 'I am so glad that I escaped with Mr Aikens's help that I can scarcely care for Miss de Bourgh. But it saddens me too. I think we were becoming friends, for she unbent to me, at least after the beginning. It was only when she remembered her place, or her mother reminded her of it, that she became unbearable again. If she had not such a mother, she might have been likeable, for she can be very earnest. But she was jealous of all of her perquisites, for she could never be sure whether they were bestowed upon her because she was Anne de Bourgh, or only Lady Catherine's daughter.'

'Surely as good a moral as any, that too much consequence can be as great a trial as not enough,' Lizzy said. 'I believe that as little a consequence as Longbourn and Meryton gave us, it was quite as much of a blessing as we could manage.'

'I quite agree. In fact, a little less Longbourn and a bit more Meryton would be a comfort just now,' Mary said. Lizzy fell in beside her and they continued on to the village in companionable silence. The rays of the afternoon sun lengthened over them and the insects danced in the golden light. It was peaceful but Mary was ill at ease.

'Lizzy, did you know that Charlotte has changed?'

Lizzy sighed. 'I had seen it. I feared as much, that her marriage to Mr Collins would cause her to lose her good nature and common sense. But to do otherwise would have been disloyal, you see.'

'She upbraided me for receiving Mr Aikens and gave me to understand that I had lost her esteem. I made it clear that she had lost mine for marrying Mr Collins, and so I fear we can no longer be friends. I am not sure that I can be friends with any of the Lucases now, because I am sure that even if Charlotte doesn't tell them what came between us, Mr Collins will. And for that, Lizzy, I grieve most deeply.' Mary stopped, overcome with tears. 'I am so sorry, if it comes between Charlotte and you.'

'Oh Mary.' Lizzy put her arms around her and Mary sobbed into her shoulder. 'I lost Charlotte the day she married Mr Collins. She forgot all sense that day, while you seem to have gained the understanding she gave away. And she should apologize for scolding you. You did the very sensible thing, to receive a friend in a house where you were a guest. The old Charlotte would have understood that. But she is Mrs Collins now, and she has adopted her husband's sensibilities as a good wife should. So for that we should commend her. But we don't have to esteem her for it.'

'I don't know what is wrong with me,' Mary sobbed, now quite wetly. She lifted her head and wiped her tears with her handkerchief. Lizzy held hers out when Mary's had given its all. 'I am either so happy as to break into tears or I am miserable and I break into tears.'

'Either way, we can hardly continue into Meryton,' Lizzy said, and Mary gave a watery smile. Her nose was very red. 'I propose that we return home, very slowly. You have no doubt not been told the news of Lydia?'

From the look of her, Mary had not. Well, thought Lizzy, it will take her mind off her own troubles.

'Oh dear,' Mary said. 'Is it bad?'

'It's Lydia,' Lizzy sighed, and she related the tale. Mary's tears soon dried in her astonishment.

'And Mama doesn't know? Or Papa?'

'Not yet. I came to find you first. I will tell Papa directly we get home, and will leave it to him to tell Mama. I know she will think only that it means Lydia will be able to visit, and she will want to attend the lying-in. But I cannot think that Papa will let her.'

'I think he should,' Mary said. Lizzy looked

at her with surprise. Mary had been full of sermons when Lydia had eloped. What had changed? 'It might be time for him to forgive Lydia, Lizzy. She is a foolish, simple girl. If she repents, should she not be embraced? The prodigal son, after all, was forgiven.'

'I don't think Lydia has repented,' Lizzy said. 'Darcy and Bingley said she was shockingly hoydenish when they saw her. She was always a flirt. Now she is quite loose.'

'All the more reason to welcome her home and restore her to her family. Only that, together with her child, can make her see that she must mend her ways.'

'This is Lydia, Mary. She has ever been spoiled and selfish, and we have been given no indication that she has changed. And there is the matter of Wickham. He does not love her, and it may be, with Lydia behaving as she does, that the child is not his. It's no longer about Lydia returning home, or Lydia returning with her child. She is Mrs Wickham now.'

'What will you recommend to Papa?'

'He'll do as he wishes, as he always does.' Lizzy could not keep the irritation from her voice. She loved her father, but he scarcely exerted himself unless pushed. 'I can only tell him what I can.'

Mary nodded. She gave voice to one last

uncharitable thought. 'It is too bad that Wickham has no more inclination for soldiering than he had for the church. That would have solved one problem, at least, if he were as bad a soldier as he was a churchman.'

'He would have been vastly more agreeable and accommodating,' Lizzy said. 'Alas for us, it is one more failing of his.'

25

Mrs Bennet took no notice of Mary's swollen nose and damp eyes but rushed upon her daughters as soon as they came into the house.

'Lizzy! Where have you been! Your father has been looking for you. Go to him at once.'

Lizzy squeezed Mary's hand and went to her father's study. The door was closed; she took a breath and knocked firmly on the door.

'Come in,' he said, and she went in to the room.

Her father sat at his desk as usual, placed so as to catch the light from the window. He looked up at her and then looked back at his book.

'Hello, Papa,' she said, and went over and kissed him. He did not respond in his usual warm fashion, and Lizzy regarded him with a questioning tilt of her head.

'I see,' she said at last. 'We have quarrelled. Or at least, you have taken some offence. I am innocent of any insult or misdemeanour.'

'Hmmph!' he said. 'I am angry with you, it is true. You did not come to Longbourn to take long walks with your silly sister and yet so you have done.'

'You are quite incorrect, sir. I came to see Mary,' she said. 'Who is not as silly as you would like to think. Kitty, I agree, is still quite without sense, but she is young and if given encouragement, she will grow out of it. That is, if *you* give her encouragement.'

He hmmphed again, but Lizzy said firmly, 'No, Papa. It is time you own up to your position. What can you expect of Kitty and Mary and Lydia if you only laugh at them and turn your nose up at them?'

'Do not speak of Lydia to me.'

'Oh, but it is of Lydia that I am here to speak.'

He looked at her. Her tone had changed from exasperation to seriousness, and now that she had got his attention, he was over his pique.

'What is it?'

Lizzy related the tale once again.

He was silent for a long time, then shook his head and made as if to return to his book. Without looking at her, he said, 'You are a married woman, my dear, so you know that this was to be expected. We cannot save Lydia from herself, though we have done our best, and I continue to do so every quarter, payment remitted.'

'Father, let Lydia lie in the bed she has made. But should her child be punished for her sins or for those of Mr Wickham?'

'Lizzy, it is all right for you to say these things. You are, not to put too fine a point on it, richer than we could ever have imagined. But Lydia's wantonness has put Kitty, and yes, Mary, in very grave danger of never marrying as comfortably as they should. They cannot be expected to marry as well as you and Jane have. I have nothing to give them. Nothing, because Lydia has taken it all. So you may count me a very bad father, but I assure you, I feel the lack keenly every year as my pockets become leaner. Kitty's only hope now is that she may be thrown into company that is more foolish than she, so that she marries as well as she can. And Mary. I thought Mary was settled as best she could be.' He threw up a hand. 'And yet, she managed to confound even those expectations.'

Lizzy pursed her lips. Had her father invested more in his paternal responsibilities when they were younger perhaps they would not find themselves in this position now. But who could say that even if he had exerted himself he could have overturned his wife's influence? Lydia was Mrs Bennet's favourite and the daughter most like her. Was it fair to think that anything could have been done?

At her long silence her father smiled and took her hand. 'So I see I have silenced you. Good. Now we can be friends again, and you can tell me more of this Mr Aikens. Is he a fool and in love with Mary?'

Lizzy smiled. 'He is an unusual young man to be sure. He sees her as a friend, and he makes no distinction between his friends. He may be in love with her. It's hard to tell. But Mary, I fear, has fallen greatly in love with him, and so you now have another daughter with a broken heart and who will become more interesting to you.'

Her father got up and stood at the window, looking out over the expanse of lawn, where the slanting rays of the sun, filtered through the trees and crossed over the grass a sight that made Longbourn so dear to all the Bennets. 'I should never have let Mary stay at Rosings. Your mother persuaded me to be worried at her lack of prospects, and Mary herself seemed determined upon that course. But Lady Catherine is as unkind as she is high-born. Even as we drove away, I knew it was wrong.'

'Mama was set on it. The connection was a good one.'

'Yes, for Rosings. But not for Mary.'

Mr Bennet's simple declaration for his family and his daughter relieved Lizzy's unsettled heart. So she did not have to scold her father for his neglectfulness: he had begun to see it for himself.

'You should tell her that, Papa. She will want to hear it.'

Her father became brisk. 'Yes, yes, I suppose I should. It is not easy to apologize to one's daughters. And you should not ask so much, you know. It is unseemly for a daughter to have so much understanding.'

Lizzy knew he wasn't truly angry, so she gave him a kiss and left him. Before she closed the door behind her he called out, 'Lizzy!' She turned.

'This Mr Aikens. Where can I find him?'

'Darcy has his address.'

'Good. Tell my son-in-law if he would so good as to provide me with it I would like to thank the young man who came to my daughter's rescue. And send for Mary to see me.'

* * *

Mrs Bennet could scarcely contain her nervous excitement. Hardly had Lizzy left her father than her mother found her and carried her off to the parlour. Lizzy ordered tea from cook, made sure that Mary knew that her father wanted her, and then sat with

302

her mother, who vented her nerves in wild, disconnected talk.

'I own that I cannot understand how Mary could act in the way that she did. For Lady Lucas said that she was quite wild to Charlotte, and said some dreadful things, and Mr Collins said that Mary showed a most unattractive fixed determination and would not be moved. And that Mr Aikens! A farmer! Coming up to the front door of Rosings to pay a visit to Mary! What on earth could she mean by allowing it! How had she met him! How could she have done such a thing! I am afraid, Lizzy, that we may no longer be welcome at the Lucases.'

'Mama,' Lizzy said, pouring tea for her mother. 'I will speak to Lady Lucas myself and explain all.' By which she meant that she would smooth ruffled feathers, though she was not sure that she would be able to do so. 'But you must stand by Mary. She did nothing wrong, And Mr Aikens is a respectable gentleman. He is a bit unpolished perhaps, but he has a good heart and is from a good family. Darcy quite likes him.'

Mrs Bennet had once disliked Mr Darcy, but as he was now her son-in-law, she had transmuted those feelings to ones of awe. If Mr Darcy liked Mr Aikens, then that ought to have been enough for her.

'But Lizzy,' she said, almost with a moan. 'The Lucases do not like Mr Aikens, and Mr Collins said that Lady Catherine was quite outraged.'

'Mama, but Darcy does, as do I. Mr Aikens is a fine young man, and he is a good friend to Mary.'

She would not say more. She could not betray Mary's confidence. Her mother, if she knew that Mary had formed an attachment, would be unstoppable, to everyone's humiliation. Mrs Bennet had a disgruntled expression as she thought for a long time. It was difficult for her not to blurt out what she felt or thought, and Lizzy sipped her tea and waited. When her mother spoke, it was with continued confusion and upset.

'I am quite angry with Mary,' she said. 'She should not have friends like this. She should not have friends *at all*. What does she mean by befriending men who are liked by some and not liked by others? It's very confusing, Lizzy. You should tell her, my nerves cannot put up with this.'

'Mama, if Mary made an unsuitable friend I would have warned her. But she has not. Mr Aikens is a fine young man.'

'Well. He might be. And perhaps he is if, as you say, Darcy likes him. But Lizzy, he has caused so much trouble that I cannot like him. Why couldn't Mary just have done what she has always done? Why has she changed? I knew when she stopped playing the piano that it was nothing good.'

Considering that they had all heard enough of Mary's piano-playing, Lizzy lifted her eyes to the ceiling.

'Mary has quite altered, it is true, Mama. But I think it is a good thing. She is well-read, and she has a good heart. She no longer sermonizes and she has learned to show some compassion. She was a good friend to Anne de Bourgh, even though that friendship was scorned. She has a good friend in Mr Aikens, for all that you do not like him. Her society has widened and that is all to the good. I don't know that the box she put herself in and that we kept her in was quite enough for her.'

'Lizzy! If you are saying we confined Mary, that is not true. But it was easier when we knew she would play pianos for dancing or not require anything but her books and her sermonizing. She was just Mary.'

Having just proved Lizzy's point, Mrs Bennet set down her teacup, her eyes wide with new perception.

'Lizzy! Why did we not make Mr Collins fall in love with Mary! They would have been a perfect match!'

'Mama!'

'Oh, Lizzy, what were we thinking. For of course you turned him down, and I was so angry with you, but I am not so any more, for you were right, for Mr Darcy is so much grander and richer. But it would have been the easiest thing to turn Mr Collins's head towards Mary! For even though she is the plainest of you girls, she is much better looking than Charlotte. Oh, Lizzy, if you had only suggested it, we should not have to worry about the entail or Mr Aikens at all! Mary and Mr Collins! Mary and Mr Collins. How tiresome that we did not think of it before.'

Lizzy watched her mother mourn the lost opportunity with an unladylike expression. A knock on the door caught the attention of both, and Mary came in. Her nose was still red and her eyes were watery. Lizzy suspected that her interview with their father had brought on a renewal of tears. But she managed a smile at her mother and her sister and picked up the teapot. Mrs Bennet wasted no time in regaling her with her new perception of a lost opportunity. Lizzy tried to stop her but it was too late.

'Mary! What do you think Lizzy and I have just decided! *You* should have married Mr Collins! What do you think of that?'

Mary stared at her mother and set down the teapot so hard that it made the tea things rattle upon the tray.

'Marry Mr Collins!' she said. *'Marry Mr Collins!'*

Mrs Bennet stopped short at her daughter's anger.

Mary sat back and looked at her mother. She spoke with great deliberation. 'Mr Collins would not have me, first because I was plain. Then he would not have me because he could not bear a wife who had more of a vocation than he did. All he has ever done since I have met him is tell me that it is unseemly for a woman to take such an interest in reading and philosophy and to have an opinion. I confess that I wondered why he never so much as looked at me when he came here looking for a wife. Now I know. He couldn't bear the competition.

'And I thank Heaven every day that he never did consider such a proposal and that you never did, for we would have been in the deepest misery from the very first day of our wedding.'

Mary had done the one thing that Lizzy had never thought possible. Upon the conclusion of her daughter's speech Mrs Bennet was bereft of words.

26

Mr Bennet's conference with Mary had little openness and much hesitation on both their parts. Mary was much intimidated by her father, and Mr Bennet could hardly apologize for his sins when they were so much a part of his character that he could not even see his faults. It had all been so clear when Lizzy told him how much Mary needed his admiration, much more muddled when he sat awkwardly with his daughter and desperately wished them both elsewhere. Still, he managed, rather respectably, to ask about her experience without revealing much confusion and boredom. For her part, Mary pitied his discomfort and was as forthright as possible. She was glad to be home, she said, and sorry that she caused so much embarrassment to all of them, but she thought the blame lay with Lady Catherine, and if there were any fault on the Bennet side, it was that they thought rather more highly of Lady Catherine than perhaps they should.

'I admit I could not understand what she meant by her invitation,' said Mr Bennet, 'but I could not find a reason to decline.'

Mary smiled and took her father's words at face value. She knew he meant not that he couldn't understand an invitation directed at *her* but one that was directed at any one of them.

'I think she meant it in a most disgusting way,' Mary said. 'To put a Bennet in her place.'

Her father smiled and waved a paternal hand at her.

'Yes, yes, it's over now,' he said. 'You must stay here with us, Mary. It's become too quiet about the place without your piano.'

'I no longer play, Papa,' she reminded him. As she said it, she rubbed her fingers. What a few moments of contentment she had stolen, just before she was exiled from Rosings, in playing the piano in her room. Perhaps — perhaps, she could return to her old habit, taking from it only pleasure in the application of herself to something difficult, and asking nothing in return. But after insisting for so many months that she had given up music, could she begin anew? What did that say of her pride and vanity, that she would lock herself away from such a small accomplishment?

Mr Bennet looked at his daughter for a long moment. Perhaps he understood something of her confusion. Then he patted her lightly on the shoulder. 'That's all right, my child. You'll pick it up again, when you want to. You'll see.'

He meant it not as a sop to her vanity, but as one who had perhaps set aside a beloved occupation, only to take it up as a comfort later in life. For the first time, Mary felt that her father saw her for who she was.

★   ★   ★

The quietness that Mr Bennet rued was soon broken and longed for once again. There was a clattering of hoofs along the short drive that led to the house then came a knock on the door. Mr Aikens had arrived. He was led into the parlour, where he saw Mrs Bennet and Lizzy and bowed to them.

'Mrs Darcy! Good to see you again! And you must be Mrs Bennet!'

He pumped Mrs Bennet's hand enthusiastically. 'A pleasure to meet you, ma'am!'

'Mr Aikens, so good to see you,' Lizzy said, hoping to lure him to a chair. But he ploughed on in his enthusiastic way.

'I've come to see how Miss Bennet has settled in. Is she at home?'

At that moment, Mary slipped through the door. She curtsied awkwardly. Mr Aikens dropped Mrs Bennet's hand to shake hers. But he also tried to bow at the same time, and he made a comical picture.

'Home safe and sound,' he said, rising from his bow. He didn't let go of her hand. 'This is a nice room. Good view of the park. I remember when I visited Lucas Lodge and rode this way. Thought, what a nice prospect. Small but neat. Well collected. Well-bred place.'

It was very like Mr Aikens to liken a house to a horse, but Mrs Bennet didn't know whether to be flattered or outraged.

'Thank you sir,' she managed faintly. 'It is nice, but the entail — '

'Mr Aikens!' Both Lizzy and Mary spoke together, quite loudly, to stop their mother. Mary finished first. 'It is but a very small park, with a view of the village. Would you like to see?'

He smiled broadly and Mary led the way, trying to still her beating heart. She told herself they were merely friends, but the look she cast Lizzy was filled with both hope and fear. Lizzy smiled encouragingly but was filled with almost the same hope and fear. She did not want Mary to suffer a broken heart — having experienced such discomfort herself, she knew they were not to be wished upon any one.

She and her mother watched them go, then her mother turned to Lizzy. 'I declare,' she said, but could come up with nothing else.

'That was Mr Aikens, and he does leave one breathless.'

Her mother went directly to the heart of the matter.

'Lizzy! Does he mean to ask for Mary?'

'I cannot speak for him, ma'am, but I suspect that he may.'

Mrs Bennet sat down. 'Does he always behave so?'

Worse, Lizzy wanted to say, but she decided not to frighten her mother. Instead, she sat down with her and took her hand. Mrs Bennet fanned herself with the other.

'I own I do not understand you girls. I must admit I thought you surprised me the most when you married Mr Darcy, but Mary far exceeded you all. This is most unexpected, Lizzy.' She got up. 'Well, I will go to Mr Bennet and tell him to expect another wedding. You can be sure he will be as astonished as I am.'

Lizzy watched her go, and sat alone in blessed silence for a moment. If Mr Aikens broke Mary's heart, she wouldn't send Darcy after him. She would box his ears herself.

★   ★   ★

There was no danger of heartbreak unless a heart broke with joy. Mr Aikens and Mary strolled down the path around the small park, and then by agreement stood by the tree where Mary had met Lizzy earlier that day.

'I've been thinking,' Mr Aikens said. 'About what you said, that you liked me even though I can't sit inside for more than a minute and my boots are always muddy. And I thought, well, if she can like me for that, maybe she wouldn't mind if I asked her to marry me.'

Mary was confused at first — it was hard to tell whom Mr Aikens was talking about. He looked at her so hopefully that she finally understood that he meant her. She spoke slowly, for she wanted to make sure that they both understood one another.

'I do not mind,' she said. 'If you don't mind that I like to sit in the evenings and read. Perhaps we can do that together?'

'Don't like reading,' he said, crestfallen. He soon brightened. 'Oh! But you could read to me! I like a good story or a rousing bit of poetry. I might like to find out how that book ended, the one you read to me before. I can't get it out of my head.' He took her hand. 'I could teach you to ride! It's easy enough. You'll like it!'

'I would learn to ride,' she said, after a taking a deep breath to steel herself. Horses were so . . . large.

'Capital! It's decided!'

He gave her a kiss and Mary felt a stirring of nerves such as she had never really felt before. When he pulled back he looked worried again. 'Are you sure? I wouldn't want you to marry me only because you feel sorry for a fellow who isn't clever.'

'I don't feel sorry for you. I only worry that you feel sorry for me.'

He looked at her blankly and she plunged on. 'I am not pretty, and I am not much in society, and I am afraid that I am not very accomplished.'

He laughed. 'Listen to the pair of us. We're both trying to find reasons why we shouldn't love one another. I think that's better than trying to find reasons why we should. I think you are quite pretty, even if other girls look prettier, and I don't care about style. As for accomplished, I've heard you play the piano and you always have your nose in a book, and that is accomplished enough for me. You don't laugh at me because I can't tie a cravat or I wear the wrong jacket. I'm a plain fellow myself.'

He was not plain. He wasn't as handsome as Bingley, whose good humour dressed him as becomingly as his best clothes, or as Darcy, whose air of consequence did the same, but he was a good, solid man none the less.

'I think perhaps we set each other off well,'

Mary said. Her nerves set themselves dancing again. Was she really engaged?

'A matched pair,' he agreed. 'May I kiss you again?'

She supposed she should say no, but she didn't.

'And now,' he said, when they broke their kiss after she had lost all sense of time. 'I suppose I should ask your father for your hand?'

'Yes, I think that's how it's done.' But she wanted him to wait so that she could savour the moment. She, Mary Bennet, was engaged to be married. Like Lizzy and Jane! And Lydia. The thought of Lydia cooled her excitement a little. She didn't think she had been duped, but what if Mr Aikens were more like Mr Wickham, and less like her other brothers-in-law? Her awareness of the present moment came back, but this time it was tinged with a little uncertainty.

Perhaps some of her thoughts showed on her face, because Mr Aikens looked worried.

'Maybe you should see the house first, before you decide. I haven't done much with it. I am more likely to be out and about than indoors. It might be a bit cluttered. And perhaps not quite as neatly kept as you might be used to. I think there might be an old harness in the drawing room.'

Mary considered his words, not to keep in

a state of anxiety, though that was its effect, but to answer him the best she knew how.

'I don't think,' she said, in the face of worry, 'that the state of your house is a matter for concern. Rather, it is this. I don't know whether you remember some of the things Lady Catherine said that day?'

He shrugged. 'I didn't care for anything she said and it has all slipped right out of my mind.'

Mary took a deep breath. 'She mentioned my youngest sister. Lydia.' She told him of Lydia's dreadful marriage and what it had brought down upon the family. 'I should have told you before you proposed, so that you could take it into consideration before making your offer. I would understand if you chose to withdraw . . . ' she faltered a little.

He was quiet for a moment. 'I can't fathom it,' he said at last. 'What has it to do with you? You haven't eloped with some rogue.'

'You don't mind?' Mary said. What kind of man was she to marry, that he didn't care about her fallen sister? She could see Mr Aikens greeting Mr Wickham and Lydia with his open-hearted acceptance and no hint of disgust and condescension. Would it not do the ne'er-do-wells good? She suddenly wanted to see it, more than anything.

'I think, Mr Aikens, that you are a good man, though we don't really know each other well enough to speak for our characters. For that, I think, our engagement should be quiet so that we might become better acquainted. And even if you don't mind my sister and her bad husband, your mother might.' Most mothers did mind such things.

He laughed and bent his head for another kiss but she evaded him sternly with a hand on his rumpled cravat. 'My mother will be so happy that I have married that she would accept a hundred bad brothers-in-law. But if you wish for a long, quiet engagement, I can only agree.' He spoke with a mixture of hope and disappointment. 'You see, you are cleverer than I am. I think of something and there! I must have it. But you think about the consequences.'

'Mr Aikens, you are trying to make me feel sorry for you,' Mary said severely. He looked sheepish. 'I do assure you, I quite like you. But I am by nature cautious and I cannot just take this leap as if I were Hyperion, sir.'

He laughed. 'No, you have a quieter temperament. Much more peaceful a ri- er, well, yes. We will have to practise going in harness together.'

'So you will have to be patient, sir. And it

may be that you find out something about me that you don't like.'

'I doubt it,' he said, but he was cheerful again. 'But I will give way in this. I have a feeling it won't be the last time.'

Many a loving dictator has let power go to her head. Fordyce warned against it. *How unamiable, and how miserable, must we pronounce the passion for ungentle command, for petulant dominion, so shamefully indulged by some women as soon as they find a man in their power!'*

Mary saw the danger from the start and vowed to avoid it. She had several marriages to study and would choose the best examples from each. Her father and mother; Lizzy and Darcy; Jane and Bingley; Charlotte and Mr Collins. Each one had strengths, even that of Charlotte and Mr Collins.

He took her hand again. 'So. A quiet engagement. I will talk to your father and we will get to know each other.'

★ ★ ★

'Well, Mrs Bennet,' said Mr Bennet later, after his permission was asked for and given. 'Congratulations are in order. I do not think there is a mother in all of England who has managed to marry off so many daughters in so short a space of time. Kitty had better watch out.'

'Oh Mr Bennet, what foolery! For you know *I* had nothing to do with Mary! I cannot hope but that he is a suitable husband for her, for she has gone and done it herself. I do not understand her. First she stops playing the piano and then she visits Rosings and is thrown out of the house, and now she is engaged! Whatever will she do next? I don't like the unexpected, and she has become quite unexpected.'

'I imagine that she has become unexpected to herself as well,' Mr Bennet said. 'But what do you think of your newest future son-in-law? Where does he fall — somewhere lower than Darcy, I think. But is he above Bingley or below him? I can't work it out. I expect I will have placed him once I get to know him better.'

'It doesn't matter what I think of him, for Mary has gone off and chosen him though we have only met him once. But he doesn't seem very like Mary at all.'

'He doesn't read, or sermonize, if that's what you mean. I think that is why they will do well together. She will read and he will listen and if they are both wise they will find a place where they can meet.'

Since such a thing had not happened for

Mr and Mrs Bennet, he could be forgiven for letting a note of wistfulness enter his voice. Mrs Bennet did not notice, for she had the last word.

'Mark my words, Mr Bennet, Mary will do something even more unexpected before the week is out. I only hope for my poor nerves' sake that we can discover it beforehand.'

27

The day Kitty came home, with extra trunks and hatboxes, and wearing a new bonnet and gown, Longbourn resounded with her mother's joyful greetings and Kitty's excited retelling of her adventures in London. Jane had implored her little sister not tell their mother about the tigers and hoped for the best. Kitty kept her promise at first, mostly because she was too full of her own tales to tell about her London trip. She and her mother had an animated reunion, and when Mary came in from walking with Mr Aikens and gave her sister a kiss, their mother said,

'And what do you think, Kitty, but that Mary has some news? Tell her, Mary!'

Kitty looked up from her trunks, her eyes bright. It would be hard to say that she noticed something different in her sister, but since their mother had never before said anything about Mary in such a way, she was interested for a moment.

'Well, Mary?' she said. 'Have you ever seen such a bonnet?' She held it up. It was a ridiculous creation.

'Never, and it's astonishing that you

bought such a thing. I'm engaged, Kitty.'

'I didn't buy it. Bingley did, and you should have seen Caroline's face — ' Kitty stopped talking though her mouth stayed open. She looked from Mary to Mrs Bennet. Mrs Bennet had an eager smile on her face, mixed with encouragement and some remaining bewilderment.

'Now Kitty, you should give your sister a kiss! Aren't you happy for her?'

'Mary, engaged!' Kitty said, instead of obeying her mother. 'Engaged! What for?'

Mary glared at her sister.

'Kitty!' Their mother cried. 'Don't be a silly girl. She is engaged to be married. He is an unusual young man, rather energetic I should think, but Mr Darcy thinks highly of him, and so your father thinks we all should.'

'I do think highly of him, and my opinion is the only one that matters,' Mary said. 'No need to kiss me, Kitty. That's an ugly bonnet, and you will look like a mushroom should you wear it.'

She left them to their astonishment. The last thing that she heard as she walked out was a gasp from Kitty and her mother's irritable remark, 'Oh Kitty! She's right, it's a ridiculous bonnet.'

The peacefulness at Longbourn with just Mary and her mother and father at home was now enlivened with Kitty's presence and the house was almost as animated as when all five daughters had lived there. Kitty did not take long in telling their mother that Wickham had visited in London, and Mrs Bennet lost no time at all in telling Mr Bennet.

Mrs Bennet faltered when she saw the look on his face.

'Mr Bennet,' she said softly, 'I know that Lydia has done much wrong, but can't we forgive her — just for a little? It has not hurt our girls so very much after all, has it? Even Mary is engaged now, and soon all of these sons-in-law will outweigh the one bad one.'

'Mrs Bennet, I have not your optimism. Mr Wickham is so very bad, it would take twice as many good sons to make up for him, and unfortunately our daughters are only allotted a husband apiece. He did not come to London just to leave his card at Bingley's. He came to ask for more money. He thinks nothing of bleeding us dry, and for that we cannot forgive Lydia, no, not even just a little.'

His wife did not remonstrate. Instead, Mrs Bennet sat quietly in the chair across from her husband, and he could see how old and strained she was. When she spoke he could hardly hear her.

'I miss her so,' she said. 'My youngest, my

dearest, my Lydia.'

And for a moment so did Mr Bennet. He remembered her, his youngest. They had been so hopeful that she would be a boy, and save them all from the entail. And he had no doubt that they had doted so on her because of that disappointment. But she — such a fat, greedy, bossy little thing, even then! All her sisters had cosseted her, and it had done her no good at all. The house had never been peaceful, not since Lydia's arrival.

'Do not think about Lydia, Mrs Bennet,' he said. 'She is not your daughter any longer.'

★ ★ ★

There was more news, of course. At dinner Kitty had to hear the whole tale of Mary's stay at Rosings, and she squealed with laughter.

'I will tell Maria Lucas at once, for she will think it the funniest thing!

'No, you will not,' Mary said crossly. 'Stop it, Kitty.'

Kitty made a face. 'You are never any fun, Mary.'

Mary had quite enough. 'At least,' she said, 'I didn't get tipsy and almost eaten by tigers.'

As this was news to Mr and Mrs Bennet and had been told to Mary in confidence by Lizzy, there was a resounding gasp around the table. Mary put down her fork but couldn't help a small, satisfied smile.

'I'm sorry, wasn't I supposed to say that?'

'Mama!' Kitty cried. 'Mary!' It was hard to tell what she meant — she was torn between expressing her anger at Mary and denying the charge. Mr Bennet threw down his napkin.

'What else, Kitty? Do you have anything else to tell us? I know you have very little sense, but I expected more of Jane and Bingley. Well, not Jane perhaps. But Bingley.'

'You always think I'm so bad!' Kitty said, sobbing. 'But Mary got turned out of Rosings! Why isn't she bad?'

Her mother tried to contain her tears. 'Now Kitty, you are no worse than Mary, and indeed, we were very upset with her, but now she is soon to be married and so we must be happy for her.'

Kitty merely redoubled her tears. Mr Bennet looked as if he wished he were anywhere but at dinner with his loving family. Mary looked out the window and wondered whether she had made a mistake in asking for a long engagement.

★ ★ ★

Her misgivings deepened when Mr Aikens was called away home. He came to visit before he left, sitting but tapping his booted foot incessantly while he talked to her. Mrs Bennet kept looking at it, then looking away, and her breathing was strained. Kitty looked sullenly upon this new future brother-in-law. Mr Aikens still tried to have a private conversation with Mary under the eyes of her chaperones.

'It can't be helped,' he said. 'My farm is my income, and so I must be careful to oversee my lands as best I can. I am in need of a good manager but have found no one who takes the care I require.'

'I understand,' Mary said, though her heart sank. He had the freedom to come and go as he pleased while she had to sit and be quiet. A thought struck her. 'Perhaps Darcy could recommend someone.'

He brightened. 'Capital idea! That is just the thing! We will do well together, you'll see!' He leaned forward and kissed her. Mary froze as still as a statue. Of a sudden he remembered who else was in the room with them and drew back. 'Ah. I do beg your pardon. I forgot you were there, ma'am.'

Kitty looked as if she were going to burst with laughter or horror. Mrs Bennet was left speechless. Her wrinkled cheeks flamed red and she swallowed hard. But she could not look at Mr Aikens or her daughters.

Mary looked down at her interlaced fingers, and wished she could sink through the floor. Mr Aikens coughed uncomfortably, then rose to his feet with relief. He made a quick bow, said his goodbyes and left them in their uncomfortable tableau. As soon as he was gone, Kitty shrieked and threw herself down on the sofa, muffling her face in a cushion. Having recovered from her emotional outburst, Mrs Bennet looked at her daughter.

'Mary,' she said with all the calm she could muster. 'You must marry Mr Aikens. You must marry him at once. I will brook no more delay.'

Mary set down her hated needlepoint and stood up. 'As you wish, Mama.'

And then she too fled from the room.

28

A long quiet engagement no longer being wished for by any of the parties, the news was announced to as great a fanfare as the middle daughter of a respected gentlemen in a small village could reasonably expect. That is to say, that hardly any persons outside the small acquaintance of Longbourn and Meryton could have been interested. Of those, a few can be of concern to us: the Lucases, the Collinses and Lady Catherine and her daughter. What Mr Collins thought was conveyed at great length in wordy letter to his cousin, Mr Bennet, who merely lifted his eyes to the ceiling and tucked the letter under some papers in his study. Lady Catherine was not silent upon the matter, but allowed her displeasure to be conveyed by Mr Collins. Whatever Anne had to say or think remained with Anne.

In the general excitement the Lucases gave their hearty congratulations on hearing the news and relations between the two families lost their stiffness. Sir William responded with genuine pleasure, because weddings meant balls, and he loved to see young people dancing; Lady Lucas felt some envy. She still had daughters remaining, and while Charlotte had managed her own affairs admirably (although Lady Lucas remained a little uneasy about it), it was not clear that Maria would manage so capably. So many months ago, when Thomas Aikens had visited Lucas Lodge as a friend to her many sons, she had looked upon him as affording the likeliest opportunity for Maria, despite his very singular character. Lady Lucas had probably never heard the word *irony* in her life, but even she had to allow that there was something uncomfortably *à propos* in that a young single gentleman with connections to the Lucas family had become engaged to a Bennet.

Still, Lady Lucas managed to tell Mrs Bennet over tea that she was so glad she had been able to introduce Miss Mary and Mr Aikens. 'For do you remember, Mrs Bennet? He visited us last year and Mary played the piano. I could see something when they spoke, I could see it. And don't you know, I remember it so well, I must have marked something in my mind then.'

Mrs Bennet, feeling gracious, allowed Lady Lucas credit for introducing Mary and Mr Aikens. She even forgave the Lucases their not entirely unexpected surprise at Mary's making any match at all, though she complained crossly to Mr Bennet later that it wasn't as if Mary had a squint and a hare-lip.

'She is a Bennet, after all, even if she is not as pretty as Jane.'

Lizzy and Jane sent their felicitations and vowed to help the young couple with their start in life. The letters between them lacked self-congratulation, because they both knew that when it came to matchmaking, there was very little art to it, and a great deal of luck. Kitty was only excited that here was another wedding at which she could be the object of some attention as the sister of the bride, and, despite her adventures in London, that was still all she cared for.

★   ★   ★

With the wedding approaching, Mary and her mother and father took a journey to meet Mr Aikens and to see her new home for the first time. Mr Aikens was so anxious to make sure that she would be pleased that he rode beside the carriage on Hyperion, telling her that she could make any changes she wished, any at all, and had he mentioned that the chimneys smoked and he put up with it, but he would ensure that this inconvenience would be remedied forthwith.

Once again Mary was struck by the ease with which she could become a dictator, since she was deferred to so often. She had to remember what had become of Lady Catherine, who given so much deference on account of her breeding and her character, abused her power.

The house was at the end of a long lane, which was rutted and overgrown. But her father noted the good pastureage and the sturdy hedges, and he and Mr Aikens fell into a long conversation about husbandry of the rustic sort.

The carriage turned a corner and they could see the house. It was very different from the one at Longbourn. It was smaller and, as Mr Aikens said, was old and run down. But it was sound and comfortable, with a pleasing façade of warm stone. When they alighted from the carriage, several hounds came out to meet them, and Mr Aikens greeted every one, calling them by name. He pushed open the door and let them in.

This will be my house, Mary thought, looking around everywhere. It had an old-fashioned elegance, but she could see by the rugs and the furniture that it was meant for comfort. Yes, she thought. I can make this pleasant. The chimneys smoked, as promised, but they could be cleaned and patched. There were three pleasant open rooms downstairs and smaller, serviceable rooms upstairs, and a view of the farm that had a charming sort of wildness. There was one room to which Mary took an instant liking. The rug was faded and stuffing came out of the sofa, but she envisaged herself and Mr Aikens spending evenings in there together and she knew she could be happy.

Not happier than Jane, for good dear Jane was the sort of person who deserved to be happiest of all, but happier than Lizzy, for she had a grand house to live up to. Instead, Mary thought, I have a house that exactly suits me.

For once Mrs Bennet bustled around as happily as if *she* were getting married. She had a great many plans for restoring the house, and her ideas were economical and sound. She was in her element. Mr Aikens listened and agreed to many of her ideas, and so, to her astonishment, did Mary. Mrs Bennet had two grand sons-in-law, and one wicked one, but Mr Aikens gave her what she truly wanted; a chance to be in some measure a part of her daughter's life.

Mr Aikens watched Mary hopefully from the doorway.

'I do like it,' Mary said. 'I like it very much.

It suits me as much as it suits you.'

He came over to her and took her by the shoulders. 'Then why are you crying?'

★ ★ ★

There was much to be done. Mary had no trousseau for she had never had any interest or skill enough to sew one. Jane and Lizzy conferred and put one together themselves.

The wedding was held on what proved to be the first frosty day of winter. The only sour note was that Mr Collins had assumed that he would officiate, and he sent a long letter to Mr Aikens, whom he had met under such unfortunate circumstances, and to Mr Bennet, explaining that he would be happy to join the couple in blessed matrimony and in some small way make amends for their sins against Lady Catherine de Bourgh. Mr Aikens read the first sentence, and unable to make any sense of it, tossed the letter aside, thinking no more of it and having forgotten who Mr Collins was. Mr Bennet, on the other hand, said to himself in his study, 'Good God. We can't allow this.' He wrote to Mr Collins sternly warning him that he would be welcome at the wedding but that the service would be held at the village church in Longbourn.

The day dawned. Mary stood in her wedding dress, closed her eyes and swallowed many times, hoping she would not faint or be ill. Her sisters and mother bustled around her; she let them curl her hair and arrange her veil and she hoped that it would soon be over.

'Are you not happy, Mary?' Kitty asked artlessly. 'You look as pale as your gown.'

'Now hush, Kitty!' her mother told her. 'You'll only make Mary more nervous than she is. Oh my dear, you look as pretty as a picture. Who would have thought it, Mary? You have a very good figure, you know, and that makes up for all kinds of showier beauty. Though Jane is the loveliest still. But try not to think of that. Dear, you are pale. Remember to pinch your cheeks.' She took matters into her own hands, taking Mary by surprise and causing her to flinch.

'Mother!' Lizzy and Jane both said. Remonstrating with her, they managed to get Mrs Bennet to leave off frightening her daughter to death before the wedding.

At last the moment came. Mary felt an unexpected peace when she walked up to the altar, with Mr Aikens waiting for her. He gave her a smile, she smiled in return, and her nerves settled at once, though it was still hard to be the focus of so much attention from all of her friends and neighbours. There was Charlotte and Mr Collins, sitting in the Lucas pew. There were her family, with the exception of Lydia and Mr Wickham. The curate opened his mouth to begin.

There was yet another delay as a great noise was heard at the entrance of the church. Mary and every one else turned around to look. In came Lady Catherine, quite grand in her travelling garments. Behind her came Anne, with a look of resoluteness, and behind them, restored to her former place, stood Mrs Jenkinson. Anne stands straighter, Mary thought. And when Anne met Mary's eyes, she gave the smallest of smiles. Mary smiled back, but her face was hidden by her veil.

The congregation watched as Lady Catherine and her daughter made their own processional up the aisle to the front pews. There was no room, so Sir William and Lady Lucas gave up their places and squeezed in next to the Bennets. There was yet more of a delay as the de Bourghs settled themselves. As they did, Mr Aikens looked very hard at them but a hand on his arm from Darcy managed to settle him down.

He and Mary turned back to the altar, and allowed the curate to compose himself.

What composure Mary had found when she saw Mr Aikens waiting for her was now lost. She heard nothing of the service. She could not concentrate and found her mind wandering. Time after time she had to drag her attention back to the present moment. Mr Aikens too, seemed more nervous than usual, if that were possible for him. Perhaps aware of the young couple's discomfiture, the curate rushed through the service as if he thought they would flee before saying their vows.

And then it was over. Mr Aikens put a ring on her finger, they signed the book, and Mary walked out a married woman, accepting the cheers and felicitations of the guests. The cold air felt good on her fevered cheeks and she was handed into the carriage with Mr Aikens beside her. They were bundled with furs, a hot brick was placed at her feet, and they set off to Longbourn House for the wedding celebration. Still in a daze, Mary looked about her and caught sight of Anne de Bourgh, accepting the thanks and good wishes of Mr Collins to herself and her mother, as if the day had been graced all the more by their deigning to participate.

There came a lull in the general hubbub, and Lady Catherine's voice rose clearly into the air.

'I did not want to come, but Anne insisted. Anne can be very strong-willed.'

Mary and Anne looked at one another. For a moment the young woman hesitated and then she said something to her mother and came by herself over to the carriage, the crowd parting for her.

Anne looked quite well. She was still thin and pale but her eyes were bright and her pelisse and bonnet framed her so becomingly that one could see her only as a young woman, not a sickly girl.

'Mrs Aikens, I wish you every joy,' she said, holding up her hand. Mary leaned down and took it.

'Thank you, Miss de Bourgh. I am so pleased that you came today. Will you — can you come to the celebration at Longbourn?'

Anne gave a most mischievous smile. 'I think so,' she confided, and Mary knew that however it had happened, Anne had achieved a measure of independence at last. Anne de Bourgh turned to Mr Aikens and conveyed her congratulations as well as a pretty apology for their last meeting. Then she left them both and the carriage pulled them towards Longbourn. Under the covering wraps she and Mr Aikens held hands.

The de Bourghs did come to the wedding feast and Lady Catherine sat silently for some time until her nature got the best of her and she could be heard remarking to all and sundry her opinion of the ceremony, the feast, and the expected outcome of such a marriage; then, as the punch flowed, she began discoursing on the countryside, the household, the furniture, the servants, and, finally, the French. All in all it was a successful reception, in that at least one guest gave the rest something to talk about for years to come.

Mrs Bennet sat and took in everyone's congratulations on getting her least likely daughter married. Mr Bennet gravely spoke with his sons-in-law, including his newest, and longed for everyone to be gone so he might have his peace and quiet. Mr Collins could be seen eyeing Longbourn until Charlotte made him stop.

Mary found the crowds unbearable. When the time came for the carriage to take them home — her new home — she was relieved and thankful. So they were once more tucked into the closed carriage, with warm bricks at their feet and wraps all around, and were sent off with cries of well-wishing. When they left Longbourn behind, she sighed with relief. Mr Aikens sat next to her, and her nerves rattled pleasingly.

'Well, Mrs Aikens, we have done it at last,' he said. He gave her a sound kiss, so that she could not speak, but only think, We have indeed. And then she could think of nothing else for rather a long time.

* * *

So it was that several days later, Mr Aikens and Mary sat together in the small parlour, a fire burning merrily on the hearth, not a bit of smoke coming into the room. Mary read out loud from *The Mysteries of Udolpho*, which had become a favourite of her new husband's. He told her that he had never forgotten when she had read it to him at Pemberley, under the trees, sitting on his coat to keep out the damp. He could even sit quite still, only tapping one foot, as he listened, and made her start all over again from the beginning, saying that he wanted to have the whole thing fixed in his head before continuing with the tale. He exclaimed often over its strange twists and had a great deal of advice for the characters, often interrupting to say that the author could not have met such people in her life, she must have made them up out of whole cloth, they were completely out of his experience.

But after a while, Mary's voice grew strained, and Mr Aikens said, 'My dear, I think it's time for bed. We keep country hours here.'

Mary smiled, marked her place and got up. She placed the little book on the shelf beside the mantel, next to Fordyce's *Sermons* and her father's book on the plants and animals of England. It was not a grand library such as was found at Rosings, or even as good as the one at Longbourn, but it was a start.

'I agree, Mr Aikens. Time for bed.'

We do hope that you have enjoyed reading this large print book.

Did you know that all of our titles are available for purchase?

We publish a wide range of high quality large print books including:
Romances, Mysteries, Classics
General Fiction
Non Fiction and Westerns

Special interest titles available in large print are:
The Little Oxford Dictionary
Music Book
Song Book
Hymn Book
Service Book

Also available from us courtesy of Oxford University Press:
Young Readers' Dictionary
(large print edition)
Young Readers' Thesaurus
(large print edition)

For further information or a free brochure, please contact us at:
Ulverscroft Large Print Books Ltd.,
The Green, Bradgate Road, Anstey,
Leicester, LE7 7FU, England.
Tel: (00 44) **0116 236 4325**
Fax: (00 44) **0116 234 0205**

Other titles published by
The House of Ulverscroft:

THE RAKE'S CHALLENGE

Beth Elliott

Weary of society life, Giles Maltravers, the rakish Earl of Longwood, decides to flee it. Meanwhile, Anna Lawrence, nineteen and inspired by Lord Byron's poems, also determines to escape and seek a life of travel and adventure. Then, when Giles rescues Anna from her first escapade, despite her resolve to demonstrate her independence, he finds himself rescuing her from one potential disaster after another. He cannot live without her and Anna has come to love him with all her heart, but she hides a secret and can never be more than a friend to Giles ... Can their love yet prevail?

HENRY TILNEY'S DIARY

Amanda Grange

Growing up in an abbey with an irascible father, a long-suffering mother, a rakish brother and a pretty sister, Henry Tilney's life bears more than a passing resemblance to the Gothic novels he loves to read. And Henry is undoubtedly cut out to be a hero. Yet he cannot find his heroine — until, that is, he meets Catherine Morland. With her refreshing innocence and love of reading, Catherine is the perfect match. But will the scheming of Henry's father and the scandalous behaviour of his brother destroy their happy ending?

THEODORA IN LOVE

Ann Barker

After her father's death Theodora Buck-leigh's new adopted family want to give her a London season. But though she is a pretty girl, Theodora has limped from birth, and dreads exposure to the social round. She takes evasive action, accepting an invitation from Dorothy Wordsworth to stay with her and her poet brother, William, in Dorset. Here she will find love, danger and intrigue. Might Coleridge and the others be engaged in treason? Can Theodora's chaperone, Alex Kydd, rescue her from this dangerous company; and even if he does, could there ever be any more between them than friendship?

THE KYDD INHERITANCE

Jan Jones

In Regency England, Nell Kydd is at her wits' end and it's easy to see why. Her father is dead, her brother, Kit, is missing and her loathsome uncle, with his mismanagement, is wrecking the family estate. She must contend with a perturbing lack of funds, an unwelcome proposal of marriage and a mother who lives in a reality of her own. Cue the arrival of the unsettling Captain Hugo Derringer: an old schoolfriend of Kit's who blows hot then cold, and is discovered at odd times — in odd places — asking very odd questions. How far can Nell trust him?

LORD WARE'S WIDOW

Emily Harland

Lady Georgiana Ware is delighted to be the object of the Earl of Thornbury's admiration, so when her hopes of being his wife are dashed, she flees south to the seaside resort of Sidmouth to recover her dignity. She is dismayed when his lordship follows her, determined to correct her opinion of him. Georgiana may find him handsome and charming, but she doesn't trust him one bit. However, can Georgiana conceal her growing feelings for this seductive man? More importantly, can Lord Thornbury penetrate Georgiana's defences and help her to realise that things are not always what they seem?